CU00871945

DREAMING *of* WATER

DREAMING

— *of* —

WATER

BELINDA BRETT

PIATKUS

Copyright © 1997 by Belinda Brett

First published in Great Britain in 1997 by
Judy Piatkus (Publishers) Ltd of
5 Windmill Street, London W1

The moral right of the author has been asserted

A catalogue record for this book is available from the British Library

ISBN 0-7499-0384-8

Set in 11/12pt Times by
Action Typesetting Ltd, Gloucester
Printed and bound in Great Britain by

To my husband and my brother

Chapter One

They drove bumpily along the pot-holed track towards the farmhouse, which rose from the level land, like a lone ship at anchor. Above, in the great width of the sky, towered grand castles of cumulus, iridescent as the inside of oyster shells. Frances, accustomed to the grey lid of the London sky, peered eagerly through the windscreen at the light-filled expanse, which seemed to stretch all around as well as infinitely upwards, and felt suddenly expectant, alive to possibilities. Free.

She was to look back on that March day with a painfully sharp recollection of her first sight of the place that would become her home. But she could not have known how misleading was her state of heightened emotion, how delusive the peaceful scene before her. She was to wonder if anything could have stopped her from plunging onward. But the strength of her desire, her need, for a different life, a fresh start, made her see, in the soft contours of the Suffolk countryside, and the sturdy outline of Willow Farm, the promise of a quiet refuge and, with the changing seasons, the chance to recover. And so, enchanted with her personal interpretation of the prospect before her, she listened to no word of caution.

'It's wonderful,' she exclaimed.

'Wait till you've seen inside.'

'I don't mean the house – or not just the house – I mean – well – everything – the space, the colours, the light.'

'East Anglians take it for granted I suppose, but there are some who say they get claustrophobia anywhere else.'

1

'And you?'

'Not yet.'

'Perhaps you haven't been here long enough.'

'I was born here.' He switched his eyes briefly from the road to glance at her through spectacles with tortoise-shell frames.

'I was born here too, but we left when I was five.'

'So I don't suppose you remember it all that well.'

'It's hard to work out what I can actually remember and what I've been told.'

'Enough to bring you back anyway.'

'Yes.' To find a safe haven, she thought, her eyes fixed on the farmhouse. 'My mother was happy here,' she said. Mother had always described life in Suffolk with such warmth, there seemed to be a kind of glow surrounding the place.

He said, 'I went away for a time.'

'I'm not surprised you came back.' She still felt expectant, eager. She wanted the feeling to endure.

'The country doesn't suit everyone, you know, least of all people who have lived in towns all their lives. Here we are.'

He stopped the car and they got out. Close to, there was a serenity about the farmhouse, a sense of permanence acquired by the seeping away of the centuries. A tumbledown wall marked its boundaries. A large single cast-iron gate lay flat on the ground beside a rotten post. Frances nudged the rusting bars with the toe of her shoe. 'I wonder what happened to the other one? Someone fancied a grand entrance. How extraordinary. Elaborate gates are completely out of keeping with this place. Just as well it's gone.'

'A wooden gate and picket fence would look much better,' he agreed.

'Still, it seems the place hasn't been messed around inside,' she indicated the estate agents' details in her hand. '"Retains original features" – just what I want – "some updating of domestic services required".'

'That is certainly true,' he said.

The house was sheltered from the wind on its north-east side by an overgrown copse of hawthorn and willow. A sea of nettles rippled against the crumbling plastered walls, choking the remnants of a cultivated garden that dropped down to a patch of marshy ground.

'"Sixteenth century",' she read out loud. '"Small Suffolk farmhouse."'

She gazed all around her at the rolling acres, faintly tinged with green. 'There must have been quite a bit of land with the house once.'

'That's right. I suppose you'd have called him a yeoman farmer, the fellow who built it to raise his family in and farm a few fields. Now all the land round here belongs to the chap who lives in that white Georgian manor house we passed a mile or two back.' He looked closely at Frances, as if he couldn't quite make her out. 'Would you be alone here much?'

'I live alone.'

'Ah.'

She felt his flicker of interest and surprise. 'It's a bit isolated for a young woman living on her own.'

Frances said firmly. 'That could be its main attraction. I've had your details after all. I wouldn't have asked to see the place if I hadn't been interested.'

Unruffled, he pressed on. 'Not only is it in an isolated position, the house has been let go and, well, you could hardly call this a garden. The present owners bought it for weekends and holidays – but they hardly used it.'

Inexplicably drawn to the place, she said defiantly, 'I like it. It's interesting: it feels mysterious. Think of all the people who have lived here – all the things that have happened here.'

'I could find you something much more suitable – perhaps in a village – there's plenty of property about at the moment.'

She turned away from his earnest face and gazed, enchanted, at the murky pond edged with straggling alder and last year's reed-mace and willow-herb. 'I've always wanted a pond. I don't want to live in a village. I like the isolation. There's a difference between being alone and being lonely, you know.'

'Hmmn.' He shuffled his feet. 'You haven't seen inside yet.'

'Just listen to those birds,' she said, ' I expect they're building nests, and soon there'll be masses of wild flowers – look daffodils!'

My daffodils, she thought, darting down the bank to touch their slender stems and the pale yellow and green of their budding flowerheads, her light shoes sinking into the soggy

3

ground, just as the sun sent out a brilliant shaft of light from behind billowing clouds.

'Mind you don't slip.' He looked down at her from the top of the bank. 'It's damp with that pond – and there's a stream the other side of the gate – you'll get flooding when there's any heavy rain. No central heating.'

Scrambling up the bank with wet feet, she said crossly, 'I'm the one who is supposed to be pointing out all the faults, not you.'

'I don't want to sell you something unsuitable you might regret.'

'Do you usually tell your customers what they want?'

'The point is, they don't always know what they want. They think they do. I've sold plenty of properties to Londoners who fall for the dream of getting away from it all and within six months they go mad from boredom and clear off back to the City.'

'I'm never bored and maybe I need a dream.'

'OK.' He took the key from his pocket. 'Originally thatched of course.' He shot a narrowed eye at the steep pitch of the wavy pantiled roof, fitted the heavy key into the old-fashioned lock and pushed open the thick oak door.

Felix would approve of this house. The thought came involuntarily, spreading hurt all through her body, for the lack of him. She wished she didn't know that Felix wouldn't consider it worth re-thatching this house, that he'd want to keep the wavy roof line, whatever needed doing to it.

'Timber-framed.' The lime plaster between the oak beams had been colour-washed a pale green. The ground floor was brick, bedded in sand. In the kitchen, an enamel sink, pock-marked and yellowed, stood on brick piers below a casement window. Plywood cupboards lurched against a wall. An ancient solid fuel stove squatted in an alcove. Felix would clear out that old stove and put in an oil-fired Aga. He'd re-enamel the sink and he'd get rid of that dreary green. And how long will it be, she wondered bitterly, before Felix is rinsed right out of me?

A large open fire-place in the main room held a charred log and a pile of damp ash. The winding stair, built round the central chimney stack, rose to a first floor with three good-sized bedrooms and a bathroom. Most of the windows were rimmed with dark splodges of damp. Layers of flowered wall-paper were peeling away from the walls. There was the sweetish smell of long closed rooms. The bathroom contained an overhead-cistern WC with a wooden seat and an enormous cast-iron bath standing on claw and ball feet, its enamel, like that of the kitchen sink, discoloured and chipped.

'What a wonderful bath!'

'You'll need to put on a life-jacket before you get in there.'

Relieved to discover he was capable of making a joke, she responded with a giggle, 'I'm not *that* small!'

The stair wound on up into a dusty attic where they disturbed a hen blackbird from her nest in the rafters. She beat her way on frantic wings out through a broken dormer window. The wide oak floorboards were pricked here and there with worm-holes, and cobwebs festooned the dark beams. Frances stood by an open lattice looking out at the Suffolk countryside stretching away in a gentle sea of green and brown under the wide sky, and thought of Constable and the infinite variety of his cloud studies.

'When the wind blows, which it does most of the time, you'll get a lot of dust from those fields – in dry weather.'

'What's a bit of dust – compared to diesel fumes. I'll leave the garden wild – for the birds – but I'll have to get rid of those nettle and brambles,' she said, looking down on the tangle of them.

'How handy are you with a scythe?'

'Only ten miles from the sea.'

'Think of the mud when it rains. No bus service. Do you have a car?'

'Yes,' she lied, planning to get one immediately, as she followed him down the stairs. 'I'll light fires in that open fire-place: I'm sure you can get logs quite easily.

'Chimney's bound to smoke.'

She was angry now. 'This is getting beyond a joke. You'll be telling me the place has got subsidence and a live-in ghost next.'

'I don't mean to upset you. But, seriously, wouldn't you prefer a renovated cottage in a village? I've just the thing in Walderfield, half a dozen miles away. You'd still be in the country – but not out on a limb like here. Let me show it to you – take fifteen minutes to get there.'

'I've made up my mind – this is what I want. And you like it really – I know you do.'

'Of course I like it – it's just the thing for a young couple with a child or two who will have the time and energy to do what's necessary to renovate the place and who'll have each other for company.' He studied her, a serious expression on his fresh-complexioned face, 'I've a feeling you'll regret it: it's a very big project.'

'And I have exactly the opposite kind of feeling. You know, when you walk into a place, straight off, if it feels right.'

'What else can I say?' He spread his arms wide in defeat.

'Say you're pleased. You're making a sale after all.'

'OK. I'm pleased. You know you'll have to offer the asking price. They bought it at the wrong time and they'll hang on to get what they want.'

'Right.'

'Are you in a position to go ahead straight away?'

'I exchanged contracts on my present house last week. I want to move as soon as possible.'

'It's hardly habitable. You'll need to get some work done here first.'

'I can camp in one room – and summer's coming.'

'You'll want a decent survey.'

'I know.'

'Look – I don't have to be back at the office this afternoon. Why don't we go and have a cup of tea somewhere?'

The Copper Kettle in Fressenworth High Street had red plastic tablecloths and vases of red and yellow plastic tulips. A bearded man with a rucksack was eating poached egg and staring morosely out of the window; a large grey-haired woman in a Barbour jacket was drinking tea and doing the *Telegraph* crossword. Beneath her table, a black labrador tried to make itself look unobtrusive. Frances and Mark – on Christian name terms by now – were followed in by a youth and a girl clad in identical school blazers, holding hands.

Mark ordered a pot of tea and toast from a wispy young woman with bored eyes wearing a frilly apron over a droopy black dress.

6

'I'll pour.' He picked up the pot.

About my age, but a bit too conventional for me, she thought, looking at his green tweed jacket and his long grey-flannelled legs cramped beneath the table. She wondered if he was married. Behind the heavy-framed glasses, his hazel eyes had surprisingly long and dark lashes. Running his fingers through the shaggy brown hair fringing his forehead, he leaned slightly forward and asked, in his curiously quiet voice, 'Tell me Frances, what are you doing here.'

'Buying a house,' she replied flippantly.

'You know what I mean. What brings you to Suffolk? What do you do?'

'Nothing at the moment. I just packed in my job.'

'You've just come here on spec?' He made no attempt to keep the amazement out of his voice.

'Why not? It's as good a place as any. I inherited the family home and I didn't want to go on living in Sevenoaks. My mother died, you see.'

'I'm sorry.' His voice held the conventional note of sympathy.

It still seemed unreal – hearing herself say 'My mother died' – as if she'd made some silly slip of the tongue. Returning after even a short absence, the expectation of coming home to her mother lay so deep in her subconscious, each time it was a shock to find the house empty. She could still hear her name being called, in that thin, sick-bed whisper. 'Frances, Frances.' 'Mother', she would answer, hurrying down the hall, before drawing to an abrupt halt, as the truth of it came surging back.

And now, she burned with guilt for the ill-concealed irritation she had sometimes felt at being the object of so much love: for ignoring the apprehension in her mother's eyes when she planned to do something considered dangerous; riding pillion on Joe's motor-bike, rock-climbing in the Pyrenees. But it was she, ill-prepared for loss, and not her anxious mother, who had been left all alone.

Avoiding Mark's eyes, Frances said, 'My father died when I was a child, so you see I have no ties.'

'You poor thing – I'm sorry.'

She bit into her toast which was clogged with butter. 'Well – at least I can do exactly what I like.'

7

'Are you looking for a job? What do you do?'

'I used to work for an architect.'

'You're an architect?'

'No. I went to art school, so I can draw a bit. And I can do office work.'

'I know someone in Fressenworth who does interior design – but she works on her own. I doubt there's much of an opening for anyone else around her.'

'I wasn't thinking of starting up a business. I just want an undemanding job – I don't mind what I do. Perhaps your firm needs a new secretary?' She was only half joking.

'Our lot are past child-bearing and don't fancy retirement.'

'Oh well – I'll find something.'

'You're very determined.'

'Headstrong, my mother used to call it.'

'You do realise how quiet it will seem here – after London. Aren't you a bit young to opt out?'

'I'm twenty-eight – I bet I'm older than you.'

He grinned. 'I'm twenty-eight too.'

'And what's all this about opting out? I'm certainly not opting out – I'm making a fresh start. What about you? Were you opting out when you came back home?'

He seemed to be considering her words as he stirred sugar into his tea. Eventually he said, slowly. 'There was a vacancy in my father's firm and I don't much like London. It suits me here.'

'And I'm sure it will suit me too.' She looked at her watch. 'I must go – I've a train to catch.'

He drained his tea-cup, and picked up the bill. 'I'll run you to the station.'

As the London train moved slowly out of the station and began to pick up speed, she thought of her mother and the hot tears pricked behind here eyes.

'Inoperable carcinoma of the bone.' To the specialist, professionally direct, those words were commonplace, but they had pierced Frances to the soft marrow of her own bones. Now, she felt again the wasted hand in hers, fragile as a papery leaf skeleton. She saw the eyes, lifeless in the sunken sockets; saw the teeth, huge in the shrunken face as her mother stretched

8

her lips in a brave attempt at a smile. Remembered with shame the revulsion she had felt at the sight and touch and scent of the carapace that housed her dying mother.

I wouldn't be sitting in this train if Mother hadn't died, she thought – and neither would I be here if things had worked out with Felix. Her mother had known about Felix from the beginning but at first, meticulous in her effort not to interfere, had tried to conceal her disapproval, no doubt hoping the whole thing would blow over. When this did not happen, she grew more daring and began to make remarks like, 'Isn't he a little old for you dear?' and 'Felix does seem to have a lot of complications. Are you sure he really is separated from his wife?' and 'Whatever happened to that nice boy Joe?' Eventually, she became forceful enough to come straight to the point. 'You're throwing your young life away on a man who is no good for you.' But that was before the cancer. At the very end, she simply said, 'Take care – be happy.'

'Don't leave me.' Frances was a little child again, inconsolable.

When she broke up with Felix, Frances lost both lover and job. When she lost her mother, she broke up her home. My mother did the same thing, in reverse, all those years ago, thought Frances, leaving Suffolk for Kent, when she was widowed.

It was called Bradstone, the seaside town where they'd lived until her father was killed. They had never been back. When she looked it up on the map, Frances found Bradstone to be about fifty miles north of Fressenworth. As the train rocked along towards London, she thought she might go and have a look at Bradstone. Through the window of the train, she watched the houses slip away to be gradually overtaken by a patchwork of hedges and fields and winter trees.

9

Chapter Two

The survey revealed the farmhouse to be structurally sound although in need of rewiring, replumbing and treatment to timbers infested with woodworm and deathwatch beetle. Mark recommended a builder accustomed to working on old properties. His name was Ted and he was a small wiry man with a squashed-looking face and grizzled hair. He seemed competent but, given the opportunity, over-fond of a chat.

Once the chemical treatment of the timber was finished, just over four weeks from the time she had first seen it, Frances moved in. The furniture stacked under plastic sheeting on the ground floor, she camped out in the largest bedroom while Ted and his team of relatives knocked the place about all round her. She bought a Peugeot hatchback and a pair of Wellington boots and looked for a job. None of the farmers needed a secretary (they already employed their wives). The market town, though well stocked with interesting speciality shops, needed no extra workers, clerical or otherwise. Mark failed to persuade his senior partners that the office staff should be increased. Then on a bright April morning, two weeks after her arrival, attracted by the sight of a carved oak coffer in its window, Frances pushed open the door of the only antique shop in Fressenworth. A bell tinkled, sounding exactly like a cow bell. The shop was gloomy, with a powdery smell of old wall-hangings, dusty furniture. When her eyes had adjusted to the lack of light, she was able to examine the coffer. She traced its flat carved foliage with her finger, lifted its lid and sniffed the musty interior, and thought how well it would fit into her new home. There was no one in the shop, just the sound of typing, hesitant and of the two-finger variety. She opened and closed the door again, to tinkle the bell. The typing stopped and an elderly man, stooped and white-haired, came through from a back room, polishing his glasses.

'What can I do for you?' He was curt, unsmiling.

'How much is this?'

'The oak coffer. Eleven hundred.'

'Oh dear – that's a bit much for me I'm afraid.'

'It's nicely carved.' He was not defensive, but wanting her to see the merits of the chest for herself.

'It's lovely. May I look round?'

'Please yourself.' He went out of the room leaving the door open. The sound of typing resumed.

Frances, disconcerted by his abrupt manner, looked round the room, which was larger than she had at first thought – the lack of light and the overcrowding appearing to diminish it. Apart from the very front of the shop, no attempt had been made to arrange anything. The place was crammed with dusty furniture, artifacts of tarnished brass and copper, dingy pieces of china. Yet, despite its shambolic appearance, this was no mere junk shop. The dust and the lack of an attempt to display it properly did not conceal the quality of some of the furniture. Labels written in stately script described some of the pieces and the prices were high. In a dark corner she came upon a lacquer decorated long-case clock. A china man rode a little gold horse across a black landscape and in the centre of the clock face, framed by Roman numerals, was the inscription of the make: Tho. Chilton London.

Concealed behind a wardrobe of vast proportions, stood a walnut bureau cabinet. Frances stared at the halo-effect of her blond hair reflected in the darkening silvery mirror plates of the cabinet doors. She rubbed her handkerchief over the front of the bureau and the wood shone richly, satin to the touch of her fingers released from its mantle of dust.

In another room there stood rolls of rugs, a rotting tapestry, a stack of faded military prints, china figurines, some chipped and broken, all dirty, piles of decorative plates, some in sets, some not, broken chairs, a sagging horse-hair settee, tarnished brass coal scuttles and jugs, tattered and fly-blown leather-bound books. Somewhere in the background, the hesitant typing continued, staccato, absorbed. 'Hunt and Peck,'

11

Frances smiled to herself. The old man must have forgotten her. Some coloured glass goblets caught her eye, the jewel reds, greens and golds glinting through the crust of dirt. A pair of Staffordshire china dogs stared with glass eyes from the top of a serpentine chest which they shared with an open attaché case crammed with broken fans.

At the back of the second room a door led into a small passage. On the right was a closed panelled door, behind which came the scrape of a chair and then the typist pecking away. Ahead was another door. She opened it and was greeted by the scent of methylated spirits, French polish, antique timber and beeswax. An elderly man glanced up from the broken chair he was repairing.

Frances said, 'Oh – sorry – I didn't realise ...'

The man grunted something, his eyes unfriendly and grey as pebbles beneath bushy white brows. Frances backed out, more fascinated than dismayed by the curious attitude of both men.

Back in the shop a large middle-aged woman with bleached curls and fat ankles was flicking dust with her wisp of a handkerchief from a circular pedestal table jammed between a tarnished brass bedhead and an enormous cabin trunk.

'How many will this seat?'

The owner of the shop, having abandoned the typewriter, regarded her warily, as if she were a large farm animal strayed from its paddock.

'Six or eight depending on size.'

The woman shifted her weight from one foot to the other, shook out her handkerchief, held delicately between pink enamelled nails, and dropped it into her crocodile handbag. 'At dinner parties I need to seat ten – sometimes fourteen.'

'You're looking at the wrong sort of table then. You want a dining table.'

'I know what I want. I want a round table.'

'You won't find a larger circular pedestal table than this one. They didn't make them any larger. I have an oak gate-leg or a mahogany two-pillar dining table.'

'Gate-legs get in the way of your knees. This one's a pretty colour.'

'It's nicely figured wood; pollard oak.'

'And the price?'

12

'Six thousand two hundred pounds, Madam.'

'You must be joking!' She took a step backwards and the crocodile bag swung on her fleshy arm.

'William IV.'

'I don't know how you antique dealers have the nerve – really I don't.'

The old man's expression became baleful. 'Madam – I suggest you visit one of our larger urban department stores and purchase one of their reproduction George III mahogany D-ended extending dining tables, which I feel certain, even supposing you should be fortunate enough to find one, Madam, you would consider indistinguishable from the real thing, thus saving yourself many thousands of pounds.'

He opened the door and held it open. The fat woman, mottled and incoherent, stalked out of it, almost walked slap into a large van that was parked there.

Frances coughed.

Tight-lipped, the proprietor appeared surprised at her presence. He took off his glasses, polished them and put them back on. With spread hands, his voice not quite concealing his agitation, he said, 'My father, a great and apt epigrammist, used to say, "Neither cast ye your pearls before swine." I dislike the general public, but I don't usually allow myself to be so self-indulgent. And what about you? Have you found anything cheap enough for your pocket yet? You've spent long enough looking round.'

Frances tried out a smile. 'You have some lovely things.'

'Yes.' A bell rang. 'Excuse me – the side door.' The old man went into the hall and pulled back a bolt, admitting two young men dressed in working jeans.

'We come for Mr Howden's goods.'

'Margaret should have left a note,' he said testily. 'Can you come back?'

'It's OK – he give us a list.' One of them produced a piece of paper and an envelope.

'Let me see.' The owner of the shop ran his finger down the list and sighed.

'There was some pieces he bought from the Woodton Hall sale. Your van bring 'em here for him.'

'All right, all right.' The tone was getting testier. 'Yes, yes, I

13

see. Secretaire bookcase, china cabinet – that Dutch cupboard – yes – wine cooler, – yes, yes.' He tore open the envelope which Frances could see contained a cheque, glanced at it, pushed his spectacles back up his nose. 'Very well then, you'd better load it up – there's the cooler – with Howden's label on.' He pointed to a rectangular lidded box, ornately carved, pilasters either end topped with acanthus leaves and ending in lion's paws with spread claws. 'The bigger stuff's in the back.' He gestured at them dismissively and watched unsmiling for a minute or two.

Reluctant to leave, Frances pretended to examine a dingy seascape hanging on the wall. The young men grumbled to each other. 'Why can't 'e go for a bit more of the smaller stuff – set of dining chairs, a few little tripod tables – he's 'ad a run on bookcases and cabinets and heavy foreign cupboards – bloody hell – feel the weight of this cooler Tony.' They heaved it up, grunting.

'Probably lead-lined.' The owner of the shop turned to Frances, acknowledging her presence this time without surprise. 'Never stop moaning, young people today. Have a much easier time than I ever did. Don't know when they're well off.'

'I suppose they're lucky to have jobs. I can't get one.'

'No?'

Frances looked at the dusty disorganised furniture, remembered the two-finger typing and, watching the two young men making heavy weather of an unwieldy wardrobe, she said quickly, 'I don't suppose you need anyone do you? To help in the shop?'

'I have an assistant,' he looked vaguely around as if to conjure her presence – 'but she's away at present.'

'I couldn't help noticing you were doing your own typing – from the sound of it that is.'

'Hmmn.'

They both moved out of the way as the two young men struggled along with the bottom of the secretaire bookcase.

'Perhaps– until she comes back – you could do with some temporary help. I've always been interested in antiques. I can type and I could look after the shop for you.' She had a flash of inspiration – 'Help with the customers.'

14

'In the old days.' He looked into the middle distance, as if back into his own memory. 'In the old days my business was mostly trade – other dealers – export – but now – things are difficult and I have to rely more on retail customers. Some who come to my shop are – well – ignorant with regard to fine furniture. Margaret deals with them usually.' He paused, as if he didn't quite know how to finish the sentence.

Frances smiled encouragingly. 'Why not let me help out – just until Margaret comes back?'

There was a silence and they both watched the two young men loading the bookcase into their van. The man took off his glasses, polished them and put them back on again. He examined Frances critically and his cool grey eyes were shrewd. 'You say you can type?'

'Yes.'

A gleam of interest sparked. 'Maybe you could tidy the place up a bit – give the furniture a dust now and again. Margaret doesn't like to do that and I can't afford to employ a cleaning woman.'

'Oh, I could make your shop look wonderful – so many beautiful things.'

'With someone here, I could get out and do a bit of buying. You could mind the show-room for me perhaps – just while she's away. I can't pay you much, mind.'

'I wouldn't expect a London salary – just the going rate for round here.' She smiled at him, trying to coax another spark from those sharp light eyes, but they remained cold as lake water, though his mouth stretched into something resembling a smile.

'Very well – I'll give you a trial. You can start nine o'clock Monday. And you'd better be on time.'

She was delighted. 'You won't regret it.' She held out her hand. 'My name is Frances Lambert.'

He took her small hand in his dry old palm. 'Benson,' he said, 'Tommy Benson.'

'Thank you Mr Benson. See you on Monday.'

She stepped lightly out of the shop and the two lads tying down Mr Howden's furniture leaned out of the back of their van and gave her a wave.

15

Chapter Three

Mr Benson turned out to be an ideal employer. Once he had explained the running of the shop to her, he left her alone: to type up his letters in their Edwardian English, and to reorganise the showrooms however she wanted. He seemed happy to be relieved of the responsibility of bringing order to the heterogeneous collection of furniture and objets d'art, and appeared pleased with the result. He would run a hand over the carving on a chair back, stroke the lustrous surface of a rosewood table, examine the tiny drawer of a walnut bureau. 'Very fine – very fine,' he would murmur to himself, as if he were rediscovering valued possessions. Frances thought it odd that a man with such evident love of beautiful things could abandon them in dark corners, allowing dust to clog their decorative mouldings and blur their graceful contours. Occasionally, he would say, 'Margaret bought that.' Thus, Frances learned that Margaret had been responsible for the purchase of a black fragment of oak tracery, an ochre Staffordshire pottery lion, a solid mahogany drop-leaf table and the red walnut bureau that stood in a corner of Mr Benson's office. 'Margaret has a good eye,' he told her, and a guarded look came over his face and he tilted his head as if he was unconsciously listening for her. Frances assumed, though nothing was directly said, that Margaret was ill.

She cleaned and polished and rearranged the furniture, enlisting the grudging but skilful help of Sidney, the ill-humoured restorer, in moving the heavier pieces. She tried to engage him in conversation but to all her questions he merely replied yes or no. His relationship with his employer appeared to be equally taciturn. No doubt they communicated on some

16

subtle extrasensory level, born of long association.

There were not a great many customers during her first week, but one afternoon a young woman accompanied by two rowdy little boys burst into the shop and immediately fell in love with a gilded Regency chair. 'I've got to have it – it's so elegant,' she said, ignoring her sons who were rolling around the floor poking each other and laughing. It seemed a reckless choice to Frances, but it was her first sale.

When Mr Benson discovered she was responsible enough to deal with customers, he started to leave her in charge. At the end of her first week, he went out one afternoon to do an insurance valuation. In the middle of her second week, he said, 'I'm off to view a sale. I may not be back until after lunch. You'll be able to manage won't you my dear? Ten per cent off for trade.'

It was the trade who worried her. Mr Benson had been gone about half an hour when a gingery man dressed in a check jacket and baggy corduroy trousers, strolled in, stopped short in surprise at the sight of Frances sitting behind the desk and asked in a gruff North Country accent, 'Margaret about?'

'I'm afraid not.'

The man's eyes were full of curiosity.

'Can I help?' Frances tried to look knowledgeable.

The man pondered a moment or two. 'I've got something for her,' he said, hand on the inside pocket of his well-worn jacket, 'When do you think she'll be back?'

'I don't know.'

He looked closely at Frances, with a puzzled expression. 'What are you doing here?'

'I work here.'

'Oh!' His eyebrows shot up in surprise.

'I've taken over from Margaret – just for the time being.'

'I see.' His hand moved swiftly away from his inside pocket, but not before she had had time to spot the wad of bank notes protruding from it. He stroked his ginger-stubbled chin.

'Would you like to leave – whatever it is – and I'll see she gets it when she returns.'

'Oh that won't be necessary.' He quickly buttoned his jacket and, glancing around the showroom, exclaimed, 'I can hardly recognise the place. What's been going on here?'

17

'Just a bit of sorting out.' She thought he might have acknowledged the improvement as well as the change.

'It'll be some surprise for Margaret. When did you say she'll be back?'

'I didn't. Can I give Mr Benson a message – or would you like to wait? He'll be back soon.'

'No need for that. I'd better be off.'

'Can I say who called?'

'Don't trouble yourself, my duck,' he said, and shot out of the door.

How very odd, she thought. Presumably the money she'd glimpsed was intended for Margaret, and the man didn't want to deal with Benson. He had departed rapidly at the mention of Benson's imminent return. Why? she wondered. At that moment a sinewy woman with bobbed grey hair came striding into the shop bringing with her a whiff of the golf course. 'My husband will be sixty in a month and he's always lusted after a stick barometer – do you have one?'

'We do,' said Frances, relieved to find she was able to remember seeing it.

After half an hour of praising the special qualities of stick barometers, which fortunately she had heard Mr Benson doing the previous day – this being a particularly fine one, of an earlier date than the ones shaped like banjos, in good working order and of a rich mahogany – she was delighted to make another sale.

Margaret's absence puzzled her. It appeared to have been unexpected and precipitate, judging by the number of customers expecting to find her in the shop. Working at the old electric typewriter which stood heavily on a small green baize-topped table, she was conscious of touching the keys Margaret's fingers had pressed. Sitting at Margaret's double-sided mahogany pedestal desk, she rested her elbows, as no doubt Margaret had done, on the tooled leather surface, used the telephone that sat there, scribbled messages on the memo pad, the carbon copies of which bore the imprint of Margaret's scrawling, impatient hand: messages concerning furniture sales, repairs, prices, requests for specific items, for valuations. Writing in this book, imprinting the carbons with her

18

own rounded handwriting gave Frances an uneasy feeling. Margaret's desk had two drawers in the top and four short drawers down each pedestal, all of them crammed with papers. During the first week, Frances ignored the contents of the desk, but one morning, because Mr Benson was asking for the sales book and also searching for some calculations Margaret was supposed to have made concerning the cost of repairs to a breakfront bookcase, she knew it was time to tackle the task of sorting it out. She started with the two centre drawers. These contained unfiled correspondence, copies of invoices and statements, bundles of black and white photographs of pieces of furniture, a roll of sticky labels bearing typed descriptions of each piece. There were old sale catalogues, Lot numbers ringed and priced, plus notifications from the auctioneers of prices achieved. Frances sorted out the photographs and stuck the right label onto each one. Then she filed them and some of the paperwork in the metal filing cabinet in Mr Benson's office.

In the top drawer of the right-hand pedestal she found a small blue hard-backed book containing lists of letters and numbers with names and dates beside them: purchases, she supposed. Every drawer overflowed with a jumble of rubbers and pencils, biros and paper clips, Sellotape and compliments slips, stamps and envelopes, notebooks and memo pads crammed with Margaret's flamboyant handwriting and her illegible Pitman's shorthand. Among these things, Frances found more personal reminders of Margaret: a broken pair of pink-framed sunglasses, a paperback copy of *Lace*, half-eaten tubes of Polo mints, three stained handkerchiefs, a bunch of keys, a gold cigarette lighter which did not work, a squashed packet of king-size Benson & Hedges. An empty gin bottle. A half full box of tissues held a nail file, eyebrow tweezers, a pot of green eye-shadow, a jar of vermilion nail lacquer and an atomiser scent spray of 'Femme'. Now, more than ever, Margaret's presence permeated the shop – in the faint suggestion of her scent, in the floating strands of dark hair that clung to the pink comb in the cloakroom, with the lipstick of the same brilliant red as the nail polish, lurking under the typewriter; in the small black patent leather high-heeled shoe wedged beneath the pedestal desk.

The telephone rang just as Frances was retrieving Margaret's shoe. She stood it on the desk and picked up the receiver. Before she'd had time to say more than 'Hello,' a rough voice, without any kind of preliminary greeting, launched angrily into 'What's happened to my chest of drawers?'

'I'm sorry – please could you explain. What chest of drawers?'

'Margaret? That's not Margaret.'

'No. My name is Frances Lambert.'

'Where's Margaret then?'

'She's away at present. I'm looking after things here for the time being.'

'She should have arranged delivery of my chest of drawers.'

'If you give me your name and a few details, I'll see what I can do.'

'When'll she be back?'

'I'm not sure. If you hold on, I'll put you through to Mr Benson – he'll be able to help you.'

'No need for that. I'll call again.' And the receiver was banged down.

Someone else who didn't want to talk to Mr Benson. 'Bloody rude,' said Frances aloud, just as Mr Benson appeared in front of her.

'Trouble my dear?'

'Someone wanting Margaret – complaining about a missing chest of drawers. He wouldn't talk to you. Put the phone down on me.'

'I see.' Mr Benson looked thoughtful. 'I'm sorry about that.' She noticed he had his coat on. 'Mr Benson, I'm getting a bit fed up with apologising for Margaret's absence. It would make things much easier for me if you could tell your customers what was going on.' She looked expectantly at him but he failed to react, as if he hadn't been listening to what she was saying. 'It's difficult for me – it's unprofessional to tell people I don't know where she is or when she'll be back.'

He still did not respond.

'I mean – what am I to tell people, Mr Benson?'

'That's up to you my dear,' he said finally. 'I'm just popping out for bit – won't be long.'

20

'I'll tell them she's gone into orbit, shall I?' she called after his back view.

The next person to ask for Margaret was a middle-aged man with a shock of grey hair and hard blue eyes set in a pink fleshy face. He was wearing a navy suit and carried a briefcase, and he turned up one morning when Mr Benson was attending a sale in Norwich. 'My name is Arthur Richmond.' He handed her a business card and she saw that he was the proprietor of an establishment in the King's Road specialising in antiques and fine art.

'I'm afraid Margaret isn't here.'

'Oh really!' He seemed surprised and even more so as he looked around him. 'My word! I've never seen the old place looking so spic and span.' He paused and concentrated on Frances. 'Margaret didn't say she was going away.'

'She was taken ill – very suddenly,' said Frances. Well, it wasn't her fault she had to resort to her imagination.

'I'm sorry to hear that – nothing serious I hope.'

'Women's troubles, I believe,' said Frances. 'It may take a little while to get over.'

'Poor Margaret. No doubt she'll be in touch when she's fit. And you, I presume, my dear, are here in her place.'

'Just for the time being, Mr Richmond – my name is Frances Lambert.'

'How do you do, Miss Lambert.' He smiled charmingly. 'Well – since I'm here, I'll take a look round if I may.' He began to move about the room and stopped beside the oyster-veneered cabinet on stand.

It was easy to see why the cabinet was described as 'oyster-veneered', she thought, for the whorled knots of wood resembled the configuration of an oyster shell.

Arthur Richmond opened the doors, pulled out each internal drawer and examined them. 'William and Mary – new stand of course – how much?'

Ten percent off for trade, Mr Benson had said. Frances looked at the ticket and did sums in her head. 'Twelve thousand six hundred.'

'Hmmn.' He'd moved round and was examining a pair of small ornamental stands made of brass with two little shelves of rosewood, suitable for displaying bric à brac. 'And the étagères?'

21

She checked the price. They were marked at £1,950. Maths had not been her strong point at school. She paused before saying, 'One thousand seven hundred and fifty-five.'

'You'll have to do better than that – there's some work been done on these.' He drew a finger dismissively along the brass edging of one of the shelves and continued to the small brass pineapple finial at the corner.

'I can't give you more than ten per cent – but Mr Benson will be back soon. You could talk to him about them.'

He'd moved away from the étagères. 'What about the Pembroke table?'

The Pembroke table was a beauty. She didn't know why it was called a Pembroke table – perhaps after someone named Pembroke? She could picture an aristocratic lady in a powdered wig, eating supper off its oval surface – the two leaves extended – firelight flickering over the lustrous mahogany. She'd heard Mr Benson extolling the virtues of its reeded fluted legs to a customer the day before.

'Nice crossbanding,' she ventured, having also just learned the technical term for the narrow edging of lighter wood set across the grain. The table was marked £3,850. 'The price is three thousand four hundred and sixty-five,' she said crisply.

'Hmmn – it's right, which is more than you can say for the étagères – how much did you say they were?'

Frances tried to remember what she had quoted him. 'One seven five five.'

'And the mahogany tallboy with the canted corners?'

The tallboy was the chest on a chest and the top chest had its corners flattened off at an oblique angle. She walked over and looked at the ticket, did another sum in her head: three three five off three three five zero. 'Three thousand and fifteen,' she said.

'And how much did you quote me for the oyster cabinet?'

Her hands began to sweat. The figure had fled from her head but she wasn't going to lose face by sneaking another look at the ticket. He was trying to confuse her, the swine. And all with a charming paternal smile. She tried to visualise the black figures on the white ticket. And they came. A lot of money. 'Twelve thousand six hundred,' she said deadpan.

He opened the doors of the cabinet, pulled out all the internal drawers once more, examined each one carefully. Then he went out of the main showroom and into the back of the shop where she could hear him moving around. When he came back, he said, 'The pair of bookcases with the cupboard bases and glazed astragal doors aren't priced.'

'Let me see,' said Frances and walked over with him to examine the bookcases. Dentil cornice, she thought, the architectural term surfacing from somewhere. Edged with reeded columns.

'They're not right of course – designer pieces really.'

'I'm sorry I can't give you a price,' said Frances, disliking this soft-spoken man. 'I'll ask Mr Benson to get in touch.'

'Can hardly sell them as antique can you?'

Frances didn't respond, having nothing to say about the bookcases, which looked fine to her.

'The Pembroke,' said Mr Richmond suddenly. 'How much did you say for the Pembroke?'

Think, she told herself. Don't be fazed. 'Three and a half thousand,' she replied.

'Is that so?' They both knew this was higher than the original figure quoted. I bet you don't treat Margaret like this, she thought. You're annoyed she isn't here and you're meanly taking advantage of my inexperience.

To her relief, he consulted his watch and said, 'I've a train to catch – can you call me a taxi? I'll talk to Tommy about the table.'

After he'd gone, she went and sat down at her desk. There was Margaret's shoe standing just where she had left it. Obeying some inner compulsion, Frances found herself taking the smart little shoe in her hand and then, after kicking off her own shoe, she slipped her foot inside. It fitted perfectly. A prickling sensation ran oddly up her spine at the touch of the cold leather, as if she had half anticipated a residual warmth from Margaret's foot. Horrified, she wrenched off the shoe. Then, all in a rush, she gathered Margaret's possessions together, packed them rapidly into a box, crammed the box into the bottom drawer of the right-hand pedestal of the desk, and pushed it firmly closed.

Chapter Four

One Saturday evening, Mark took Frances out to dinner. The restaurant was Swiss. There was a cheerful log fire and everything was warm and bright and clean. The pine tables had been scrubbed to the colour of set clover honey and were laid with blue and white gingham table mats and napkins. An outsize cuckoo clock and pictures of the Alps at every season of the year hung on the walls. While they ate cheese fondue, gradually, in a guarded kind of way, they began to get to know each other. By the time they were on to their second bottle of wine Frances felt bold enough to ask Mark if he had a girlfriend. He didn't answer immediately. Then, with a half smile, he said, 'Put it like this – I don't have a serious relationship. I wouldn't be asking you out if I did.'

With her forefinger, she traced one of the blue squares on the table mat. 'I had what I thought was a serious relationship. But it broke up.'

'Poor you.'

'I'm not quite over it.'

He let this confession settle and then he said, 'Is there any chance you'll get back together?'

'No.'

She was grateful he asked no further questions but, nevertheless, felt a sudden urge to talk about it. She'd had no one to talk to for so long. 'It was all confused with my mother dying you see. I loved my mother – but I don't think I coped very well with her dying.'

'It must have been very hard.'

'He was good to me then. The man I was with.' She felt the

hot tears at the back of her eyes. 'It happened so quickly. My mother had to stay in hospital for a course of radiotherapy. When it was finished I wanted to take her home and look after her. But they wouldn't let me. She was only fifty when she died.'

Mark leaned towards her across the table and said gently. 'You don't have to put yourself through all this you know.' He topped up her wine glass.

During those final, desperate weeks, Frances was spending more nights with Felix in his flat in Pimlico than she was in the flat she officially shared with her friend Clare in Kennington. But Clare was often out with her boyfriend and when she wasn't, the two of them were in the flat. They were kind, Clare and Robert, but absorbed with each other.

It was Felix she came to after the hospital visits. The hospital visits which made her feel as if her heart was being wrenched from her body. It was unbearable – watching Mother fading away. Felix gave her strength and comfort. In bed with Felix, the future did not seem so empty. She thought, 'I love Felix'.

Mark was looking at her kindly, silently. Frances took a sip of wine and said, 'I was working for him you see. So when we broke up, I packed in my job.'

From the beginning she had felt at home in those tall light rooms, Andy and Peter solidly at their drawing boards, Felix everywhere, rolls of drawings, fabric samples, tiles, paint charts, scraps of carpeting. It was fun working for Felix. She admired his flair and self-confidence and was grateful for the way he paid attention to her ideas. She never forgot how, at the very beginning of their time together, he commended her tentative suggestion that grey walls might look good with white paint work.

It was too close, their working relationship, for them to remain at arm's length.

Felix had a client who bought a holiday house in the mountains above the Rhône. He said, 'I need to go to France to look at this house of Gerry's. It's been empty for a year and he wants it gutted and extended. I'd like you to come with me and help to get out a scheme for him.'

They flew to Lyon, hired a car and drove to Valence, where

they turned off the autoroute. At the end of a narrow mountain road, they found the house which was built of stone with a roof of rust-coloured Roman tiles. For three days she helped plan, took measurements. Felix made sketches. 'We'll put the kitchen here and build a terrace leading out of it, to take advantage of the view – they'll eat out here – a trellis for a vine to provide shade.' Mountains stretched away into the distance. 'Swimming pool below – steps down from the main bedroom.'

She looked at the blue hills and the yellow sun and imagined the kitchen with a flagged floor, cast-iron cooking pots, pottery bowls, bunches of herbs, paintings in primary colours.

They stayed in a small hotel in the valley. After dinner the first night – magret of duck and Côte du Rhône – he said, 'You look so lovely – I want to make love to you.' She felt a kind of lurch inside, thought guiltily of Joe far away in Edinburgh – looked into Felix's dark eyes, and was lost.

Mark was silent, drinking his wine. No doubt he guessed the man she was in love with was married.

Frances had always known about Esme, who lived in Sussex with her and Felix's teenage son Jeremy. But Felix said he and Esme were legally separated, soon to be divorced.

It took her a long time to realise that Felix's need for love, his skill in obtaining love far outweighed his capacity to give it. Nevertheless, he had cared for her when she was at her lowest. She remembered the feel of his hands gently stroking her face when she told him about her mother's cancer. 'You're having a rough time aren't you,' he said. And she laid her head against his chest, and wept.

But Felix was fickle and he had a low threshold of boredom. After her mother died, dependent and afraid, Frances could sense him making time for her and beginning to begrudge it. He'd done his duty, seen her through the worst, but that was over now. She was no longer able to entertain him. Diminished by his inattention, she forced him to tell her where she stood with him. He was evasive but when pressed, he told her Jeremy was smoking pot and Esme was on the verge of a nervous breakdown. 'I have to face up to my responsibilities,' he said. She couldn't argue with that and he did look pretty wretched. The worst bit was when he said, 'We'll still be working together – I'll see you every day – and there's always the Pimlico flat – we can be together there.'

'No,' she yelled. 'I won't be your bit on the side.' He seemed stunned by her rage.

A waitress in a gingham apron approached with a platter of apple strudel and Frances brought herself back to the present and lifted her eyes to Mark's.

'Well, here's to your new job.' He raised his glass. She raised hers and they clinked them together and drank.

'So how's it going then? Do you get on all right with old Benson?'

'He's not exactly forthcoming – quite pleasant. But it's an odd feeling you know, suddenly taking on someone's job while they're still supposed to be doing it. It's as if she's at my elbow, checking up on me. And peculiar people come into the shop to see her – and ring up for her. No one seems to know she's gone away. And from what little Mr Benson says, I don't think she'll be back for a while.'

'That's good from your point of view isn't it.'

'Of course, though I can only think of this as temporary. But I don't mind. I quite like not being able to look ahead and know this time next year I'll be doing exactly what I'm doing now. Security can be awfully inhibiting.'

'I don't agree. I think having the framework of a regular job and a settled home can give you the freedom to plan ahead without worrying. I'm lucky – I enjoy my job – get on pretty well with my father, considering we work together. But of course I don't live at home. I have a flat in Fressenworth.'

How interesting, she thought, that he still refers to his parents' house as home. But then, Sevenoaks had been home to her while Mother was there.

'You'll probably get fed up and clear off back to London in the end,' said Mark. 'It won't be exciting enough for you around here.'

'What makes you think I want excitement?'

'Oh I don't know. There's a certain restless feel about you.'

'But I have my lovely farmhouse you didn't want me to buy. I won't leave that in a hurry.'

'How are the builders getting on?'

'Ted doesn't approve of my plumbing and cooking arrange-

27

ments. But he's agreed to get the stove back in working order, and then I'll cook you Sunday lunch. Roast beef and Yorkshire pudding with nice thick gravy and horseradish sauce.'

'Sounds terrific. I'll have a go at those nettles for you. I think we've got a scythe somewhere hanging around at home which I can probably use without chopping off my leg.'

'Thanks.' She flashed him a smile. 'I want to plant a flower garden – and I thought I might get ducks for the pond – or even some geese.'

'Oh I wouldn't do that. Geese can be fierce and they make a lot of noise.'

'Well – they'd be like guard dogs. After all, as you kept pointing out, I do live in an isolated position.'

'It would be more sensible to fit a burglar alarm.'

Chapter Five

Frances met Victor Howden for the first time one wet April afternoon. Mr Benson was out doing a valuation and Frances had been watching the rain sweeping down in icy drifts, gusted against the windows by the arctic north-east wind. Out in the street, water hissed in muddy fountains from the wheels of cars, and people struggled to control umbrellas which threatened to turn themselves inside out. The fine soft days at the beginning of the month might never have been: a false spring.

A shadow darkened the glass door, the cowbell tinkled and he stood just inside the shop, rain dripping from his Burberry mackintosh. He took off his dark wide-brimmed hat and shook water from it, revealing hair as smooth and shiny as black plate glass, crinkled at the temples and on the thick neck. The merest inclination of his head and a narrowing of the eyes told her he was instantly aware of everything in the room, especially her. He unbuttoned his mackintosh, beneath which he wore a dark pinstripe suit. He approached. She rose and came out from behind the desk, noticing the curve of a gold watch-chain, the burgundy of a silk shirt. His hand, when he extended it towards her, was lightly furred with curling black hairs. A gold signet ring gleamed.

'We haven't met – my name is Vic Howden.'

She put her hand in his. The name seemed familiar. 'Hello – I'm Frances Lambert.' His strong grip made her own small hand feel frail. He held it for longer than was usual, as if memorising it.

'And you work here now?'

'For the time being – until Margaret gets back. But of

29

course, you must know Margaret.'

'That's right.' His eyes flicked away from Frances to a small satinwood chest that stood against the wall. He strolled over to it, opened the drawers, ran a hand inside each, stood back, scrutinised the chest as he had scrutinised Frances. 'Handles aren't original and it's a little red. Too much money of course.' He glanced around the shop and then, switching his gaze back to her, concentrated his protuberant eyes upon hers. 'There are quite a few changes here.' A pinpoint of light seemed to flare and Frances regretted her mother's training to 'always look people honestly in the eye.' She moved back a couple of steps. He acknowledged this conscious distancing with an amused twitch of his mouth. 'All right if I take a look round?' And he turned away and began to prowl round the shop.

She sat down behind the desk and watched covertly. Vic Howden. She was right – the name was familiar. She thought of the very first time she came here. Saw herself talking to Mr Benson, remembered the two young men loading 'Mr Howden's furniture'. They'd complained about the size and weight of the pieces. Mr Howden was clearly a dealer of substance. She wondered where he had his business. In his deep voice, the faintly flattened vowels held the hint of an accent – not Kent, not quite South London. He was perhaps forty-five.

It was a relief when he went out into the hall. She heard him in the room behind, turning keys, opening drawers, swivelling table tops. For someone familiar with the place, he seemed to be spending an inordinate amount of time examining the stock. Perhaps her reorganisation had revealed goods he hadn't seen before, or perhaps Mr Benson had bought several new pieces since his last visit. He spent the best part of an hour looking round. When he returned to the front showroom, he came and stood in front of Frances as she sat at Margaret's desk. 'Tell Benson I'll give him five grand for the satinwood chest – I'll call him.' He took out his watch on its gold chain. 'One o'clock – what do you do for lunch, Frances Lambert?' He fixed her with glossy eyes.

Appalled, she felt the stirrings of sexual attraction. Why? He was awful. Much older than she and arrogant.

'I have to stay in the shop when Mr Benson's out.' She felt

30

herself flush and dropped her eyes.

'Another time?'

'I probably won't be here.' She fitted a piece of paper into the typewriter. Howden shrugged into his Burberry and picked up his hat. 'I hope you will,' he said. 'Goodbye for now.' He walked over to the door, opened it and went out without looking back. She watched him cross the road and get into a silver Mercedes estate car parked on a single yellow line.

'What did he want?' asked Sidney with rare loquacity, coming through from the workshop just in time to see Howden's departing back view.

'To look round. He might buy the satinwood chest.'

'Would choose to come when the guv'nor's out.'

'You think he did it on purpose?'

'Maybe. They done business for years – very pally with Margaret.'

'Mr Howden?'

'That's what I said.'

'Perhaps he came in to see her then.'

'She bid for him. Mr Benson don't like it, but he can't stop her. Margaret do what she want.'

'If he knew her that well – he'd know she wouldn't be here. Where is Margaret?'

Sidney's face took on a stubborn set, the jaw clamping tightly shut, the eyes suddenly opaque, more than ever like beach pebbles. 'Ask Mr Benson. I can't stay here all day gossiping.' He turned and went out of the room, the rubber soles of his shoes squeaking on the linoleum.

Frances had Ted build her a small terrace on the western side of the farmhouse, where it would catch the afternoon sun. It was constructed from weathered paving stones she found in a demolition yard. One Sunday evening she and Mark were lounging companionably there in the old cane chairs she had bought from the shop, watching the sun slip down the sky, spilling orange light over the fields of young corn. They had eaten what should have been Sunday lunch, but turned into supper because they'd spent all day working in the garden. Frances had weeded and dug over the one discernible flower bed. Mark, stripped to the waist, had scythed nettles. Looking

31

at him now, his long legs stretched in front of him, arms resting loosely in his lap, she remembered how the sun had struck silver sparks off the flashing blade, and how the sweat had shone on the corded muscles of his arms and back as he swung the scythe with increasing confidence, felling swathes of sappy nettles. She hadn't watched anyone scything before. It called to mind farm boys in nineteenth century English landscape paintings and, more fancifully, bronze statues of Greek athletes. He's got a good body, she thought, well proportioned, strong. He is good looking in an almost classical way. But I do not, at present, find him physically attractive. She liked him. He was dependable, pleasantly easy-going, uncomplicated. The sort of person who makes a perfect friend. The claret he'd brought along, to drink with the meal, had made her comfortably drowsy. She glanced up at his face, preparing a friendly smile. He was watching her. Their eyes met. And there it was. Without either of them saying a word or moving a fraction, the atmosphere became charged. She could not stir – even to raise her glass to her lips. She did not want this. She did not want to be wanted – to be affected by it. She thought involuntarily of Vic Howden's glossy eyes. There seemed no getting away from sex. And then, with a sudden rush of longing, she thought of Felix. Panic set her heart racing and freed her locked muscles. Clumsily, she scrambled to her feet, banging her thigh against the table. 'I'll put the kettle on – make some coffee.'

He smiled a little wistfully, 'If that's what you'd like.'

She brought out the mugs of coffee, steaming in the cooler air. The sun had almost dropped to the horizon. A fish leaped in the overgrown pond and a blackbird called from the depths of the hawthorn thicket. They sipped their coffee in silence. After a while, Frances said, 'Tell me Mark – how well do you know Margaret?'

'Margaret?' he sounded surprised. 'She's just someone who's been around for ages. I see her when I go in to the shop. I have dealings with her from time to time. The old boy buys goods from the sales we run and occasionally sells through us too. She bids for him. I sometimes think he gives her too much leeway.'

'What do you mean?' She found herself thinking about the odd people who turned up at the shop looking for Margaret and managed to avoid being referred to Benson.

'Oh – nothing specific. He's getting a bit slack I suppose and she's been with him for yonks. He's something of a recluse now and I think he's probably let her get the upper hand. Poor old sod. I suppose he feels he can't manage without her.'

'Well he is, isn't he,' said Frances sharply. 'Managing without her.'

'That's right.' He smiled at her good-humouredly. 'And, you must admit, the place looks a lot better since I've been there to sort things out.'

'I believe that's always been a bone of contention between them. Benson's too mean to employ a cleaning woman and Margaret would never consider that kind of thing to be part of her duties.'

'How old is she? What does she look like?'

'Oh forty-ish. Quite smart. I think the word is gamine. Very small. Black straight hair with a fringe. Sometimes wears glasses, tinted with gold frames. Talks very fast.'

'Married?'

'Margaret? Good Lord no. Very much the single woman – not spinsterish though – independent. Something rather tough about her.'

'Attractive?'

'If you like that sort of thing.'

'Men friends?'

'I daresay. I really don't know.' An irritable tone had crept into his voice.

'Where does she live?'

'Oh some village the other side of Halesworth I believe. I'm bored with talking about Margaret. You are far more interesting – why don't we talk about you?' He put out a hand and gently took hers. She didn't resist him but when he slid his other arm round her shoulders and eased her towards him, it felt wrong. She tensed. Caught her breath. He removed his arm. She relaxed and leaned back in her chair. It suddenly seemed very quiet. The birds had stopped singing and there was not a breath of wind. Behind Mark's glasses, his eyes were unreadable.

33

Chapter Six

'You'll have to go and bid for me at Royton Park – I'm not up to it.' Mr Benson was wheezing into his handkerchief. A heavy cold had kept him home for a couple of days and now he looked as if he should still be in bed. His thin wrinkled cheeks, normally pale, were faintly flushed, his sharp grey eyes watery and bright. His breath rasped in his lungs and his back was more bowed than usual as if it was painful for him to straighten up.

'Shouldn't you go home Mr Benson – you look as if you've got a temperature.'

'I'm all right,' he said testily. 'Now here's the catalogue – I've marked the lot numbers. Identify yourself to the auctioneer when you arrive – say you're bidding for me – they'll give you a number. I've marked the items I want you to bid for and the prices to go to.'

'I've never been to a sale before.'

'Well then it'll be a little adventure for you won't it.' Mr Benson blew his nose. 'Don't get carried away and go on bidding above those prices mind – and get yourself some lunch – there'll be someone doing food.' He thrust into her hand the catalogue, a map with Royton Park marked on it and a crumpled ten-pound note. 'Run along then.'

Half an hour later, Frances turned off the main road as instructed, and followed a narrow rutted track flanked by fields. The car clattered over a couple of cattle grids and then she was driving through park land. Ancient trees, beech and oak, chestnut and ash, were just coming into leaf. In bleak contrast, a line of dead elms stood like black skeletons starkly against the pale sky. A lake glittered, flat as a looking glass. The classical façade came into view behind cedar trees, imposing, pedimented. A few days previously this house had been bought by a consortium of farmers, along with 3,000 acres of farmland, and the last descendant of the nobleman who built the mansion in the mid eighteenth century, left it for ever to end her days in a home for gentlefolk.

Sunlight warmed the grey stone and Frances saw the tall pillars of a colonnade, the glint of a glass conservatory, decorative stone balustrading, and then the utilitarian canvas of the marquee in which the contents of Royton Park were to be sold.

She parked the Peugeot in a muddy field, lining it up with the Volvo estate cars favoured by dealers. Pleased she'd put on flat-heeled shoes, grasping her catalogue, she set off over the soft ground, through the terraced remains of a formal rose garden, to the marquee. The auctioneers were Mark's firm, Harrison and Draper. Would he be here? An efficient-looking girl wearing tinted spectacles and a red blazer sat at a table to the entrance to the marquee. She gave Frances a bidding number. 'Mr Draper's over there.' She waved a well-manicured hand towards the auctioneer's rostrum, around which milled a group of people holding sheaves of papers. Mr Draper, tall, dark-haired, soberly suited and forty-fivish with lean cheeks and astute eyes, acknowledged she would be bidding for Benson Antiques, and registered the unfamiliarity of her face without comment. Mark was nowhere to be seen, and she felt rather relieved he wouldn't be here to see her make a fool of herself. Nervously, she examined the unfamiliar surroundings and faces.

The sale would start in half an hour. People crowded into the large marquee where rows of folding chairs faced the rostrum behind which stood some of the furniture to be sold, as it did also around the perimeter of the tent. Wardrobes, tables, bureaux, cabinets, chests of drawers, stacked chairs, sofas. Another tent contained more and there were trestle tables laden with china, glass, books, pictures and household utensils. Clothes hung forlornly on rails. Faded velvet curtains, rolls of carpet, oriental rugs lay upon the ground. The dealers prowled, pulling out drawers, examining veneers, measuring widths and heights, turning over chairs. Women in quilted anoraks and head scarves searched for bargains. Men in tweed jackets and boots, accompanied by labrador dogs, rested on shooting sticks, and young mothers tried to keep control of little children. Frances watched and listened.

'Uncle Eric has a wash-stand just like that – what do you think it'll make?'

'Jenny, come and look at this woodworm.'

'Not a complete set of course.'

'Feet aren't original.'

Frances examined her catalogue. Having previewed the sale, Mr Benson had ringed lot numbers and put a price beside each one. He had marked eleven items: a couple of tripod tables, an East Anglian press chest, a mahogany bow chest, a satinwood inlaid card table, a rosewood whatnot, a mahogany demi-lune sideboard, a walnut kneehole writing desk, a rosewood sofa table, a walnut canterbury and an English lacquered cabinet 'in the oriental taste'.

The next thing was to identify the pieces. She found the kneehole writing desk first. She ran a hand over the cracked walnut veneer, lifted the folding top, folded it back, let down the secretaire front and pulled out one of the small internal drawers in what she hoped looked like a professional manner.

''Ello darlin'. A touch on her arm. She turned. Smooth black hair, sharp boot button eyes, baggy striped trousers and a dusty black coat too long for his short frame. A cheeky smile. 'Don't remember me do yer?' He held out a hand. 'Ronnie Fletcher – I come into the shop the other day.'

How could she forget him? 'You sold Mr Benson a table.'

'Mahogany drop-leaf – nice condition.' He was pumping her hand. 'Benson 'ere?'

'No.'

'Going to introduce us, Ronnie?' They were joined by a taller man, a fur-collared parka over his thin brown suit, a check cap on his brown hair. He clapped Fletcher on the arm, looking appreciatively at Frances out of slanting pale blue eyes.

'This young lady's here for Benson – what's yer name darlin'?'

'Frances Lambert.'

'Frances – that's a nice name. I'm Trevor Briggs – pleased

36

to meet you.' He shook her hand. 'Have you taken over from Margaret then?'

'That's right.'

They regarded her enigmatically. She stared back – enigmatically – she hoped.

'Nice piece.' Ronnie stroked the kneehole desk tenderly with stubby fingers.

'Yes.'

He lifted the top, folded down the front and pulled out a drawer, turning it over thoughtfully. 'Benson interested in it?'

'He might be.'

'And you,' he said. 'Are you interested in the goods or the money?' He smiled knowingly and winked one of his sharp black eyes.

Not knowing what to make of this question, she tried to assume a considering expression.

Trevor filled the silence hastily. 'Careful Ronnie – perhaps this young lady isn't familiar with the sale room like Margaret is. First time you've bid at a auction, is it, Frances?'

She looked back steadily, deciding to bluff. 'I wouldn't say that.'

Ronnie said, 'She knows what she's about Trevor. Are you workin' today, darlin'?' Again the knowing smile and when she didn't reply immediately, he added, 'Margaret do as a rule.' He replaced the desk drawer, traced the outline of the little brass handle with his forefinger.

'Of course,' said Frances recklessly. 'Just pretend I'm Margaret.'

'We'll keep an eye on you Frances – you'll be all right.' Trevor grinned, displaying a mouthful of teeth too even to be natural.

'You'll have to excuse me now,' she said. 'I want to look at something else.'

''Course you do – ta-ta for now then Frances.'

She moved away thankfully, spotting the lacquered cabinet. Ronnie and Trevor melted into the crowd, but ten minutes or so later she saw them standing in a group of dealers all thumbing through catalogues. There was a slim young man with a brown moustache and a weasel face wearing a sports jacket; another young man, well set-up wearing laced leather boots over

37

skintight jeans, a long suede coat, unbuttoned, showing a red and white spotted scarf knotted at the neck, and on his head a black homburg hat. He was smoking a cigar. A fat middle-aged man with a red face, wearing cavalry twill trousers and a vast shapeless pale jacket, sucked at a pipe and stroked his small goatee beard. A swarthy man leaned upon a silver-topped cane, gesticulating with his free hand as he talked. At his side, like a bodyguard, bulged a huge man in a tight brown suit with a colourful kipper tie.

As, covertly, she watched the band of men, she saw Ronnie say something and glance in her direction. As a result of what he said, all the men in the group turned to look at her. She felt hot with embarrassment. An exhibit, like the furniture, conspicuous, unprotected, threatened. She made herself examine the little gold Chinese figures on the chest before her, touch the twisting oriental trees, the plumed birds, the ornamental bridges and pagodas of another country.

The buzz of conversation subsided. The sale began. Frances sat down on a folding chair, with the catalogue, a ballpoint pen and Mr Benson's list. The tent flapped in the gusty spring breeze and there was a muddy smell of trampled grass.

Mr Draper was brisk and businesslike, witty and flamboyant, a calculating showman. The speed with which he raced through the lots – his very swiftness pushing up the prices – the dramatic decisive crack with which he brought down the hammer held Frances spellbound. His shrewd eyes were everywhere, a lock of black hair falling over his high forehead, the strong voice carrying to the back of the marquee.

He sold the pictures first. The eighteenth and nineteenth century English and Dutch school landscape paintings 'after' Hobbema, Constable and Turner; idealised pastoral scenes. The 'Gainsboroughs' and the 'Van Dykes': stylised tableaux of poker-faced children posing in uncomfortable clothes with animals or musical instruments; languorous ladies with alabaster complexions and elaborate coiffures reclining on chaise-longues; stern gentlemen in military dress mounted on stately horses. Family portraits. Frances wondered if some distant descendant might put in a bid for an ancestor. Perhaps the stout old girl with wispy hair in the shapeless tweed suit? The athletic young woman in jeans and fringed jacket accompanied by a couple of fat spaniels? The thin man, hunched as a bent stick, in khaki waterproof jacket and deerstalker hat?

'A hundred for it? Eighty? Seventy I'm bid – five – eighty – five – ninety – five – a hundred – one hundred pounds I'm bid – one hundred and ten against you seated now – twenty – forty – fifty – two hundred pounds – two hundred pounds at the back there – two hundred pounds only – are you all done now? I sell at two hundred pounds.' Two hundred pounds for a melancholic man and a dappled grey horse with pricked ears and watchful eyes. Somebody's great grandfather.

The sale progressed, carried along swingingly by its own momentum. She marked in prices, comparing them with the listed estimates in the loose-leaf front of the catalogue. There was plenty of latitude, either way.

By twelve-thirty, Mr Draper had sold 200 lots. He was half way through the china and glass. It would be an hour before any of her lots came up – time to get something to eat.

There was a queue for refreshments, so she went into the garden to look at the house. She wandered through a dilapidated Victorian conservatory dotted with dead plants and broken stone seats. Once it would have burgeoned with palms and luscious creepers. Water would have cascaded from the stone fountain, now cracked and green. She left the sad conservatory and crossed a balustraded terrace leading to the Tuscan colonnade. Built on to the house in the late eighteenth century, this had been partially destroyed by a fire which swept through it one and a half centuries later, leaving its fluted pillars black and flaking. On the west side of the house the windows were shuttered, blank as closed eyes. Peering through a crack in an ill-fitting shutter, she saw a high room with a carved mantel, an ornate plasterwork ceiling and dusty floorboards. A broken broom lay beside a pile of rubbish.

In the catering tent she bought a slice of mushroom quiche and a cup of coffee and took them into the rose garden, where stood some rusty garden furniture. She sat down upon an iron chair among roses tangling over a broken trellis, and bit into the quiche, feeling the sun warm on her cheek.

'Hullo Frances Lambert.' A shadow blocked the sunlight. Vic Howden stood smiling down at her. 'May I join you?'

Surprise turned the quiche into an unswallowable lump, preventing her from replying, and in no time he had pulled up a broken chair and sat down, setting a glass of whisky on the table. He fixed his eyes upon her face. 'I saw you sitting quiet as a mouse marking in the prices.'

She felt acute discomfort.

He took a mouthful of whisky, looked into her face and said, 'Ronnie and Trevor tell me they've had a word with you.'

'Yes.' As she spoke Ronnie and Trevor appeared as if he had conjured them, emerging from a tunnel of overgrown rose arbour like hunting animals, loaded with cans of beer and plates of sandwiches. Ronnie winked at her. Trevor smiled and raised his cap, and they both nodded respectfully at Howden before settling down on a rustic bench in a patch of sunlight, and opening their beer cans.

'I understand you're working,' Howden said with deliberation.

Why did they all treat her like a child? 'That's right,' she said.

'Good.' His eyes were still fixed upon her face and she felt her cheeks redden. 'Just checking.' He smiled, took a large cigar from his pocket, unwrapped it and lit up.

Watching him, Frances heard Sidney's voice echo in her head. 'Very pally with Margaret. Gets her to bid for him. Benson don't like it. Margaret always do what she want.'

'I believe Margaret is a friend of yours, Mr Howden,' said Frances.

'What makes you think that?'

'Oh I don't know.' Frances waved her hands around airily. 'Something I must have picked up.'

He said, 'Dealers know each other – it's a small world – I've done business with Margaret over the years. Clever woman.'

The gold signet ring on his little finger gleamed in the sun. Smoke from his cigar swirled between them. She thought about referring to the uncertain date of Margaret's return, but was reluctant to reveal her own ignorance. Howden raised the cigar to his lips and drew on it. Then he pulled out the gold watch on its chain and examined it. Among the casually dressed majority, he seemed oddly formal in his suit of grey

40

flannel complete with waistcoat.

'Come along my dear – we'll miss our lots.'

As she rose, smoothly he took her arm and guided her back to the marquee. She felt imprisoned by his light grip. Her apparent intimacy with Vic Howden was not lost upon Ronnie and Trevor who paused in their consumption of sandwiches to smile knowingly. Once in the sale tent, Frances extricated herself and chose a seat two-thirds back and to the left of the auctioneer. Howden was behind and to her right. Ronnie, Trevor and the other dealers stood at the back. With quickening heart, she opened the catalogue. Twenty lots to go before the kneehole desk. When she took up her ballpoint, her palms were sweating.

Mr Draper, raucous, commanding, jacket dashingly open, was enjoying himself. 'Lot four hundred and sixty-eight – the walnut kneehole writing desk with folding top and secretaire drawer with fitted interior.' There was an anticipatory stir in the tent – this was an important piece. A lad in a white coat pointed to it with a stick.

'Who will start me off now? Two thousand for it – two thousand – two thousand I'm bid – two thousand five hundred.' (Mr Benson had marked it £6,000.) 'Two thousand five hundred – eight – two thousand eight hundred – three thousand, three thousand I'm bid – three thousand two hundred.'

The adrenaline spurted sharp in Frances's stomach. She held up her catalogue.

'Five – eight – three thousand eight hundred, three thousand eight hundred – standing at the back, three thousand eight hundred – nine.'

She couldn't see who was bidding against her. 'Four thousand, four thousand for the eighteenth-century kneehole writing desk.'

Frances waved her catalogue.

'Four thousand I'm bid – any advance on four thousand – four thousand then – it's with the lady seated – are you all done now?' He waited a moment, looked round expectantly and then, 'The walnut kneehole desk for four thousand pounds to the lady.' He brought down the hammer.

Frances brought down the hand clutching the catalogue, and held up her bidding number with the other hand. Draper cried

'Benson' in a ringing voice and the desk was hers for £2,000 less than Benson's figure and £3,000 less than the top estimate in the loose leaf at the front of the catalogue. Flushed with success, she marked the lot number with a triumphant tick and £4,000.

She bought the demi-lune sideboard for £2,100 and the rosewood sofa table for £4,000, each time feeling a dart of excitement as Mr Draper pronounced 'Benson' in his carrying voice. She got the card table for £1,200 and the bow chest for £300. Everything she bought went for considerably less than Mr Benson had indicated. After a while the hot glow of success tempered to a cold sweat of apprehension. It shouldn't be as easy as this. Bidding for the Norfolk chest, she suspected she was the only serious bidder. At the raising of her catalogue the competition seemed to fall away. In a couple of hours she had bought all the pieces Benson had singled out, well below his estimates.

Uneasily, she watched Draper continue to conduct the sale with practised flamboyance. The black moustached man with the silver-topped cane bought an enormous George III D-ended extending dining table and a set of eight nineteenth century Chippendale style dining chairs. And then she watched the battle between this man and Howden for a mahogany bureau cabinet with a splendid broken pediment, the cabinet top edged with fluted pilasters topped with carved Corinthian capitals. Howden lost but he made his adversary pay £17,000 for it. Lighting up a cigar, Howden didn't look like a defeated man. Her stomach contracted with something akin to fear as she watched the careful hands shielding the flame, the full lips encircling the rounded end of the fat brown cigar.

Suddenly, she had had enough. She left her seat and queued with the other buyers to collect her receipts from the auctioneer. The sale was drawing to a close, dwindling away in a dribble of minor artifacts. Mr Draper's replacement – a thin young man in a blue suit – sold off the rolls of dusty Persian carpets, the faded velvet and chintz curtains, the pink hunting coats, the forlorn box of medals and ribbons, the bearskin busby in its tin box, the ceremonial sword and the malacca walking sticks, the bowlers and top hats.

She reached the head of the queue, and explained that

Benson would settle the bill the next day. The girl acknowledged the familiar name. Frances collected the paperwork and turned to go.

'You done well.' Ronnie Fletcher was waiting outside the marquee. 'We'll load up for you.' He was confidential, intimate.

'No thank you,' she said coldly. 'Mr Benson will be sending the van to collect our furniture tomorrow.' She walked briskly away from him. He followed, touched her arm. 'You've got to get it away.'

She shrugged him off.

'Sorry darlin' but you wasn't thinkin' of clearin' off was you? Without offerin' your lots?'

'I don't know what you're talking about.' She was suddenly sick with apprehension.

'Ronald dear boy where are your manners?' Skilfully, Vic Howden disentangled Frances from Fletcher's anxious hands.

Panic bubbling up, Frances dodged away from Howden and stumbled towards the field where the cars were parked. The two men followed. She heard Howden mutter something to Fletcher who dropped back. She reached her car and got out the key. Howden was behind her. 'Don't rush off my dear.'

'Why not? I've finished my business,' she said briskly.

'Miss Lambert. Frances. I may call you Frances? You know perfectly well you haven't finished your business here today.'

'I don't know what you're talking about,' she said, with more bravado than she felt.

'You did very well.' He put his hand on her arm as she made to fit the key in her car door. She shook him off, catching her breath. Howden said calmly, 'Come on now, it's a bit late in the day to plead the innocent. I don't know exactly what you said to Fletcher and Briggs, but they were confident you knew what you were doing.'

'I said nothing.'

'You seemed quite clear about our arrangement at lunchtime.' The smile stretched, revealing gold fillings. There was a gleam of amusement in the glossy eyes. 'You're just pretending, aren't you? You're just pretending you didn't know what was going on. You can't really expect to get away with that, my dear.'

43

A flash of insight flared in her brain. She lifted her head defiantly and looked him in the eye. 'I know Margaret used to bid for you Mr Howden. But I was bidding for Mr Benson. And now I'm going home.'

'No, my dear. You were bidding for *me*. And you are *not* going home.'

His smile was smooth and he pitched his voice low, as if reasoning with a disobedient child. 'It was a good try.' And now there was no mistaking the underlying note of menace, 'But you wouldn't have bought those pieces for anything like that money if I'd not known you were settling.'

On the periphery of her vision she became aware of Ronnie and Trevor and several of the dealers she had noticed earlier at the sale. She caught a glimpse of a brown moustache, a long suede coat brushing laced boots, a round red face. They were gathering like cruising sharks.

'Settling?' She heard the quaver in her voice, as she tried once more to fit the key to her car door with trembling fingers. He didn't attempt to stop her this time. He just said, in that same silky voice with its undertow of menace. 'You'll be putting your goods up.'

'Putting my goods up?'

'At the Knock-Out – the Settlement – along with the rest of us.'

Put your goods up. Offer your lots. Realisation came with a gut-wrenching spasm inside. Unwittingly, she must have got herself involved in something she had only vaguely heard of: a Dealers' Ring.

Howden laid a hand on her arm. It was almost a caress. 'There's nothing to worry about my dear.'

She shrank from him. She felt weak; sick. He released her arm and smiled a sly smile.

'Mr Benson wouldn't like it.'

He laughed. 'Old Benson won't want to fall out with me. And you can't pretend he sent you out cold, without giving you the low-down.'

She saw Mr Benson's ashen face, the spot of red burning on each cheek, heard the rasping cough that shook his hunched shoulders. And now she was angry. Desperate to find a way out of this nightmare. 'You know perfectly well he left everything to your friend Margaret – it's all her fault.'

'Come along my dear – we're wasting time.' He took the key from her hand, unlocked the car door and held it open for her. She got in and he bent down and handed her the keys. 'You'd better follow me. I'll wait outside the park just before the turning to the main road – silver Mercedes estate.'

'Where are you going?' She hated him.

'*We* are going to the KO of course.' He straightened up and closed her car door, sealing her inside. She watched him walk away across the grass, assured, confident.

In a fury she started the engine and drove off through the park. Questions swarmed in her mind like bees. Buried at the centre, huge as the bloated queen, lay the ultimate question. Did Vic Howden really believe she had agreed to cooperate with him, or had he merely taken advantage of her lack of experience and her misguided decision to brazen out her ignorance?

What had she done to mislead him? There was that peculiar conversation she'd had with Ronnie and Trevor, before the sale started. Something about working, 'Are you working today?' Margaret usually did, he said. 'Pretend I'm Margaret' she'd said. At lunch, Vic Howden had said, 'I understand you're working.' Oh what a fool I've been, she shouted out loud as she approached the end of the park and spotted the silver Mercedes waiting there. But why not ignore Howden and just go home to have it out with Benson? Leave him to negotiate with that horrible man? It would be a perfectly justifiable action. Benson should have prepared her. He must have known something like this could happen. I'll run away, she thought. Go back to London: Now.

The Mercedes was moving out of the park, signalling left. A decision seemed to have been made involuntarily because, instead of heading for home, she found herself turning left, as if mesmerised by the shining silver car. She gripped the steering wheel, unable to deny the pulse of excitement that was beginning to overcome her fear.

Chapter Seven

For forty minutes Frances followed the Mercedes along quiet country roads, and drew up beside it on a roughly levelled piece of ground surrounded by trees.

'This way.' Howden led her down a steep track to a deserted marina. 'It's nice and quiet here.' Down a wooden ramp they went, to a line of pontoons. 'The season hasn't started yet and only a few of us leave our boats in the water all year round.'

He was wearing sailing shoes – incongruous with his formal suit. It seemed to add a touch of farce to the clandestine set-up.

There were perhaps a hundred boats floating in the marina, their sails furled and covered, cabins padlocked, tillers lashed, curtains drawn behind portholes. Waiting for summer. On the other side of the broad river she could see fields, a round-towered church, a line of trees. Exposed by the falling tide, mudflats, filmed with water, glistened by the river banks. In midstream the current ripped out to sea, tearing at the mooring buoys.

She walked along a pontoon following Howden, as if in a dream.

'Here we are. This is my boat.'

So this was to be the venue for the KO. A forty-foot motor-sailor exuding money: two masts and a black hull; the name *Calypso* in curly gold letters on the stern.

'She's based on a traditional boat design.' He placed a proprietorial hand upon the deck. 'But she's got a powerful engine and she sails well. When the weather's bad, I furl the sails, close myself in the doghouse, and then I'm safe and dry and I can go anywhere.'

Surprised at his spontaneous enthusiasm, Frances clambered after Howden over the guard rail on to the teak deck. She knew a little about boats, having done some dinghy sailing, but never had she been aboard a sea-going vessel like this.

He unlocked the door of the doghouse which led to the main cabin. She followed him inside and sat down on one of the seats piled with soft cushions. The surface of her skin seemed alive, over sensitive to her clothes and to the air, and she found she was breathing too quickly. She tried to steady herself while Howden brought out bottles and glasses and placed them on the table in the centre of the saloon.

She remained silent. Then, as if in reply to some favourable comment she might have made about his boat, he said, 'I get a lot of pleasure from her. Come here most weekends in the summer. Sail up the river – or go out to sea.'

The boat rocked as the others climbed aboard. They settled themselves round the table: Ronnie and Trevor, the young man with the brown moustache whose name was Dick, the man with laced boots and the black Homburg – removed to reveal wiry curls – introduced to her as Patrick. And the fat red-faced older man, smelling of stale pipe and sweat, whose name was Billy.

Frances eased her tense frame back into the plush cushions and waited. Ronnie and Trevor regarded her warily. Howden, pouring tumblers of whisky, glanced towards her and said, 'There's gin if you'd prefer it.'

'I would, thank you.' Frances looked at the generous quantity of spirit in the tumblers. They'll all get drunk now, she thought with a shiver of fear. And what will I do then?

Ronnie slurped his whisky, smacked his lips and said 'Who's in the chair?'

Trevor said, 'How about Vic?'

The others murmured their assent to what was clearly a regular arrangement. Howden had taken off his jacket and tie and undone his waistcoat. His normally smooth hair was slightly ruffled; he was enjoying his undisputed authority.

'Comin' to sit near me then darlin'?' Ronnie patted the space beside him.

'I'll stay here, thank you.' She was positioned on the left of Howden who had produced a slim gold pen and a thick black notebook. To the right of Howden sat Dick, chewing a fingernail, and on the other side of Dick, Billy was drinking with concentration, a couple of cigars on the table in front of him. Next to Billy came Ronnie, trying to catch her eye, then Trevor, who lifted his glass and winked at her. Between herself and Trevor lounged Patrick, the top of his curly head catching the last of the sun's rays which threw a wavery reflection from the water into the cabin. Billy offered a cigar to Howden. These were lit, and then, into the anticipatory silence, Trevor flung a jocular remark. 'We was expecting champagne squire.'

Howden jerked his head up but didn't reply. Trevor checked himself and smiled obsequiously. 'Only joking Vic. Just remembering that cooler what I brought abroad for yer.'

'Is that so?' Vic's voice was cold, his eyes malevolent.

Chastened, Trevor dropped his eyes and cleared his throat.

Billy, oblivious, said belligerently, 'Let's get on.'

Howden opened the black notebook with purposeful fingers.

Frances took a large mouthful of gin and tonic and felt her stomach clench in anticipation for she knew not what. Cigar smoke prickled in her nostrils and as she breathed it in she was aware of the tension tightening like a steel brace around the circle of men.

Like a ringmaster cracking a whip, Howden banged on the table. 'We'll start with the rosewood breakfast table. That was your lot wasn't it Patrick? Fifteen hundred under the hammer.'

'Correct.' Patrick looked up from his catalogue.

'It's worth more than that, isn't it?'

'Just a little more,' said Trevor, who was sitting on Patrick's left. 'Another fifty pounds.'

'Ronnie?'

'All right then – sixty.'

They were looking at Billy, who said rapidly, 'I'll go seventy.'

Dick was next. Holding his catalogue under the table top, he wrote something on it before looking up. 'Very well, eighty.'

Howden swept round the table with narrowed eyes. 'I'll put on a hundred,' he said.

They were looking at her. Six pairs of male eyes watched

48

and waited. She felt like a child who has strayed into some mysterious ritual for grown-ups. A female child snared by a band of adult males. From the lazy complacency in Howden's eyes she realised he had been perfectly aware of her naivety all along and had manipulated her to his advantage. Why had she not been sensible and gone home straight from Royton Park? Impotent rage burned through her sense of vulnerability and isolation. She could not risk making even more of a fool of herself by entering the bidding. Trevor looked at her inquiringly. She shook her head. Then it was Patrick's turn again, and they had completed one round of bidding. She was reminded of a poker game.

Patrick said, 'Very well, a hundred and ten.'

Trevor looked thoughtfully and then he said, 'All right – a hundred and twenty.'

Ronnie barely hesitated, 'A hundred and thirty.'

Billy took a slurp of whisky and went to £140. Dick, examining his fingernails, said slowly. 'Well I suppose I'll go to a hundred and sixty.'

Howden contemplated them once more, 'Two hundred.'

They skipped over her in the second round and Patrick said, steadily, 'Two hundred and ten.'

Trevor shook his head, 'That'll do for me.'

Ronnie said, 'That's enough for me.'

Billy said, 'I'll take the money.'

'I'll take the money.' What did that mean? Frances wondered. 'Are you interested in the goods or the money?' That was what Ronnie had asked her at Royton Park. What money? She took a large mouthful of gin. It was all very confusing.

Now there were only three left in the bidding. Howden, Patrick and Dick. It was Dick's turn. 'I don't know,' he said, 'I'll have to see.' He appeared to make a calculation on his catalogue, hidden beneath the table, and then hesitantly, he said, 'All right then two hundred and twenty.'

Howden, keeping his eye on Dick, went to £250 without much hesitation. Patrick, who was watching both the other men, put it up to £280. Dick said reluctantly, 'Three hundred I suppose.'

'Three fifty,' said Howden, still watching Dick. It went

49

round once more and after Howden had bid £450, Patrick came out of the bidding. 'I'm going for some fresh air,' he said. Trevor followed him up on to the deck. Dick, taking advantage of the opportunity to be even slower while this was going on, said, 'All right then, I'll go four eighty.'

'You'd better have it then Dick, since you want it so badly,' said Howden. 'I'm out.' With his gold pen he added something to the calculations he'd been making in his black book.

Suddenly they remembered she was among them. Howden poured gin into her glass, overconsciously solicitous. Ronnie winked at her, 'Wanted fillin' up darlin'.' He nodded towards her catalogue and tapped his own, and she realised he wasn't referring to her drink but to the rosewood breakfast table which appeared to have had almost £500 added to the hammer price during this private sale. And now it belonged to Dick, instead of Patrick who had 'bought' it at Royton Park. So did Dick have to buy it from Patrick at the new price? The original £1,500 plus the extra £480?

Patrick and Trevor came back into the cabin and poured themselves more whisky. The Knock Out continued. Sinking back unobtrusively, Frances watched as the competition between these men stirred up a volatile mix of antagonism disguised by humour. They auctioned four tea caddies, three chests of drawers, a games table, a corner wash-stand, a china cupboard and a set of eight Regency chairs. As the money went on, she could see that the main buyers were Howden, Patrick and Dick. Ronnie and Trevor bought nothing at all. So what was in it for them?

Billy got one of the chests but only, she guessed, because Howden, who took the other two, didn't want it. Patrick got the tea caddies. The corner wash-stand and the china cupboard went to Dick, and Howden took the chairs and the games table. They were half way through the second bottle of whisky, and Billy was the only one who showed signs of being drunk. Frances, automatically emptying her own glass, began to feel an alien presence taking over her body and mind. It was rather a relief. She grew fascinated, observing the cross-currents of pure machismo. Howden was Mr Big. Up to a point no one would antagonise him. Weasel-eyed Dick played his game of deliberate indecision. Patrick's expressionless pale eyes seemed to operate like a wide-angled camera lens. Margaret must be some woman, she thought to be able to contend with this lot. *And here I am, in her place.*

The combination of cigar smoke, whisky fumes and over-heated bodies formed an ever more dense and pungent atmosphere. A far-away feeling began to sweep over Frances. Terrified she was about to pass out, she struggled to her feet and escaped up on deck. The fresh air rushing into her lungs knocked her off balance. She swayed and clung to the rail. Then, slowly everything stabilised and she was able to force her eyes back into focus. It was nearly dark. Inside the cabin someone switched on a light which spot-lit the strip of water between the boat and the pontoon. She watched the ripples, bright as knives.

'Are you all right?' Trevor's voice was kindly. He and Ronnie were sitting in the cockpit nursing their drinks.

'I'm OK thanks. Just needed a breath of fresh air.'

'Your lots is coming up next,' said Trevor.

'Ah.' She didn't know how else to respond.

Ronnie said, 'Even if you don't want the goods, you could make yourself a bob or two.'

'Make yourself a bob or two.' *Of course.* That was it. That's what they'd been doing. Making themselves a bob or two – just by being there – just by helping to buy the goods in the first place – just by being present at the real sale – just by bidding. Someone would have to pay them. The eventual buyer? Hanging on to the inspirational surge in her over-stimulated brain, suddenly she thought she saw it. Saw the Knock Out. How it operated. What would Mr Benson say if she returned with 'a bob or two'. But no furniture? Or – suppose she pocketed whatever cash she might make. Told him the pieces went for too much money at Royton Park? No, he'd be able to check it out. Anyway she'd never dream of doing such a thing. That would be out of the question. What did Margaret do? Her mouth went dry.

'All right to go back in, are you Frances?' Trevor touched her arm lightly.

'I'm fine now thank you.' She was determined to show no sign of weakness.

They went back into the cabin and took their places round

the table. From the heat in her cheeks she knew her face must be bright red. They would see it glow like a ripe tomato. But they couldn't know how her heart was drumming against her ribs and how she didn't dare write on her catalogue for fear of her shaking hand.

'So – we come to your lots now my dear.' Howden turned to Frances who was sitting next to him. His eyes, very close, taunted her. 'We'll start with the kneehole. We all know it's right and it went for four grand. Patrick?'

On Frances's left, Patrick said, levelly, eighty quid.'

By the time it got round to Howden, on Frances's right, £160 had been added. 'One eighty.' He turned to Frances: 'Well?'

Focusing beyond his eyes, she said, clearly, 'Two hundred for me.'

A collective sigh seemed to issue from the men seated round the table, followed by an increase in the tension binding them together.

'Two hundred and fifty,' said Patrick.

Trevor looked thoughtful. 'All right then – three hundred.'

Ronnie whipped a quick glance all round. 'Three fifty.'

Billy's face was shiny with sweat. He took an extra deep slurp of his whisky and said, 'I'll go four hundred then.'

Perhaps Dick really didn't want the kneehole? Eventually he put on another fifty.

Howden took a little time to increase the bidding. 'I'll make it five fifty.'

And now they were watching her. She tried to keep her voice steady. 'Six fifty.'

Patrick wrote himself a note and said in his usual level tone, 'Seven fifty.'

The bidding had gone round twice and now it was back to Trevor.

'Trevor?' Howden looked across at him.

Trevor glanced at Frances. 'I'm out.'

'So am I,' said Ronnie, immediately.

Billy lifted the tumbler of whisky to his mouth with an unsteady hand. 'Another hundred on that.' His voice was thick with alcohol.

'I'll go the same.' Dick drummed his fingers lightly on the table.

'Very well,' said Howden, 'I'll put another two hundred on.'
Frances tried to unscramble the sums in her head. Her heart
was beating so loud and fast it interfered with the workings of
her brain. She scrawled wobbly figures on her catalogue.
Benson's limit was £6,000. Howden's last bid had put the price
of the kneehole up to £5,150, she gulped her gin and looked
round. The portholes were black now. Anticipation quivered
through the circle of men. 'Another two hundred,' she said,
and felt their ill-concealed surprise.
'I'm still in.' Patrick looked up under his eyes at Frances.
'I'll go another two hundred.'
'Billy?' Howden's voice was matter-of-fact.
Without raising his eyes from his tumbler of whisky, Billy
shook his head and it was Dick's turn.
Dick assessed Vic and he looked at Frances with his weasel
eyes and then back at his fingernails. 'No more for me,' he
said slowly.
It was Howden's turn to bid. She couldn't see his eyes for
the cigar smoke he exhaled, but she knew he wanted the kneehole desk. 'Another two hundred,' he said from behind wreaths
of blue smoke.
Her heart was pounding loud as a two-stroke engine, as she
scrawled figures with trembling fingers. One more bid and
perhaps she could secure the desk for Benson. 'Two hundred
more for me.' Her voice came out loud and high. If she got it,
that would make the price £5,950.
They were all out except for Howden, Patrick and herself.
Patrick shot her a calculating look. 'I'm out,' he said.
They all watched Howden. For a breathless moment, she
thought she would be returning to Benson with the kneehole
desk. Then, casually, he said, 'I'll put the same on again.'
It was between the two of them. She stopped breathing. She
longed to continue, but Benson had set £6,000 as the limit for
the desk and it wasn't her money. Slowly she let out her breath
and turned to face Howden, inches away from her. His eyes
were opaque as the black portholes. He held his gold pen
loosely in his right hand and on his full lips was the faintest
hint of a smile. She'd make him wait. She drew a face on her
catalogue. Looking up slowly, she said, 'No more for me.'
Everyone shifted in their seats with the release of tension, as

Howden claimed the kneehole desk.

From the other side of the table, Billy glared at her. 'Sitting in the right place my girl, weren't you.' His face was blotched red and purple and he stank of sweat, whisky and stale cigars. What did he mean? Her heart was thumping a little more slowly now, but she burned with a revelationary excitement. Presumably Howden would have to pay her, or rather Benson, for the desk she'd 'bought' for £4,000. And he'd also have to fork out the extra £2,150 that had just been added to the original price. Judging by the calculations the others were making on catalogues and scraps of paper, everyone got a share of the money put on in the Knock Out. 'Sitting in the right place my girl.' She'd been last to bid before Howden. Because she'd put the most money on – she must qualify for the biggest share of the pay-out. Yes. That must be right.

The Settlement continued on into the night. As if in response to some powerful drug, Frances grew high on the tension of the exhilarating game. Danger no longer seemed to threaten, but rather to stimulate. Recklessly, she entered the bidding for all the pieces she had supposedly bought at Royton Park.

She succeeded in claiming the demi-lune sideboard, calculating its eventual cost to be no more than Benson had expected to pay for it in the first place. She did almost as well with the card table, but lost the Norfolk chest to Patrick, who also got the tripod tables. Vic took the sofa table, the walnut canterbury and the bow chest: Dick the rosewood whatnot. Billy took the Chinese lacquer cabinet, but his surly expression told her he wasn't comfortable with his successful bid. From the sly smile flickering over Dick's face, it looked like Billy's gamble hadn't paid off and by staying too long in the bidding, he'd got landed with paying out money for goods he didn't want.

By the time they finished, it was nearly three in the morning. She was exhausted and, with the sale of the last piece, began once more to be affected by the dense atmosphere in the cabin. They were all drunk, Billy the only one obscenely so.

Howden, his shirt half undone, exposing black chest hairs, studied his black book and worked his calculator. Trevor prodded Ronnie who had fallen asleep. Patrick leaned his head against the plush upholstery and blew smoke rings. Dick, watching Howden, made his own calculations. She willed herself invisible but, as if deliberately to show he knew what was in her mind, Howden raised his eyes and fixed a highly conscious male gaze upon her. Hot with discomfort, she struggled to her feet. She was aware they'd all been peeing over the side. Now she needed to relieve herself urgently.

'You'll find everything you need in the aft cabin,' said Howden. He stood up to allow her to brush past him and his eyes continued to follow her as she went out of the saloon and through into the aft cabin.

There were stainless steel fittings including a shower unit in the washing compartment, along with scented soap, nautical hand towels and a bottle of spray cologne.

The cabin contained a large, duvet-covered double bunk. She glanced at her reflection in the mirror on the fitted dressing table opposite the bunk. Her eyes were red and seemed to have sunk into her head. Her hair had darkened and smelt of smoke.

Beside the dressing table, built-in shelves held books. Glancing at them, she saw a mixed collection of sailing books, almanacs, popular novels and books on antiques. Unconsciously, her hand moved towards a copy of *Whitacker's Almanack*, which protruded slightly. She pulled it out, opened it, and was confronted by pages of tidal atlases. She made to return the Almanac, but it refused to slip back into its space. Puzzled, she reached behind the row of books and her hand came into contact with some obstruction: something differently shaped, both hard and soft. She grasped it and pulled out a woman's shoe. Light and delicate, it was a small black patent leather high-heeled shoe for a left foot. She stared at it with stunned recognition. Its partner rested in Benson's shop. There was no need to slip it on her foot to confirm it would be a perfect fit.

A burst of laughter sounded from the main cabin. Unhesitatingly, Frances crammed Margaret's shoe into her oversize shoulder bag, zipping it out of sight. Then hurriedly, she slid the books back into their places upon the shelf and returned to the saloon.

Burning with curiosity as to how Margaret's shoe came to be concealed behind a row of books in Vic Howden's rear cabin, she watched in a daze while the man concentrated on his calculator and his black book, his labours orchestrated by jokes and disputations, as they sorted out who owed whom what for which piece of furniture, and each made sure he was getting his fair share of any pay-out. Bank notes were changing hands.

Through the thin leather of her shoulder bag, Frances traced the shape of Margaret's shoe, both hard and soft beneath her fingers.

Chapter Eight

'You can always leave my dear – if that's how you feel.' Benson regarded her coolly from the other side of his desk upon which rested a bundle of bank notes. 'But before you go, we had better get this little matter straightened up.' He consulted the Royton Park catalogue in his hand. 'Now, you tell me you kept the sideboard and the card table. But you couldn't hold the kneehole, the sofa table, the canterbury and the bow chest against Howden. Patrick took the Norfolk chest and the tripod tables; Dick the whatnot, and you lost the lacquer cabinet to Billy, which is just as well.'

He glanced down at the bank notes, and then up at Frances. 'There will be some remuneration when I have checked it all out.'

She was filled with rage. 'I don't want your dirty money. You set me up. I've broken the law on account of you.'

'I assure you, Miss Lambert, I didn't intend that this should happen.'

'You sent me there – totally unprepared – like – like a lamb to the slaughter. It's just not good enough Mr Benson.'

'I can only repeat, it was not my intention you should participate in the Ring.'

Frances was exhausted. Her head in the relentless grip of a hangover headache. Sorting through the blurred images of yesterday, her inner self knew she need not have cooperated with Vic Howden and his cronies. But there was no avoiding the fact that, once she had gone along with the situation she found herself in, she had become intoxicated with the racy tension of it all. And now she was uneasy and ashamed. It was

57

a relief to off-load her troublesome conscience on to Mr Benson.

'Perhaps I will – leave – I don't like working for a dealer who operates in a Ring. I don't care for the KO, Mr Benson.'

'I see you have picked up the terminology – just as you have picked up with remarkable facility – the ability to settle.' He allowed himself a bleak smile. She thought suddenly he looked a frail old man. 'Why do they allow it? Those auctioneers? They must know.'

'They want to sell things. How do you value a work of art? An antique is worth what anyone's prepared to pay for it. The bidding is open after all.'

'There were some good things at Royton Park and they went too cheaply on account of Vic Howden and his horrible Ring.'

'They could have been put on reserve – people can always get independent valuations. They don't choose to pay the money to get proper advice from a reputable dealer.'

'Are there any?'

Mr Benson's pale grey eyes turned dark as the North Sea in winter.

She said, 'The auctioneers estimated prices, after all.'

'Harrison and Draper aren't fine art specialists – they sell anything – houses, farm machinery, cattle, pigs. Anyway, estimates are often fairly approximate. You can't value an antique like a modern artefact and many auctioneers don't have the knowledge.' Mr Benson passed a hand over his eyes tiredly. 'Miss Lambert – if you feel you have been unfairly treated then you should go. I would like you to know that I do not support the activities of the Ring. But you should also understand that dealers won't push prices unrealistically high by bidding against each other – that wouldn't be any good for anyone. Of course there are bargains to be had – if you know what you're doing – and we all make mistakes. You can spend a lifetime learning about antiques. Antique dealing is a business like any other. It has its successes and its failures. For all those making a decent living, there are plenty of others going out of business. And, like everything else, it has it share of crooks among the honest men.'

'Vic Howden,' said Frances.

Benson's mouth tightened and she saw his old fingers involuntarily dig into the desk top with a pressure that made them look more bloodless than ever.

'It's all very well for you to say you don't operate in a ring Mr Benson, but you must know that Margaret did. She was part of their set-up. They thought I was just carrying on where she left off – or at least that's what they pretended. You can't tell me you didn't know about Margaret.'

He mustered his strength and now his eyes were bright and piercing as the points of steel blades. 'I think you've said enough Miss Lambert. Please go.' His cheeks were paper white; sweat beaded his brow and darkened his silver hair. He stood up as if to command her, swayed and sank back again, failing to conceal his unsteadiness.

Frances felt sudden compassion. 'You're ill – you should be in bed.'

'I'm all right.' Spots of red flamed in his cheeks as he continued, unable to control the emotion in his voice. 'Margaret is a clever woman. She knows my opinion of Victor Howden. I've never inquired about her personal relationship with the man; and neither have I felt it necessary to investigate any deals she may have done with him. It could be, she's fiddled me over the years.' His voice dropped as if he was talking to himself. 'But then I've allowed her the opportunity – given her the responsibility.' He stopped and started again, his voice levelling out. 'I'm an old man now Miss Lambert – not in the best of health. I do not feel the need to excuse myself.' He had regained his dignity. 'Now – perhaps you will let me know whether or not you wish to remain in my employ.'

'And perhaps you will let me know for how long that is likely to be?' countered Frances. 'When is Margaret coming back?'

'I can't tell you that.'

'Mr Benson, you're not being fair to me. If she's ill, is she going to get better? If she's gone away somewhere, is she coming back?'

'She was called away – suddenly. She will be back.'

'Wasn't that rather odd? Must be a couple of months ago now.'

Benson appeared sunk in thought.

'Have you been in touch with her?'

The old man came to with a start, shaking himself out of his private contemplation. 'Miss Lambert,' he said briskly, 'I'm really not prepared to discuss this matter any further. I'm happy to employ you for the time being – it's entirely up to you whether or not you decide to stay.'

She smiled, wanting to cheer him up. 'There's nothing else for me around here. I'd like to stay on if that would suit you. But don't expect me to attend any more sales for you.'

'Very good.' He rubbed his dry old hands together. 'Run along then – I'll see you tomorrow.'

She sensed he was already regretting his revelations.

Frances drove slowly home. So, Margaret wasn't ill. She'd been called away, suddenly, mysteriously, leaving the imprint of her presence almost palpably in the shop and one high-heeled shoe on board Vic Howden's boat. Her thoughts about all these puzzling matters were so absorbing, it wasn't until she was opening her front door, she remembered she was to have dinner with Mark. Hurriedly she washed and changed into a plain black dress. She was tying a green silk scarf round her neck when he arrived, wearing a blazer with brass buttons, in place of his habitual tweed jacket. He refused her offer of a drink and ushered her stiffly into his car. He stared pointedly through the windscreen as he drove, making no attempt at conversation. Frances, noting the tension in his forearms and the strength with which he gripped the wheel, sat quietly watching the fields and hedges slip by.

In the bar of the small restaurant, which specialised in fish and smelled of garlic, he relaxed enough to ask her what she would like to drink. She swallowed cool white wine and wondered at the stern set of his mouth. After a while, in order to break the silence, she said, 'I saw your Mr Draper yesterday – at the Royton Park sale.'

'I know.'

Silence.

'I see,' she said.

He wouldn't look directly at her and she felt irretrievably let down. She had not realised Mark's approval was so necessary to her and she was hurt that it could so easily be withdrawn. Impulsively, she went in for the attack. 'What did he say then? That sharp-eyed showman?'

'I don't really want to tell you.'

'I'd much rather you told me and stopped being so horribly pompous.'

He did not look up from his wine glass.

'Come on. I want to know.'

'All right then. Charles Draper said some "dizzy little blonde" bidding for Benson got herself mixed up with the local Ring.' He looked at her now, flushed, embarrassed. 'How the hell did that happen?'

She stared angrily back at him. 'It just did.'

'I can't believe you got yourself involved with that scum.'

Refusing to defend herself with feeble excuses, voice rising, she said, 'If Mr Draper doesn't approve of the Ring, he should do something about it.'

'I could tell you.' Mark paused before continuing. 'But I don't suppose there's much point.'

Gaining confidence, Frances said, 'I would have thought there was something auctioneers could do ... Obviously they don't choose to.' She made an expansive gesture with her arm, spilling wine from her glass. 'Anyway, it seems Margaret has been doing business this way for years. I expect you knew that.'

'What Margaret does is not relevant.'

'Mark, I didn't realise.' She wanted him to look warmly at her again. 'Honestly, I know it sounds silly, but I didn't realise. If it hadn't been for Vic Howden none of this would have happened. He made them think I was bidding for him. I didn't understand what was happening until too late and then I couldn't get out of it.'

'Of course you could.' Instead of softening at her confession, his voice was thick with bitterness. She thought of Mr Benson's similar reaction at the mention of Howden.

'Vic Howden has a shocking reputation. One look at him and I'd have thought you could tell what a crooked bastard he is.'

'That's not the point,' she said, taken aback by his strength of feeling. 'I told you – I didn't have chance against him. Margaret is the connection. You must know that. He saw an opportunity of carrying on as before.'

'Just forget about Margaret.'

Frances thought of Margaret's shoe, back at the farmhouse, lying at the bottom of her shoulder bag. She wondered whether she should tell Mark about it, but decided the least said about the happenings on Howden's boat the night before, the better, and contented herself with remarking. 'Those two had a very close relationship.'

'Margaret and Howden? So I believe.' Mark stabbed a sauté potato with his fork and put it down again on his plate.

'She's gone away you know – Benson said.'

'You told me she was ill.'

'I was only guessing. She left in a rush – I've no idea why.' He poured more wine.

'Mr Benson doesn't like Vic Howden either.'

'No one ought to like Victor Howden. Look – I won't go on any more – it's your life. But you want to watch what you're doing.' His expression was serious and she was aware of a shift in their relationship. Mark seemed almost wary of her, as if in his eyes she had acted out of character.

Back at the farmhouse, she asked him in and prepared coffee.

'You'll be nice and warm next winter,' he remarked, examining a radiator waiting to be fixed to the wall.

'Yes and I'll have you know the chimney doesn't smoke,' said Frances. 'We tried it out the other day.'

'They've made a reasonable job of re-enamelling the sink.'

'The bath comes back next week – I can't wait.'

They sat down with their coffee, she on the big old sofa she had brought from Sevenoaks, he on one of the easy chairs. She put on a tape, and watched him as he listened to Mozart, his hand shadowing his face as if he was protecting himself from her. Later, as they said goodbye in the doorway, he slipped an arm round her shoulders, smoothed back her hair and kissed her gently on the cheek. For a brief comforting moment, she rested against him, breathing the warmth of his body, feeling the roughness of his cheek against her forehead.

After he had disappeared into the night, she took out Margaret's shoe and examined it. There was a long scratch scored into the shiny patent leather. Turning the shoe over in her hand, she felt the thinness of the leather sole – in need of repair. She ran her hand inside and to her surprise, her fingers encountered a piece of crumpled paper wedged in the toe. She pulled it out and flattened it. There, before her eyes was Margaret's familiar scrawl, spider black on the scrap of paper. *'Vic – have gone away with N.H. No doubt Carla will console you. M.'*

Mr Benson said she'd been 'called away'. And would be back. He must know where she was. It was very silent in the farmhouse. So silent, she could hear her own heartbeat and the blood surging in her ears like distant surf. The elegant shoe, the message in that flowing, decisive hand, conjured Margaret – small, dark, clever – vividly before her. It was a triumphant message and in it Frances saw confirmation of Margaret's intimacy with Howden, and her bid to be free of him.

Who was N.H.? Did Mr Benson know about him? It must surely be *him*. And who was Carla?

Next morning she took the shoe to the shop with her and put it in the bottom drawer of the desk along with the box which held the rest of Margaret's personal belongings.

Over the next few days, Margaret was seldom out of her mind. Why had her shoe been hidden behind those books? And who had put it there? If it was Howden, when would he find out it had gone?

Mr Benson retreated, as she had expected, into his former reserve and there were no more conversations about Margaret, but between them her shadow hovered – a substance almost too real to be ghostly. She considered showing him Margaret's note but then decided to keep it to herself.

On an impulse one drowsy afternoon, she opened the bottom drawer of the desk and took out the shoe and the box. She re-united the shoes, standing them together on the floor. She threw the half-eaten packet of mints into the waste-paper basket, pulled out the wiry strands of dark hair from the pink comb, and was suddenly discomforted by her own prying eyes, but at the same time consumed with the desire to discover more. Certainly, she knew a great deal more about Margaret than she had when she first put these abandoned possessions into the box, but everything she knew posed further questions.

There seemed a dreamlike quality in the warm, moist air of

the late afternoon. Mr Benson had locked his office and gone out to see a customer. Sidney was in the workshop stripping down a pine mantel. No customers lurked in the shop. There was something eerie about the sight of the empty shoes on the floor. They seemed almost about to take on a life of their own and Frances could not help imagining them propelled by Margaret's determined feet around the familiar showroom, with a staccato clack clack of the stilettos. She felt Margaret beside her, objecting to having her belongings disturbed.

There came a small sound, something between a click and a tap. Frances whipped round in agitation, but nothing was there. When she looked back again at the shoes, she could half fancy they had moved and a sudden change of light – it must have been the sun slipping behind a cloud – gave the impression of a shadow passing. With galloping pulse, she jerked her eyes round the room but caught only a glimpse of her own distorted reflection in the gilded convex mirror. She let go her breath, involuntarily held, and tried to gain control of her wild imaginings. Margaret's anger seemed to fill the air. Frances tried to rationalise these confused sensations. Perhaps somehow, she had projected her own animosity towards Margaret on to Margaret's feelings towards her. But Margaret couldn't reciprocate when she didn't know Frances existed. It was ridiculous to believe that Margaret didn't like her. What she knew of Margaret, she disliked. And yet, that little pile of personal possessions moved her; pathetic clues to a personality. Along with the defiant note – Margaret's pen had scored deep into the paper – they brought to life Margaret and her dealings with Howden, endorsing the depth of her commitment to him: accomplice and lover. N.H. must be a powerful man to break that bond.

Frances took out Margaret's blue hard-backed book and laid it on the desk. She examined the columns of numbers and letters and tried to make sense of them. They were lists of purchases bought at auction. Each sale was listed and dated, beneath which were lot numbers and prices marked with the letter H. or the letter B. Could it be that Margaret was bidding at auction on behalf of both Benson and Howden? Employed by Benson – 'I've given her the responsibility' – rewarded by Howden 'very pally with Howden'. She imagined how Howden might view the sale, mark the catalogue, and leave the rest to Margaret, saving himself the trouble of turning up to bid. Would he sometimes leave her to take part in the Settlement? What about any competition there might be between Howden and Benson for certain pieces? With whom would Margaret's loyalty lie? Sidney's words echoed in her head, 'Margaret do what she want.' She saw the spots of red burning on Benson's dry old cheeks: 'It could be she's fiddled me over the years ... I've allowed her the opportunity ...'

Frances turned the pages of the small hard-backed book. The last entry was dated 27 March. *Woodton Hall Sale on 26 March.*

Lot 233 Sec. Bookcase £5,000 H.
Lot 300 Pr. Vict. Rosewood Cabs. £4,500 H.
Lot 410 George III Mah. Tallboy £1,800 H.
Lot 420 Mah. Pembroke Table £2,100 H.
Lot 436 Dutch Mah. Armoire £3,100 H.
Lot 450 Mah. Wine Cooler £1,500 H.
Lot 461 Sundry framed prints £50 H!!!!

Frances looked at this last entry which Margaret had marked with a row of black exclamation marks. There then followed a list of articles she had bought for Mr Benson at this sale, each marked with a B. A rosewood circular breakfast table, a mahogany writing table, a landscape by Crome, four George III table candlesticks and the brass jardinière with leopard mask that now stood in the hall. Yes. Benson sold that breakfast table last week; the landscape which was only 'after Crome' was hanging in his office, and the writing table was in the workshop awaiting repair by Sidney. She put the book down and searched among the piles of old sale catalogues. Eventually, she found the one for Woodton Hall: Draper again. She flipped through the shiny pages. Margaret had scrawled prices and comments in black biro: 'v. nice; ace; too dear and !!!!!!!!'

March 26 – Margaret's last sale, thought Frances. Her handwriting, sprawling blackly across the white pages of the catalogue, echoed the flamboyant 'a's and 'm's and the snaking 's's on the crumpled scrap of paper hidden in the shoe. '*Gone away* ... Carla will console you.'

The day after the Woodton Hall sale – 27 March – Margaret had carefully entered the respective purchases in her blue book and disappeared. That was six weeks ago. Frances slid her fingers over the smooth surface of the catalogue, tracing the pale sepia outline of the Hall, overlaid with the printed information: Tuesday 26 March. Very soon after that date, she, Frances, had come into Benson's shop for the first time, attracted by the oak coffer in the window. She rested her head in her hands, remembering: Benson getting the better of the bossy woman who was complaining about the price of a dining table, 'Neither cast ye your pearls before swine' – the woman furiously crashing out of the shop almost colliding with a van; the two lads loading the furniture: 'We come for Mr Howden's goods'. She remembered how they had complained about the large and unwieldy pieces. Frances studied Margaret's list of furniture bought at the Woodton Hall sale and remembered: the secretaire bookcase in two pieces, the awkwardness of the tallboy, the massive armoire, the wine cooler, rectangular, lidded and richly decorated with acanthus leaf carving and lion's paw feet. That had been a Friday because it was the following Monday – 2 April, when she started to work for Benson. She had only missed meeting Margaret by three or four days. No wonder her presence was almost tangible. Margaret's breath had still been in the building.

The list of figures and letters raced across the ruled pages of the notebook. Frances shut her eyes and still she saw them. She shook her head angrily, willing them to disappear. The shop door opened, signalled by the tinkling of the cowbell. She put the book back into the box, grabbed Margaret's shoes and stuffed the whole lot into the bottom drawer of her desk, pushing it firmly closed.

She knew instinctively who had entered the shop before she looked up from her task. It was almost as if her thoughts had summoned him: Vic Howden, sportively suave in a light coloured linen jacket and navy blue trousers, a silk scarf of purple and gold tucked into the collar of his open-necked shirt. He came towards her smiling with confident familiarity, prepared only for a friendly welcome. Margaret had been so much in her mind, linked with Howden, Frances almost expected her to materialise, tripping in behind the man, on those determined stiletto heels, ready to repossess her desk and the typewriter and the telephone and Mr Benson. She blinked, focusing her eyes with an effort.

'Sleepy?' Howden presented himself to her, the light summer clothing emphasising his swarthiness. He drummed his fingers on the front of her desk and she found herself staring at the initials engraved on his signet ring. No doubt his shirts were monogrammed, and his tailor-made suits would have his name woven inside. She didn't trust her voice. Her instinctive recoil was allied to an equally instinctive disturbing and unwelcome fascination for this man. As he appraised her with glossy eyes, his fingers restless on the desk top in front of her, she had to acknowledge – defying all reason – his presence engendered in her a horribly compelling kind of reckless excitement.

'It's hot out there,' he said. She stared back at him remembering his adroit management of the Settlement – the nimble fingers delicately pressing calculator buttons and shuffling bank notes.

'Mr Benson isn't here.'

'No matter. Anyone interested in the sideboard?'

'Maybe.'

Her head blazed with uncomfortable images. He smiled lazily, as if he knew she didn't want to be reminded of that night, and moved across the room to examine a pair of brass candlesticks and from there to open the secretaire drawer of the mahogany bookcase.

'How about the card table? You got that for a good price.'

She would not respond.

'Yes. You did all right.'

Did he think she'd be flattered? The unstoppable words poured out. 'You tricked me, Mr Howden. Put me in an impossible situation. It was a rotten thing to do.'

'I thought you rose to the occasion rather well.' He closed the drawer of the bookcase and came to stand by her desk. 'And what's more, you seemed to enjoy yourself.'

'That's not true.' She was furious with him for having the perception to divine her shameful feelings and furious with herself for sounding so childish.

'Calm down my dear.' He touched her lightly on the arm,

confident of his ability to placate her. 'No hard feelings. I'll just take a look at the stock while I'm here.'

'All right.' Her arm where he had touched it prickled. Appalled at her physical response to him, she watched him move round the room. His strongly built body was beginning to thicken with middle age, but he was light on his feet. Softly, he padded the showrooms, opening and closing cabinet doors, pulling out drawers, flashing a tiny torch. He disappeared into the back room and she heard him in the store. She heard him try the locked door to Benson's office. Then she heard him go through to the repair shop; heard Sidney grunt a response to a soft spoken question. The afternoon wore on. No one else came into the shop. She typed an unnecessary list to drown out the muffled sounds of Vic Howden creeping about in the sultry silence, opening and closing doors and drawers, sliding pieces of furniture back and forth. His examination was so meticulous it seemed almost as if he was looking for something. Frances was troubled. A tag-end of a question flickered at the back of her mind. She stopped typing and got out Margaret's blue book. She was puzzling over its contents when Howden came back into the room. She closed the book and thrust it into the top drawer of her desk.

'I see you still have the satinwood chest. Tell Benson my offer stands. He might as well take it – he won't do better.'

Frances made no comment. Howden went on, 'I'll take the Imari dish.' He placed it on the desk before her, where it glowed gold and blue and rusty red. She resisted the impulse to remark upon the length of time it had taken him to purchase so little while she wrapped it in tissue. Silently, he watched and her hand almost faltered as she wrote out the receipt for his cheque.

'How do you occupy yourself in Fressenworth, Frances Lambert? What do you find in this quiet backwater?'

'I'm extremely busy renovating my house, Mr Howden.'

'That must be *very* stimulating.'

'Rewarding certainly.'

'Well you can't be doing that all the time. What else do you find to interest you?'

'I don't need anything else.'

'You will.' His smile was speculative as he took the receipt from her. 'What are you doing tonight?'

Caught off guard, she found herself replying automatically, 'Nothing.'

'Have dinner with me. I'll pick you up at seven-thirty. Give me your address.'

There was a static moment, like a scene from a film freeze-framed, and then she heard someone, speaking with her voice, accept his invitation and supply him with her address.

'Ah – Willow Farm. Very good.' He smiled, turned and made for the door.

As soon as the door had closed behind him, her normal self exclaimed to the empty shop, 'My God what have I done?' There was no justification for buckling under like a spineless schoolgirl. Unless – maybe she could get him to talk about Margaret? Would that make it all right? Staring at the type-writer, instead of the familiar keys, she saw Vic Howden's well shaped hands, his fingers drumming the front of her desk, and she thought of the way his thick dark hair curled down the back of his neck.

Chapter Nine

When Howden had gone, she tried to put him out of her mind by concentrating on the filing. After a short while, the shop bell tinkled and Trevor pushed it open, an uncertain smile of some charm upon his broad face. Frances was growing accustomed to Ronnie and Trevor bringing in pieces of furniture that Mr Benson sometimes bought and sometimes didn't, but this was the first time Trevor had been in since Royton Park.

'Mr Benson's not here.'

'I've brought 'im a table.'

'So you do buy the goods sometimes,' she said acidly.

He worked on his smile. 'Can I fetch it in.'

'Oh all right.'

He went out and came back in again with the table, leaving his old blue transit van parked outside with the back doors open.

'There you are – nice little mahogany tripod – see the bird-cage support – lovely patina – that's a real nice table. Bought it off of a old lady what's moving house.'

Frances looked at it cautiously. 'I suppose you could leave it – and I'll show it to Mr Benson when he gets back.'

'Very good.' He rubbed his hands together. 'I'll just close up the van and pop back.'

'If you must,' she murmured under her breath, as he shot through the door. He returned looking cheerful. She laid down the papers she was sorting through. 'I hope you gave that old lady a fair price for her table.'

Trevor looked hurt. 'Would I do down a old lady? I've got

my good name to think of. See here Frances – I may call you Frances may I? – Won't get no business if I don't give a fair price. I've been dealing all my life – it's my work and my pleasure – you get my meaning? It's like this – someone ask me to go an' look at a article what they want to sell. Sometimes I don't want to bother to go an' look – but you never know – that might be the one thing what you've been looking for all your life – you have to go an' see.'

'The pot of gold at the end of the rainbow?'

'Got it in one. You never know. Then I ask myself this question – what do you do if you find something what's worth a lot more'n the person what's selling it think?'

'Well – what do you do?'

Trevor had seated himself in an old leather wing chair and looked likely to remain there for some time. 'You ask him what do you want for this article? But if he say something silly and you know you could sell it tomorrow for double that figure – what do you do then?'

'Tell him it's worth more?'

'If you do that, he might want to offer it to someone else – and then you lose it.'

'So what do you do?'

'That's my question – what I ask myself.'

'And I can guess what answer you give yourself,' said Frances cynically.

Trevor assumed an open and honest expression. 'You want to be as fair as you can with these people, but sometimes that backfires. I see a nice little Mendlesham chair – yew wood – elm seat – turned legs – crinoline stretcher. I offer two hundred and seventy – that's real then – the money makes it real – and then they won't sell it to you – if you say it's worth thirty quid that's a different matter.'

'I see,' said Frances in the same cynical tone of voice.

'Like I say – I want to be fair. I have a living to make and I have to think of my reputation. I like to think I'm the same with people whether I want to get something out of them or not.'

'So what about this table then?'

'In this case I know what I'm prepared to pay for it, but I ask her to name her price and then I make her an offer – a fair one what she took. Sometimes they say "Is that all?" But then they're forgetting my profit.'

'Well I don't suppose she'd have done better at auction.'

'She would not – what with transportation and commission.'

'I didn't exactly mean that,' said Frances pointedly, hearing Benson's voice in her head – 'They don't want to pay the money to get proper advice from a reputable dealer'. Looking Trevor in the eye, she said, 'Meantime the Vic Howdens of this world have it all their own way.'

'I'll you something for nothing.' Trevor screwed up his eyes earnestly. 'You want to keep on the right side of Vic Howden.'

'What do you mean – exactly?'

'I won't say more'n that.'

Frances thought, he's frightened of him. She said, 'Well, he certainly keeps you lot going.'

Trevor leaned forward in the wing chair. 'I'll tell you a story. When I was a lad I tried to buy a good clock at a sale. I bid against the Heavies – went way over what I should have – and when I went to collect my clock there was no workings inside it no more.'

'That's terrible.'

'Mind you – it's a while ago – things are better now.'

'So long as you keep on the right side of Vic Howden.'

'What else?' He spread his hands in mock helplessness. 'A chap like me can't do down a chap like Vic Howden.'

'I suppose there's always a Vic Howden.'

'I wouldn't say that. Mostly we're all just making a living – but with him it's different – it's like he wants things more'n most people – be the one what call the tune. And he's the devil for women. That's why I say you want to look out for yourself.'

'I heard he was very friendly with Margaret.'

'Too right.'

'She must be in a difficult position – between Howden and Benson.'

Trevor's face expressed grudging admiration. 'She's equal to it.' He paused. 'Mind you – Vic gave her a rough time – she has to fight to keep her end up. One time she got wrong with him I see him nearly kill a little dog she had.

72

He was loading a Chinese porcelain dish what she'd bought. Just putting it in her car when the dog got under his feet. He kicked it so hard I thought he'd killed it. Margaret went wild. If it had been his dish and not Benson's, she'd have smashed it over his head.'

She could believe Howden had a cruel streak, but she would not expect it to show itself in common violence. He seemed too urbane and sophisticated a man to kick a dog. His violence would surely be subtle, verbal, non-physical.

Trevor was saying something. Absorbed in her thoughts, she had not heard him. 'Sorry?'

'Will I see you at the Corn Hall Wednesday? There's a good breakfront coming up – just up Tommy's street.'

'I doubt it.'

'If he send you along, we'll look after you.'

'I've heard that one before.'

'Don't be like that.' He stood up and slapped his check cap back on his head. 'I'll be off now. See you Wednesday.'

The bell tinkled as the door opened and closed.

Vic Howden was late enough collecting her for Frances to wonder if perhaps he wouldn't turn up. Relief and disappointment fought for supremacy. But at eight o'clock the silver Mercedes swung into sight. She waited nervously in the sitting room while he got out of the car, walked up the path and banged on the door. She let him in, and he stood for a moment looking intently at the freshly painted walls and the colourful rugs lying on the scrubbed brick floor. 'You've certainly done a lot of work here.'

'It was in an awful state.'

'Yes.' His eyes scanned round almost as if he was familiar with her home, and settled on the fireplace where branches of lilac in a blue jug stood on the hearth.

'You know this place?'

'Not really. Are you ready? Shall we go?'

The restaurant had soft lights, apple-green paint work and circular tables draped with long white tablecloths. Gentle watercolour landscapes were ranged along the walls. They entered to the subdued buzz of well-mannered conversation among formally dressed people taking care not to clatter their

73

cutlery. Frances watched a waiter reverently present a dish of snails to an appreciative middle-aged couple, and thought, you come here to pay homage to food, not necessarily to have a good time.

As they were being shown to their table, the proprietor appeared briefly, in a Chef's hat and apron. He greeted Howden with the deference afforded to a valued customer and nodded at Frances. There was only professional politeness in his expression, but aware of this special attention singling them out, she felt uncomfortably conscious of the impression she and Howden made. She should not have worn the green dress which was cut very short and felt tighter than usual. She felt very young and blonde beside swarthy Howden, who was wearing a dark suit and a Paisley patterned tie in strong reds and blues. The age gap made it possible, but there was no chance anyone would take them for father and daughter.

Champagne on ice arrived as if by magic. The waiter poured two glasses and glided away.

'It's lucky,' said Frances pointedly, 'that I like champagne.'

'Very lucky.' He raised his glass to her.

It was a game.

The glass was smooth and cool against her lips. She felt immediate enjoyment at the taste and touch of the liquid prickling her tongue and sliding down her throat. She picked up the menu. The selection was gourmet with near-London prices.

Howden said, 'I recommend the foie gras.'

'I don't eat foie gras on principle.'

He looked up with exaggerated alarm. 'Oh dear – I hope you're not an animal rights person – or a vegetarian. You're not a vegetarian are you?'

'I'm carnivorous, like you. I just happen to believe force-feeding a goose to enlarge its liver is pretty disgusting.'

'You're missing out, my dear. But never mind. Have a canapé.' She took one, and followed it with more champagne. She should never have allowed him to hypnotise her into coming out with him – to this expensive and intimate place. He refilled her glass, watching her face as he did so. She lowered her eyes, concentrated on the menu. The waiter reappeared, pad in hand. 'Are you ready to order sir?'

'Frances?'

'Potted shrimps to start with please, and then the turbot with fennel.'

Howden said, 'You approve of eating fish then.'

'Fish are wild – they have decent lives.'

'Ah yes – swimming around in our polluted seas.' He turned his attention to the waiter, who stood impassive. 'Foie gras, followed by the rack of lamb. And I'd like to order more wine.'

Enjoying her champagne, Frances decided to pretend this was the kind of business occasion Felix had sometimes asked her to handle on his behalf. She had known exactly how to maintain the right balance of informal camaraderie and efficient formality, making careful use of her natural attributes. Sometimes it was fun. Sometimes it sickened her: the hot hand straying to her knee, the foot nudging hers.

While they ate their starters and finished the champagne, he inquired about her background, her previous jobs, her reasons for coming to Suffolk, and paid attention to her responses, as if he really wanted to get to know her. Protective of her privacy, she tried to provide him with as few details as possible. But he seemed to have an uncomfortable knack of homing in on her replies, watching her reactions and extracting information as much from what she did not say as what she did. His protuberant eyes shone weirdly in the candlelight. She tried not to look into them. Vic Howden. Lover of Margaret. Lover of Carla, whoever Carla might be. Did he have a wife? He must surely have been married at some stage but it was hard to imagine him in a domestic role, helping with the washing up or mowing the lawn. As if he had divined her thoughts, he suddenly said, 'I'm not married at present,' and touched the white table napkin to his full red lips.

'Oh really!' Startled, she blundered on without thinking. 'Well – I don't usually have dinner with married men – except when it's business.'

'So – you don't need to pretend this is business.'

While she was trying to think up a witty response, the waiter arrived with their main course. The turbot, creamy white in a swirl of terracotta sauce, decorated with fronds of dark green fennel and set off by a curve of wild rice, looked like a still life painting. In her mouth, the fish was succulent and tasted delicately of aniseed. The rack of lamb, dark brown on the outside, showed pink when Howden cut into the flesh and made the juices run. To drink there was a bottle of Chablis for her and a bottle of claret for him.

Determined to gain control of the conversation, she asked, with sudden inspiration, 'How did you get into the antiques trade, Mr Howden?'

'Mr Howden? I thought we'd moved on a bit. Or do you want me to call you Miss Lambert?'

'I suppose not.'

'Oh good.'

He mocked, but nevertheless, she balked at calling him Vic. 'Come on – tell me – how you got into the antiques trade.'

'What do you want to know that for?' He leaned back and watched her lazily with narrowed eyes.

'How do you learn about antiques?'

'You just pick it up: by trading. There's no formal training for antique dealers – you don't take courses and pass exams. You can read books and go and look at furniture. You'll have to come and see my showroom in Kelvedon. I've a wonderful eighteenth-century double-dome walnut bureau cabinet at present. Best you've ever seen. Superb patina. Original mirror plates – well I'm pretty sure they're original. Far less money that you'd see in Bond Street. And a George III oval Pembroke table – they're rare you know. Shell inlay. And I'd love to show you my Russell Flint watercolours.' He smiled, as if he was visualising them.

'Russell Flint?' The name rang a faint bell.

'Don't generally deal in pictures, but I was lucky enough to drop on to a set of signed prints. Originals are worth forty grand – if you can get hold of them. He painted pictures of luscious women. Had a model called Cecilia he was specially fond of – English girl, but looked Spanish. He'd dress her up in Flamenco gear. Beautiful girl – flashing eyes, long black hair, olive skin, gorgeous figure.'

'Russell Flint. Is he still alive?'

'Unfortunately not. Very popular artist. You see cheap prints of his paintings about.'

She had a sudden memory of walking through Selfridges picture department and noticing a set of framed prints of a Flamenco dancer with wild black hair and swirling scarlet skirt, naked from the waist up. She ate a flake of turbot. 'So – now you have a showroom in Kelvedon. But how did you start up?'

'Twenty years ago I was in the motor trade. But I lost interest in cars. Made enough money to move on – I like fine things. I wasn't born with a silver spoon in my mouth, my dear. I've had to graft for what I've got. People like you would call me *nouveau riche*. But I'll tell you what – it's good fun being *nouveau riche*. You can take a pretty young woman out to a swanky restaurant for a start.'

Crude, she thought, unpleasantly aware that she had abandoned one of Felix's principles regarding business entertaining, by overindulging in alcohol. But it was too late to worry about that now, and here, cocooned by the formality of her surroundings, she could remain in control. If she kept the conversation centred on the antique trade, maybe she could get him to talk about Margaret.

'What brings you to Fressenworth today Vic?' (There – she'd managed to call him Vic.) 'We haven't got a decent sale in the area.'

'I bought an Imari dish – *Frances*.'

'You didn't come here just to buy an Imari dish from us.'

'I had someone else to see. And since the forecast is good, I'll spend the weekend on my boat. A couple of friends are turning up tomorrow. We might take a trip out to sea.' He regarded her over his glass of claret. 'You'll have to come along some time.'

Frances couldn't help responding positively to the prospect of a new experience. 'I've done some dinghy sailing, but I've never been out to sea,' she said.

'It's a good feeling – out there bashing through the waves – no one to bother you – nothing but the sea and the sky – and the Russian tanker that's not watching its radar, and the odd container that's fallen off a ship – and a few free-floating beer cans – no, it's great, you'd enjoy it.'

Her head felt like a balloon that has too much air in it. She thought of Vic's boat and of her own part in the Settlement.

And she thought of Margaret's shoe. Had Vic noticed that it was gone from its hiding place behind the row of books? Had he known the shoe was there in the first place? She was still slightly awed by the way in which she had automatically commandeered it for herself. What else might she discover about Margaret aboard Vic's boat?

'Maybe,' she said.

The waiter cleared their plates. 'How do you like working for Tommy Benson? He's a tight-fisted old codger.'

'We get on OK. But it's a bit unsettling since I don't know how long I'll be staying. Margaret will want her job back, I expect. That is, if she ever returns.'

'Hmmn.'

'She must have left in a hurry – everything was in a muddle.'

'Some people do act precipitately.'

'You should know if that's in her character – from what I hear.' She looked him boldly in the eyes which suddenly seemed to go opaque as she added, 'I believe you know Margaret rather well, Vic.'

He didn't answer straight away and when he did, his face was impassive, the tone of voice noncommittal, 'Margaret and I have a business relationship.'

'A pretty long-standing one from what I hear, so what do you think caused her to clear off like that – so suddenly?'

'I have no idea.' His eyes had grown alive and held a calculated gleam. She wondered if he imagined she might know things about Margaret? Might guess about Margaret and him? Could she force him to give himself away? The wine might have made her brain sluggish but it had also injected a dose of dare-devilry. 'I'm sure you do really,' she said, 'Have some ideas that is.'

He was still looking at her with that calculated gleam, but somehow she felt he wasn't seeing her. 'We have a business relationship,' he repeated. 'A long-standing business relationship – only.'

'Liar,' she wanted to yell.

A bowl of green salad and a platter of cheese were slipped on to the table. The lettuce leaves glistened with oil and bore the faintest whiff of garlic. Howden scrutinised the Stilton, the Brie, the Camembert.

Irritated by his composure, she found herself going in for the attack. 'I haven't forgiven you for conning me into breaking the law, Vic. I could easily have walked off with the furniture from Royton Park, and just dumped you and your load of hangers on – and there wasn't a thing you could have done about it.'

'You didn't though did you.' He cut a triangle of ripe Brie and put it in his mouth.

'I'm not like Margaret you know – you can't play me along like her.' She was breathless with rage. 'I'm of no use to you.'

Howden finished his mouthful. 'Shame,' he said.

'You have to understand – I shan't change my mind. Why are you bothering with me?'

'Surely that's obvious?' The invitation in his eyes was so compelling, his features seemed to blur and the imagined touch of his lips and his hands was so real, it made the surface of her skin prickle with fear. 'You're a very attractive young woman – with a bit of spirit.' He leaned forward and added softly, 'I didn't force you to come.'

There was a faint singing in her head, like air escaping from a balloon. She prised her eyes away from his and helped herself to salad. Calm down, she said inside, calm down. When she felt able to control her voice, she said, lightly, 'You're perfectly right.' As long as she kept her head, it didn't matter what he thought. Silence quivered between them. Poor Margaret – beguiled and deluded, used and discarded by this ruthless philanderer. No wonder she had fled. Perhaps she was happy with the mysterious N.H. and never would return to repossess her job and her abandoned belongings. What of her home? Frances imagined a barred and empty house with shuttered windows and a garden choked with weeds. She chewed her lettuce and glanced around the restaurant, avoiding Howden's hypnotic eyes.

'Would Madam like a dessert?' The long silence was broken by the waiter returning with the menu. Frances tried to concentrate on the selection described in florid part-French. Rhubarb Bavarois with Rhubarb coulis and Almond Tuile – Honey and Walnut Parfait with Coffee Bean Sauce and Nougatine Wafer. The words began to spin in her head, making complex patterns of light and shade, sweet and sour, soft and hard, thick and thin. A faint queasiness stirred in her stomach. 'I'd just like coffee, please,' she said rapidly.

'Filter, espresso, or cappuccino?'

'Espresso, please.'

Howden said, 'I'll have filter coffee and we'd like a couple of brandies.' He stopped and added with heavy deliberation, 'Brandy all right for you Frances? Or would you prefer another liqueur?'

'Brandy's fine.'

How could she retreat from the intimacy he was manipulating her towards? She wanted to go on talking about Margaret but was unable to challenge his assertion that his relationship with the woman was purely a business one without revealing her own illicitly acquired evidence. In the end it seemed safer to remain silent: to leave the next move to him. She could see he was amused by the situation, aware she was in some kind of dilemma. He watched her thoughtfully as he rolled the brandy glass between the palms of his hands. 'I expect old Tommy's pleased with the way you've tidied up his shop. You've transformed the place. It must have been hard work sorting out all that clutter. I bet plenty of things have come to light the old boy didn't even know he had. I don't suppose he checks on much does he? I can't imagine he keeps a stock book up to date.'

'You're wrong there, Mr Howden.' She felt defensive of Benson.

'Vic. The name is Vic – remember.' He swirled the brandy round in his glass and continued in a conversational tone. 'I'm wrong am I? Really? Do you mean to tell me there's some crazy kind of order in that place after all? Beneath all that dust and old junk, Benson can lay his hands on the candlesticks he bought a year ago at a sale in East Dereham? Or the tallboy he got off an old couple who were moving house?'

The brandy, funnily enough, seemed to be settling her stomach and clearing her head. She felt sharp and tingling with life. 'What are you getting at Vic? It's unprofessional to discuss my employer's business methods.'

'I was merely speculating as to whether your spring-cleaning and superb reorganisation had revealed any surprises, that's all

– an unremembered collector's piece? A bronze, an ivory figure, a piece of carved scrimshaw? Some *objet d'art* I might like to buy?' He swallowed the last drop of brandy and looked at her over his glass. She glanced quickly at his eyes, not giving them time to latch on to hers, grateful for the opportunity to bring Margaret back into the conversation. 'Judging by the way you go through our showrooms – practically with a tooth comb – I should think you know our stock better than I do, and I'm certain Margaret offered you the pick of anything Benson ever bought.'

Ignoring her sharpness of tone. Howden said good-humouredly, 'No harm in keeping an eye out. You probably know my taste by now.'

Frances didn't reply.

'Finely made, good condition, classy.'

She refused to look at him.

They finished their coffee and Howden said, 'I think I should take you home now. It's time for bed.'

She wiped her mouth with the thick white napkin. 'Thank you. I suddenly feel quite tired.'

He didn't touch her as she sat beside him in the car, but every now and then she could feel him sneaking her a sideways look as she stared straight through the windscreen at the road ahead.

'Here we are then.' They drew up at the farmhouse and he stopped the car and switched off the engine. He got out and came round to open the passenger door while she was still struggling to unclip her safety belt. And then they were standing in the dark facing each other.

'Thank you for a delicious meal.'

'I enjoyed your company.' He took her hand and when she braced herself against him, exerted a light pressure upon her palm with the tips of his fingers before releasing her.

'Goodbye Frances. See you soon.'

And then he was off, driving the Mercedes into the quiet night. She closed and bolted the door, went upstairs and fell into bed. Lying alone in the dark, she found she could not sleep. Howden's physical presence was too disturbing to be shut right out of her mind. And there were all those questions about Benson's stock. Did he still think he could make use of

81

her there? Margaret provided the connection between them. He had blocked all her questions about the woman and yet, she had a vague sense of unfinished business between Howden and Margaret and an odd feeling that, in some unfathomable way, Howden thought she, Frances, could be of use.

Chapter Ten

The uncertain spring gave way to fine early summer weather. Frances spent the long light evenings in her garden. She planted petunias and geraniums in the reclaimed flower bed; a wisteria to grow up the front of the farmhouse, a white clematis at the back. Down by the pond, the long-leaved branches of the weeping willow trailed in the water. Spears of new green rushes sprang up. A clump of irises, deep purple, veined with yellow came into bloom. There were marsh marigolds, like huge floating golden buttercups, and among the tall grasses, swathes of deep pink willow herb. She liked the overgrown, wild feel of it. Here was a proper pond, not a manicured garden pool. Just beneath the surface of the brown water, if she looked carefully, she could make out shoals of small dark fish, pursuing their hidden lives. She watched water beetles skidding over the surface, and insects clouding the air above it. Once she thought she caught the brilliant blue flash of a dragonfly.

When she felt hungry, she would go indoors and make supper – salad or soup and cheese – to eat on the terrace, where she would watch the sun drown in an ocean of red and gold which slowly leached into the distant fields of growing corn. It was very quiet and strange sitting there alone waiting for something to happen. Mark seemed to be neglecting her. No doubt he had heard of her evening out with Howden, and if he was going to be awkward about that, she didn't feel like telephoning him. She knew no one else well enough to make contact on her own. They were all Mark's friends, met when she was out with him. For the first time since she came to

Fressenworth, she felt lonely, and unhappy memories crowded her mind. There were bitter memories of Felix. But mostly the memories were sad ones of her mother, so thin and frail, bravely struggling to move her painful limbs, gagging over the hospital food. Fading away. Desperate to nourish, Frances fed her mother teaspoonfuls of home-made soup and of egg custard, tastes of mashed banana or peeled grape. At first Mother did her best to be nourished. Towards the end, fretful, she would push Frances's hand away, 'Don't force it down my throat – I can't swallow. There's no point.'

Flowers died quickly in the overheated atmosphere. Even the hardy chrysanthemums Frances brought were withered in a couple of days. 'Don't bring any more flowers. They worry me.'

In health, Mother had loved flowers, had belonged to a flower club where she learned their botanical names and how to make an armful of spring flowers appear unarranged and natural, or a dozen yellow roses and some greenery look like a piece of sculpture, until she gave up her membership on account of a power struggle between two opinionated flower club committee members. Frances regretted that. Going to the flower club occupied Mother's spare time and kept her mind off what Frances was doing. Remembering all this, Frances felt guilty again. But until her illness, Mother seemed happy enough. Over the years there had been men friends. Frances thought angrily of Harry who melted away after the first few hospital visits.

'Harry can't bear sickness.'

Bloody Harry, thought Frances. He was probably punishing Mother because, when he wanted her to, she wouldn't agree to marry him.

What were they really like, those few years of her parents' marriage? Their time together, cut short by her father's early death, helped her mother to believe in an idyll.

An early memory – was it really a memory? – placed Frances walking along an esplanade between her parents, each hand in one of theirs. Waves curled themselves over on the shore beneath: windows in a row of houses above them caught the light. Was it imagination or memory? – the comforting warmth of her mother's and father's large hands enclosing her own small ones, the excitement of being whizzed high into the air between them.

And now, she was in Fressenworth alone. The novelty of it was beginning to wear off. Perhaps she should have listened to Mark and chosen a less isolated place for her home. The almost uncanny peacefulness of the farmhouse jarred her strung nerves. She found herself nostalgic for crowded pavements, for the panting diesel engine of a London bus, the predictable ting of its bell. Here, the endless bird song, the wind whispering through the leaves, and the unexplained secret click of a door-latch, creak of a floorboard made her strangely uneasy. She slept fitfully during the short nights, half listening for stealthy sounds – jolted sharp awake by the bark of a dog fox in the copse, by the tap of the climbing rose against her bedroom casement. Perhaps she hadn't transplanted all that well to this rich agricultural land. Perhaps like some weeds, she did better in impoverished soil. It was always a relief when dawn broke. Then the bird song seemed more cheerful than melancholic, the early sunshine promising, the scents of the countryside reassuring, and she could get dressed and go to the shop. People – even difficult customers – were a welcome antidote to her solitary state.

Patrick came in one morning, accompanied by a woman. He'd shed his black hat, and his reddish curls had been shorn close to his head. He wore skintight jeans and a loose collarless shirt and brown espadrilles. This was Frances's first meeting with Patrick since the Knock Out, and she greeted him coolly.

'Good morning, Frances,' he said with a polite smile. 'This is Carla Holmes – she's looking for some Regency sabre-leg chairs for a client. I know Benson had a set – have you still got them?'

So this was Carla. Howden's Carla. Instantly alert, Frances examined Patrick's companion. She was probably nearer forty than thirty, of medium height, slim, with a bony face and luxuriant black hair that sprang from her forehead in a well-defined widow's peak, to fall, bouncing on her shoulders like a great bunch of fine wire. High-heeled black sandals with slender straps emphasised her smooth brown legs. She looked tough, selfpossessed, sexual.

85

'Carla decorates and furnishes the houses of the rich and famous.'

She smiled. Her teeth were large, evenly spaced and toothpaste white.

Frances, dressed in a flowered shirt and short-sleeved white blouse, conscious that her hair needed washing and she hadn't bothered with make-up, saw herself dismissed as of no significance in a single all-encompassing sweep of Carla's round brown eyes. 'We've a set of six side chairs – rosewood with brass inlay – I'll show you,' she said, and led Carla through to the back showroom. Together they surveyed the chairs. Their drop-in seats had been freshly upholstered by Sidney in a striped material of dark and light grey. They looked elegant and expensive.

'Your client has a table?'

'Circular pedestal – rosewood with brass inlay.'

Of course. No doubt Carla's client had recently acquired such a table from Patrick – who probably stood to gain from a deal between Carla and Benson for the chairs.

Carla turned each chair over, examined the legs, the back splats, the carving on the rail and the brass inlay. Frances waited for Carla to find fault.

'The legs have been restored on this one, and there's some brass inlay missing here.'

'We can see to that for you.'

'They're rather dear.'

'There are six of them and they are right.' Suddenly, Frances very much wanted to sell the chairs to this supercilious, arrogant woman.

'What's your best price?'

'I can't take off anything without checking with Mr Benson.' To her own ears this sounded overapologetic and immature.

'Far be it from me to regret Margaret's departure, but if she'd been here at least she'd have given me a price for the chairs.' The tone of Carla's voice could have sliced through any of the nearby timber like a cheese cutter.

Frances took a decision, and said coolly, 'I can give you ten percent off, which is what we give the trade.'

'They're still overpriced.'

'I'm afraid I can't let them go for any less,' she said in

as friendly a voice as she could manage. 'Try sitting on one – they're comfortable as well as elegant.' She brushed a speck of imaginary dust from one pristine seat. Carla did not sit down, but she examined each chair meticulously once more, before announcing tersely, 'Very well, I'd better have them.'

Conscious of her own extreme antagonism, Frances forced a pleasant smile. 'I'm sure your client will be pleased.'

Carla ran red-nailed fingers lightly along the top rail of one of the chairs, tracing the inlay. 'I should think so.' She reappraised Frances, a tiny gleam of interest sparking in her shiny eyes. 'And I daresay old Benson's pleased to have found a replacement for Margaret so quickly.'

Likewise Vic Howden in regard to you, thought Frances, visualising the scrawled message – 'Carla will console you'. Not, surely, that Vic needed any consoling. Poor Margaret.

'For the time being,' said Frances, 'Until Margaret comes back.'

Carla looked surprised. 'I rather thought she'd gone for good.'

'Really? What makes you think that?'

'Oh I don't know.' Carla's smile was knowing, secretive, conclusive. Was she arrogant enough to assume herself to be the cause of Margaret's departure? 'Perhaps I've got it wrong.' Still smiling, Carla shook back her thick loose hair and smoothed it behind her ears, like a cat preening itself as it relishes the taste of stolen cream. 'So – how do you like working in a provincial antique shop?'

Ignoring the patronising tone, Frances replied that she liked it very much.

'Not too dull for you – after the Big City?'

'Never a dull moment. How did you know I'd been working in London?'

Carla admired her blood-red nails. 'Do you know, I really can't remember.'

It could have been Vic. But Carla was the sort of person who would make it her business to know all about everything, by any means.

Back in the front shop, Patrick had opened the glazed astragal door of a mahogany china cabinet and taken out an ivory carving of the Virgin Mary. He turned it round thoughtfully in his hands. 'Well?' He didn't look up, delicately running his fingers over the carving.

'A deal has been struck – you've earned your supper.'

Ignoring Carla, Patrick replaced the figure in the cabinet and addressed Frances. 'I see you still have the sideboard.'

The demi-lune sideboard she had acquired at the Knock Out stood by the window. 'It's on reserve,' said Frances, which was almost true.

'You were lucky to hold that,' he said.

'What has luck to do with it?'

'You're talking about some deal, I suppose,' said Carla, her voice shrill with curiosity.

'That's right – concerning Frances and your friend at a sale.'

'I don't have time to go to sales.' The fine gold bangles on Carla's arm slid down and clashed together as she put up her hands to smooth her hair.

'Why should you bother when you can rely on me and Vic to help you get hold of the right pieces at the right price?'

Carla scribbled an indistinguishable signature on the sales slip Frances had passed to her, and said 'Mr Howden's van will collect the chairs next week.'

'Don't become too dependent on the Godfather will you, Carla.' Patrick was suddenly waspish.

'I like powerful men,' said Carla, turning to Frances, 'Don't you?'

Frances thought, she can't make me out – she's too confident to feel threatened, but nevertheless she wants to discomfort me. She gazed steadily back at Carla – the smooth brown skin, the over-abundant hair, the quick competent hands. 'I like', she began, glancing towards the shop door which was opening, and just before the bell tinkled, she finished her sentence, 'I like ... gentle men.'

Mark stepped inside.

'Darling – what a lovely surprise – how did you know I was here?' Carla's smile was one of complacent familiarity, Frances's defiant mood deflated. Mark looked uncomfortable. 'Oh! I saw you in the distance, but I really popped in to see Frances.'

Frances, her self-confidence instantly restored, was gratified

88

to see Carla's eyes reappraising her. 'Hello Mark,' she said, smiling at him.

He said, with nervous haste, 'I'm in a rush – but I hope you're free on Sunday.'

'Sunday?' She allowed her voice to express uncertainty, although she had nothing arranged for the weekend.

'I'll phone.' Mark turned to the others. 'How are you Carla? Patrick?'

Carla, disconcerted, was looking from Mark to Frances. 'You know my friend Mark then?' She touched his bronzed hand lightly, making it seem like a caress. 'such old friends aren't we, Mark – but of course we're both locals.'

'And here comes another,' said Patrick, observing Trevor parking his van outside. As Trevor entered the shop, Mark said quietly to Frances – 'I'll phone about Sunday,' and shot out through the door. While Trevor and Patrick greeted each other, Carla said, 'Let me know when the chairs are ready for collection,' and lit a cigarette after offering one to Frances, who refused it.

After Carla and Patrick had gone, Frances found herself considering the extent of Mark's relationship with Carla while Trevor tried to draw her attention to an inlaid tea caddy. 'I suppose you can't give me a yea or nay till Mr Benson come back.'

'Sorry – but I can offer you a cup of coffee I'm just going to make some.'

'I'm privileged.' He grinned at her. 'I'll just close up the van.'

'I suppose you know Carla Holmes,' said Frances, watching Trevor stir three spoonfuls of sugar into his coffee. 'I haven't had dealin's with her but I do know her.'

'She seems like a tough lady.'

'I reckon you've hit the nail right on the head.'

'I hear she's friendly with Mr Howden.'

'That would figure.' He was enjoying his coffee, not paying much attention to her questions. She wanted to find out more – aware of a pin-prick of jealousy. Mark had never mentioned Carla – but then why should he? 'Is Carla at all like Margaret?'

'She's better looking and a few years younger.'

She'd be older than Mark though. Perhaps he was dazzled by her brittle sophistication. Frances sighed.

'Cheer up.' Trevor smiled at her. 'Thanks for the cuppa. I'll leave the caddy shall I? I'll drop in tomorrow when Mr Benson'll be here.'

'It's pretty.' She opened it, to distract herself from thoughts of Mark and Carla, took off the internal twin lids with their little turned ivory knobs.

'Satinwood,' said Trevor, 'Nice bit of inlay.'

She admired the frilled edge of the shell inlay. 'Where did you get it? Off another old lady?'

'It's like this Frances – this old lady ring me up to say she's got some pieces to sell. I drive twenty miles and this tea caddy's the only thing what's any good – to get it I have to take away a gi-normous Victorian chest of drawers what I pay fifty quid for and should sell for eighty – if anyone want a huge thing like that – I strain my heart out getting it down a winding staircase – and I also have a Victorian chiffonnier with the veneer all lifting off. The profit on the tea caddy have to take account of all that.'

'I see.'

'Like I say – I want to be fair – I have to make a living and I have to think of my reputation. I like to think I'm the same with people whether I want to get something out of them or not – take this woman I went to see last week. She have this chair she want to sell. Her husband used to sit in it before he died. And she keep seeing him sit there. Well she started to pipe her eye. You don't know whether you say the right thing but you do your best. I offer her a hundred for the chair – what she paid two-fifty for new – and she wouldn't take it. When it come down to it it's the hard cash what count.'

'Perhaps she suddenly realised she couldn't bear to part with it at any price – and you making an offer for it made her realise.'

'Well, she had a mirror what'd been hung over a radiator – all the plaster was cracking and coming out – horrible thing – I offered her thirty pound for it – I told her it'd cost a hundred to put it right and I wasn't going to do it because the thing wasn't worth a hundred.'

'What happened?'

90

'Sold it yesterday for forty-five quid.'

'So you made a bit of profit then.'

'I tell you Frances – I work hard for my bit of profit – don't do my back no good neither – humping great bits of furniture about.' He rubbed the base of his spine.

'Oh dear. I'm sorry.'

'Everyone have a bad back in this business. You get used to it. But it hasn't half played me up lately. I reckon humping Vic's wine cooler aboard his yacht's what really done my back in – lifting the so and so up off the trolley on to the deck – months ago now ...' He rubbed the base of his spine once more and sucked in air between pursed lips making a hissing sound. 'And it still isn't right.'

'What does the doctor say about your back?'

'Don't go near no doctor. You got to learn to live with it. You look a bit peaky yourself if you don't mind me saying. You want to get out and have a bit of fun.'

'Yes.' Perhaps she and Mark would have fun on Sunday. Go somewhere. If he'd decided to dismiss her dealings with Howden, things should get back to normal. And really she had no right to be bothered about his friendship with Carla.

'Well ta ta for now,' said Trevor. 'Thanks again for the cuppa.' And off he went, tipping his check cap to her as he closed the door.

After Trevor had gone, a vague memory surfaced in her mind: Howden's weighty goods being loaded the day she came into Benson's shop for the first time. At the Knock Out, Trevor referring to the 'cooler loaded with booze.' Howden's antagonism. She puzzled over this for a bit and then she got out Margaret's little hard-backed book. She flipped through the pages until she came to the last one which listed Woodton Hall sale on 26 March. And there it was: 'Lot 450 Mahogany wine cooler £1500 H.'

Chapter Eleven

Speeding along in the sunshine in Mark's car, Frances felt happy. She had no idea where they were going. The undulating Suffolk countryside shone with the freshness of early summer. The sky was a blue vault, arching over acres of rippling corn, the green expanse interrupted here and there by a field of oil-seed rape in flower, startling the eye with an occasional flash of over-brilliant yellow. The roadside hedgerows frothed with hawthorn blossom and cow parsley, and through the open window came gusts of scented, pollen-laden air. Beside her, Mark seemed relaxed and light hearted. She noticed how the down on his sun-tanned forearm glistened in the sunlight, and felt a sudden urge to touch it and to lay her fingers softly on the back of his neck beneath the brown hair that brushed the collar of his open-necked shirt. I must be getting over Felix, she thought, with some surprise.

'Nearly there.' He glanced at her.

'But I don't know where "there" is.'

'You soon will.'

Ahead of them, the translucent quality of the light made her think they might be approaching the sea. To their right stood woodland, the trees every shade of green from the yellow of the limes to the blue of the pines fringing the road, which she now saw dropped down to a river. She thought of the marina where Howden kept his boat. Was it nearby? On this same river? Here, black and white Friesian cows grazed on peaceful water-meadows and the river curved, smooth as glass, sweeping round and widening into an estuary where it merged with the sea. In the far distance the horizon was a strip of ultramarine.

As they descended, the narrow road petered out into no more than a track, at the end of which, by the waterside, stood a pink-washed public house. Mark parked the car and they both got out. Boats rested, head to tide, on swinging moorings and a few idled along, sails slack in the light breeze, trailing ripples.

'It's idyllic.'

'I thought you'd like it. We'll have lunch in the pub and then I'll show you the river.'

The pub was full of yachtsmen clomping about in yellow sailing boots and blue Guernsey sweaters, clasping pint mugs of bitter. Frances and Mark escaped to the garden where, at a wooden table, they lunched on ham sandwiches and ginger-beer shandy. The river sparkled and they watched the boats slicing through the water, and listened to the flap of a sail, the creak of a rope, the metallic whirr of a winch.

'This is good. I love an outing.' She had not intended it as a reproach, but he said, apologetically, 'I've been rather busy, or I'd have got in touch sooner, but I expect you had things to do.'

'Oh there's plenty to do – I sometimes think I'll never be straight. The bathroom's still in chaos and Ted's found dry rot in the attic. But actually, Mark,' she said, needing badly to confide. 'I've been a bit sad. It's very quiet at home – specially at night.'

'Almost too quiet,' he said in a quiet and considering voice.

'But it's what I wanted. What I came here for.'

'You don't know what you really want till you get it.' He paused, then added, seriously, 'You don't have to stay there, you know. If you're frightened. I could sell that place quite easily for you – once it's done up.'

'I wouldn't dream of it,' she said, robustly. 'I didn't say I was afraid – I said I was sad. Come on – let's go for a walk.' She grabbed his hand and leaped to her feet. Soon she was following him along a path of sun-baked mud on top of the narrow, rush-lined river bank. The tide was flowing out. At the water's edge in the widening strip of glistening mud and in the shallow pools fringed with samphire, the wading birds probed for food with their long bills. Mark said they were mostly oyster-catchers and redshank. Frances recognised a heron, rising into the air with slow wing-beats.

'That's a curlew,' he said, and she glimpsed the long down-curved bill as the bird sped past. Chilled by its wild sad call, she thought unwillingly of nights alone at Willow Farm, lost concentration and stumbled. Mark turned. 'Are you OK?'

'I'm fine,' she replied. 'But oh what an eerie sound that is – the cry of a marsh bird.'

'Perhaps because these birds inhabit bleak mudflats, deserted marshland, empty beaches – their calls represent the atmosphere of those places. But today there are boats on the river – people all around having a nice time – and the sun's shining.' He put an arm round her shoulders.

'It still makes me feel sad.'

'Cheer up. This isn't like you.'

'You don't really know what I'm like.'

'Any more than you really know what I'm like.' His tone was brusque.

'Sorry.' Not wanting to hurt his feelings, she raised her hand and clasped his where it rested on her shoulder.

'You seemed happy earlier on – what's upset you? Is it the farmhouse?'

'No – I don't know.' The thought of being alone in Willow Farm could not account for the sudden feeling of desolation that swept over her with the lamenting cries of the birds.

They drew apart and resumed single file along the narrow path until they came upon a strip of sandy beach. Two boys were throwing sticks for a muddy little dog which rushed about retrieving them from the water. Mark and Frances stood and watched. Soon, the boys were waist deep in the water, the dog swimming in circles. As she watched, Frances was fired with a great desire to plunge into the river herself. She needed the shock of cold water, the forced activity of her limbs to scour away this desolate feeling – to feel happy again.

'I've a brilliant idea,' she said, 'Why don't we go swimming?'

'In there? You're having me on. It's cold and muddy – the tide's going out and there's a vicious current.'

'Oh Mark – don't be boring – you're always telling me not to do things.'

'But you never take any notice.'

'I really want to swim.'

'You haven't got a swimsuit – or a towel.'

'So?'

He dropped his arm from her shoulders. 'Well you certainly wouldn't catch me going in there.'

The boys and their dog charged out of the water with a great deal of shouting and splashing and barking and tore off along the beach.

She looked into his face which had grown suddenly stern. No, I don't really know you, she thought. You're not responding. 'Where's your sense of adventure?' she cried, stripping off her jeans and shirt. If he replied, she did not hear it, as she dashed into the river in her underclothes.

There were sharp stones on the riverbed. Mud oozed between her toes. The current tugged at her legs. She launched herself forward. The icy water knocked the breath out of her. But in a moment she was swimming strongly, just holding her own against the tide. The river pressed against her limbs. She gulped air and gave herself to it, diving down away from the light. Exhilaration came when she burst through to the surface, pushing her streaming hair away from her eyes.

'Take care,' yelled Mark from the beach.

'It's all right. I won't drown. Come and join me – it's wonderful.'

'I'm not tempted.'

She swam in circles, waving at him. Down she dived. Surfacing, she did a few strokes of crawl, a few of breast-stroke. On her back, she kicked her legs. Enclosed by the water, forcing her limbs to perform as she wanted, shutting out the sunlight, shooting up into it, she felt her sense of desolation dissolve. She felt powerful and free.

'Mind you don't get cramp.'

The cold was indeed beginning to bite. But she swam on for several minutes before heading for Mark and the beach. When she rose out of the water and scrambled to her feet, her bra and pants were transparent. Mark grabbed her icy hand. 'You're mad,' he said, as she gasped with the cold. 'Here, take this.' He stripped off his blue denim shirt, revealing his pale chest with its light fleece of brown curls. 'Let's find somewhere a bit more private.' He wrapped the shirt round her shoulders and led her up the bank and along a narrow path overgrown with bracken and brambles. 'You can get dressed under the trees.' He had her jeans and shirt in his other hand.

The path led to a wooded ridge where, majestic above the silvery willow and bush alder, stood a group of Scots pines with seamed reddish trunks. He guided her among them to an enormous and ancient oak tree. Its massive lower branches bent down to rest on the ground and its great gnarled roots arched up out of the ground like the limbs of some prehistoric animal. Soon, they were standing beneath the canopy of leaves, concealed.

'Use my shirt as a towel,' he said, unsteadily.

With her back to him, she unhooked her bra and stepped out of her pants. It would be untrue to say she felt surprised when, from behind, he took her breasts, one in each hand, and pulled her hard against him. His face was in her wet hair and he was kissing her neck and her shoulders. And then he let her go. Freed from his grasp, she turned, and saw him struggling out of his jeans. He was flushed and bright-eyed and breathing fast. Was this what she wanted?

For a moment, naked, they stared at each other. He was erect. A stranger. A voice in her head said, don't think about it. And she pulled him down on to the soft earth which smelled dankly of leaf mould. His eyes were closed. Beyond his head, up through the canopy of swaying leaves, the sun was glinting. His mouth was on hers and she could feel how his whole body was shaking. There was a moment of panic because he was not Felix, and then, he was inside her and she was moving in time with him, feeling herself beginning to come alive. And then it was all over. Lying beneath him, she felt how violently his heart raced against her breast and thought 'What have I done?'

'Oh Frances.' His voice was husky with emotion. 'Did you ...?'

'Yes,' she lied, trying to wriggle out from under him.

There was the sound of footsteps and the rustle of leaves and a female voice called, 'Barley – come here, good dog – here Barley.'

France half opened her eyes. A yellow labrador raced into view, bounded over her feet and disappeared. 'Good dog,' the voice said. 'Been after those rabbits again have you?'

Frances giggled. Mark said, sharply, 'Don't. For God's sake don't. It isn't funny.'

'Oh I don't know. When you think about it, the sex act is pretty odd – and out here – on the bare ground with people walking past – I suppose we could be arrested for indecent behaviour.'

'Well that wouldn't be funny.'

'Rabbits.' She began to laugh.

'Frances please don't. Please don't laugh.'

She stopped when she saw that he was trying to contain some strong emotion. 'OK. Let's get dressed.' She pushed at his chest with her hands. He clambered off her, brushing earth and leaves from his skin. When they'd both put some clothes back on, they sat down to rest against one of the oak tree's massive roots. In silence, they watched the river, shining like a silver sword below them. A few white sails drifted by. Exhausted, Frances closed her eyes. Bird song, inexpressibly sweet, floated up from the swampy thicket below.

'That's a nightingale,' said Mark.

'I didn't know they sang in the day.' The pure, bubbling song was oddly recognisable, crudely reproduced in a million musical boxes.

'You notice it more at night because you hear them singing alone.'

'Thou wast not born for death, immortal bird,' murmured Frances. 'Poor Keats. He died so very young.'

'Don't talk of death. It will make you sad again.'

'You told me not to laugh,' she said a little snappily, feeling now nearer to tears than laughter.

He began to stroke her arm. She remembered the feel of his heart beating against her breast and thought how separate she was from him. Unresponsive to his caressing hand, she gazed at the river, framed like a picture, by the branches of the oak. He slid his fingers up her arm, following the line of her shoulder and neck to her jaw, turned her face towards his and kissed her on the lips. Unsummoned, a tear came to her eye and fell between their faces. He released her. 'Just because I asked you not to laugh doesn't mean I prefer you to cry.'

Shamed by the hurt in his eyes, she said, 'Sorry,' and tried not to sniff as another tear trickled down her cheek.

'Women!' Now anger threaded his hurt and blunted her shame.

She blew her nose on a handkerchief she found in her jeans pocket. 'Don't say "Women" like that. That's what all men are supposed to say. They're supposed to indicate the contrariness of women in exactly that tone of voice.' She hated the chip of ice lodged in her heart. 'You know I've been hurt.'

'You seemed quite keen to forget it a little while ago.'

'It's just that it's the first time since ...' Now she couldn't avoid sniffing as she remembered the rapture of lying with Felix.

'How do you know I haven't been hurt – by some woman?'

'I don't. Have you?'

'That's not the point. Women make use of men just as much as men make use of women if you ask me.'

She wondered, was he insinuating that this was what she was doing to him? Or was he alluding to some private wound? 'I suppose it's inevitable,' she said. 'We all get hurt sooner or later.'

'Men get upset like women do,' he said crossly. 'They just don't go on about it all the time. It's all right to be emotional if you're a woman – but men must learn to hide their feelings.'

'Only because they don't want anyone – mainly other men – to accuse them of weakness.'

'Oh you have all the answers. When I was a little boy I used to envy my sister – not having to fight anyone or play rugby, and she had the nerve to say that was just what she wanted to do – well – play rugby anyway. But of course she didn't have to prove it: she was quite safe. It seemed tough – being a boy. And now, I often think women have an easier time.'

'Women don't have the freedom men have.'

'That's what we've just been talking about – freedom. Freedom to indulge the emotions. And you can be irresponsible – get some man to look after you.'

'That's not freedom.'

'It's freedom of choice. You can choose *not* to have a job. Plenty of men would like the opportunity to have babies so they can mess about at home with the kids and listen to Radio 4 – provided with a cast-iron excuse not to be successful at work. Women can decide whether to enter the race or not. Men have no option.'

'And a lot of women want to enter the race *and* have children. And nearly kill themselves in the process. OK if you're a real high-flyer, you employ a nanny – and then she's the one who gets to do finger-painting with your children while you rush home from work laden with Safeway bags and head for the kitchen. You can't be a proper mother *and* do a demanding job. It's not like that for men – they can be jolly fathers and have a first-class career as well.'

'That's obvious. That's biology.' Through the lens of his glasses, Mark's hazel eyes held a cold, superior expression.

'You don't like women very much do you?' she said acidly.

'Of course I like women. It's just that you're all so unpredictable.'

'And men aren't?' She remembered how, such a short time ago, this man with the cold superior eyes, had lain in her arms, shaking from head to toe.

He didn't respond, watching the river. Pale grey clouds appeared from nowhere and skidded in front of the sun. The nightingale stopped singing. After a while, he said, 'Tide's turned and the wind's swung round. Time to go.'

Chapter Twelve

First thing on Monday morning, Mr Benson said, 'I'll be out a good deal this week – Christie's South Kensington on Tuesday and then I've a couple of dealers to visit in the Cotswolds. 'You'll be able to manage I dare say?' He regarded her quizzically. And she remembered his satisfied smile when she told him she'd sold the chairs to Carla. 'I'll be fine.' She was pleased she'd earned his confidence, but unable to resist adding, 'So long as you make sure everything is priced.'

They both knew this was not the case currently, and was unlikely to become so. He took off his glasses, folded them up and put them in his pocket. 'I'll keep in touch by telephone my dear. Any problem will have to wait till my return.' And he disappeared into his office, shutting the door behind him.

While she sorted the mail, she wondered if Mark would telephone and, conscious that she was largely responsible for the great leap forward in their relationship, tried to think what to say to him.

She really liked Mark; was attracted to him – to his cleancut Englishness, his honesty, was moved by his apparent feeling for her, enjoyed his company – but to embark upon the intimacy of a proper relationship? She was not sure she was ready for, or wanted this. She wanted neither to hurt him nor to lose him, but there was still the memory of Felix. And there was the horrifying allure of Vic Howden's discomforting eyes, the luxuriance of the hair curling low on his neck.

'You're in a bit of a muddle aren't you my darling.' If only her mother were here. Tears burned behind Frances's eyes. Mother seldom raised her voice and seldom nagged. But there was a dependable firmness there; a confidence in what she perceived to be right. If only she could hear Mother's voice in her ears instead of just in her head – even if she chose to take no notice of what Mother might say. But she was not here. There was no one here with whom she could be natural and open, against whom she did not need to keep up a guard. She thought about telephoning Clare, sensible Clare. But Clare and Robert were married now and busy doing up their house in Clapham. And Clare was probably pregnant. Last time they spoke, Clare told Frances, confidentially, 'We're trying for a baby.'

Halfway through the morning Mark telephoned. He sounded brisk and distant, but then, he was calling from the office. 'The firm are sending me to London on a course for three days. I meant to tell you yesterday, but I forgot.'

'Never mind. I hope the course goes well.'

'Thanks.' He paused and started to say, in a softer voice, 'Yesterday was ...'

Without giving him time to finish, she rushed in with, 'I'm afraid I went a bit mad yesterday.'

There was a pause, and then he said, 'I suppose you did.'

'Well so did you.'

'It was good,' he said lightly.

Perversely, she wanted that softness back in his voice. She wanted depth of feeling. 'Look forward to seeing you when you get back.'

'Sure – I'll be in touch.' Now his voice was definitely casual. 'Must go.'

She heard the click as he put the receiver down. Her feeling of disappointment was quickly followed by one of relief. She would not have to face him again just yet.

The next few days seemed to drag. She felt lonely, both at home, and at work. Although he was there, in the back work-shop, the irascible Sidney seldom ventured out of it and, when he did, he never said anything to her.

Business was slow. The hot weather made people lethargic, almost bored. They would come in to the shop and wander round, exclaiming under their breath at the prices, and then go out again with barely a nod in her direction. Sometimes she would say pointedly, and with a cheerful smile, 'Goodbye – thank you for calling,' if only to demonstrate her visibility.

By Thursday, she had not heard from Mark, though she imagined he would be back in Fressenworth. She had been bothered by a problem with the telephone. It would ring. After answering as usual with 'Benson Antiques', there would be some kind of distant buzzing and then the line would go dead. She reported it to the engineers, who checked the line and found no fault. Could it be someone wanting only to speak to Margaret? Could it even be Margaret herself? Calling from goodness knows where?

On an impulse, she opened the bottom drawer of her desk and took out the cardboard box containing Margaret's possessions, untouched since the day she had shut them in there. She looked once more at Margaret's pink comb, at her sunglasses, the paperback copy of *Lace*, the bottle of 'Femme', the cigarette lighter that didn't work. The high-heeled shoes. Her heart began to bump unevenly as she took out the bunch of keys. There was a yale latch key and two mortice keys. Spare keys to Margaret's house? Where did Margaret live? What was her surname? Weston. That's right – Margaret's surname was Weston. She'd seen it on envelope addressed to Benson's. Frances turned the pages of the telephone book.

Weston M. Forgetmenot Cottage. How apt, she thought, as if I'd forget you, Margaret. *Forgetmenot Cottage, The Green Girdlestone*. She'd have to look at the map, but she thought Girdlestone was a village about ten miles south of Fressenworth. The keys had grown warm in her sweating hand. 'Do I have the nerve for this?' she asked herself, aloud in the empty shop.

The telephone rang. Still holding Margaret's keys, she picked up the receiver with her other hand and gave her usual answer, 'Benson Antiques'. There was no immediate response. 'Margaret?' she whispered, waiting uneasily for the now familiar buzzing and for the line to go dead. And then Felix's voice, instantly recognisable from the first syllable, sounded into the void. 'Hello Frances.'

When she managed to answer him, her voice felt as if something was chasing it back down her throat. 'How did you know I was here?' Did she feel dismay or relief?

'Can we meet?'

She didn't answer. Had he left his wife? Had her own precipitate departure galvanised him? Did she want him now? She felt sick, disorientated. But the sound of his voice had always stirred her.

'I miss you.'

What did she feel? Not nothing. She made herself say, 'I've just got over missing you.'

'Do you mean that?'

She hesitated – if he was free ... if he loved her ... Perhaps he would ask her to marry him? Strange thought. 'How are Esme and Jeremy?'

'It's difficult.'

'I daresay.'

'Are you all right?'

'I'm fine.'

'When can I see you?'

'Have you left them again? Esme and Jeremy?'

In the silence that followed, she knew how it was. Eventually, he said, 'Esme's better and Jeremy's exams went OK. With any luck he'll be off to college in a couple of years.'

Deadly insight led her to the next question. 'They're away on holiday aren't they? And you're on your own?'

'I'd like to see how you are.'

And now she saw him as he really was. Clever, charming, but shallow and weak. Dishonest with himself. Elated, she realised she didn't care about Felix any more. It was over.

'Whatever you might think about me – I want you to know that I care for you. I'd like to check you're all right.'

She found she could laugh. 'I think you're lonely. You don't like being on your own. You need a woman.'

'You don't have a very good opinion of me.'

She laughed again and asked him how things were at work. They talked for a little and then he said, 'If you fall in love, I'll be jealous.'

'If you care for me, it should make you happy.'

'I'm too much of a bum for that,' he said sadly. 'He's a lucky chap.'

'Who?'

'Don't tell me there isn't someone.'

'Not really,' she said. 'Felix, I'm all right. You were very good to me when my mother was dying – thank you for that. And I won't ever forget you.'

'Often, I think of you. Please take care of yourself.'

'You too. Goodbye Felix.'

There was a kind of sigh the other end of the line and he rang off without saying goodbye.

It worried her a little to think how ephemeral had been that imagined love. The empty feeling inside that still remained was nothing to do with Felix. It was lack of her mother, and Felix had been all muddled up with the time of Mother's dying.

Margaret's keys were still clutched in her damp palm. Decisively, she put them back in the box and shut them away once more. I'll give it a week, she said aloud, and then, if there's still no news of Margaret, I'll go there.

The afternoon wore on: hot and windless. Oppressed by the lifeless air in the front showroom, she was driven, in search of company, to visit Sidney in the workshop. He was having a tea break and reading the *Eastern Evening News*. He signified his resentment of her interruption by stretching out his hand for another biscuit from his sandwich box without looking up. She murmured something, returned to the front showroom discon-solate, and sat down at her desk waiting for something to happen. She thought of Margaret's keys asking to be used. Got up and wandered restlessly from room to room. No one came. She stared at the silent furniture and it seemed to stare back at her. In Mr Benson's office the sagging chair was a reminder of its customary occupant, as was his desk piled with sales cata-logues, correspondence and an over-flowing ashtray. She emptied the ashtray, repelled by the acrid smell of it. Loitered, lifted and replaced the heavy blackamoor figure on the carved pine mantel, peered closer at the over-restored nineteenth-century landscape painting that hung on the panelled wall, and brushed dirt from the damaged gilt-wood mirror. Her sombre reflection, staring back from the shadowy mirror plate, looked like the face of a drowned girl, peering up through a film of water.

She turned from the disturbing image and her eye was caught by the small red-walnut bureau that stood in the far corner of Benson's room. The old brass handles, delicately

104

chased, shone softly, the timber shiny as a conker fresh from its case. Impulsively, she walked over to it and swung down its fall-front, revealing the interior of the bureau, neatly fitted with a row of small drawers beneath pigeon holes, above which, a decorative fretwork completed the satisfying appearance. Frances opened the little drawers, marvelling at the ease with which they slid in and out, admiring the tiny hand-cut dovetails. Idly, she ran a finger round the fret above the pigeonholes, and put her hand inside one to feel the depth.

The telephone rang, shrill in the silent building. The sudden sound took her by surprise. She started nervously. Her hand jerked back and up, grazing her wrist against the decorative fret which, to her surprise, slid almost imperceptibly forward. With the tips of her fingers, she eased it further towards her and in a second had drawn out a slender box. The telephone went on ringing, while Frances stood there, gazing down at the secret drawer in her hand. The romance of it immediately fired her imagination to hope for a yellowed love letter, a lock of hair, a ring. She slipped her hand inside. But her eager fingers, searching right to the back of the little drawer, found nothing. Distracted by the tinkle of the door bell, she replaced the secret drawer, closed the fall-front of the bureau and walked out of Benson's office into the main show room.

'Ah – there you are.'

Vic Howden stood, suave and suntanned in nautical navy and sailing shoes. He smiled at Frances. 'All alone?'

She nodded, folding her arms. His eyes roved round the room, flicking over the furniture, noting the newly acquired Victorian walnut pedestal desk, the elaborate Art Nouveau brass umbrella stand. His eyes flicked back to Frances and he moved nearer to her. She leaned away from him, her back muscles tense. He smiled and she noticed clipped black hairs in his nostrils.

'Pretty as ever,' he said, 'But a little tired and pale. What's the trouble Frances?' He came closer and peered into her face.

She stiffened. 'I'm perfectly fine, thank you.'

'Ah – it's the peace and quiet around here getting you down isn't it? You need a change of scene – a dose of fresh air. Why not spend Sunday on my boat – a trip out to sea will put the roses back in your cheeks.'

'I'm busy this weekend.'

'We'll make it next weekend then shall we?'

Next weekend was a long way off. She could always get out of it. 'I'll have to check my diary.'

'I wouldn't dream of forcing you my dear.' He gave her a penetrating look which seemed to home in on her stomach. 'I was rather hoping you might enjoy it.' He went on looking at her.

A blush crawled up her neck and suffused her face. To her chagrin, she saw from his amused expression, he noticed. She was rescued by the telephone 'Benson antiques.'

It was a young woman asking about the cost of repairing a games table. While she talked to her, Howden went out into the narrow hall.

When she had finished, she found Howden in Benson's office, the door of which she had forgotten to lock. He was examining the red-walnut bureau with a critical dealer's eye. It was clear he had not seen this piece of furniture before. Benson's office was always kept locked when it wasn't occupied by the old man. 'How much?' The expert fingers swung down the fall, touched the little drawers, traced the fret. 'Ah – yes.' He found the secret drawer and in a trice pulled it out and held it in his hand.

'Shame it's empty,' she said. 'Have you ever found a secret inside a secret drawer?'

He looked sharply at her and his impenetrable eyes darted a curious spear of sudden interest. He slid the secret drawer back into its place and said, 'When you've seen as many of them as I have, you know that secret drawers never contain anything more exciting than an old bill. How long has Benson had this bureau?'

'I don't know. It was here before I came.'

'What's the price?'

'I'm sorry, Mr Benson hasn't marked it. That might mean it's not for sale.'

'If you don't know it already, you will learn, Frances, that everything has a price.'

'When he phones at the end of the day, I'll ask him and let you know.'

Howden drummed impatiently with blunt fingers on the

reddish wood. 'Very well.' He opened one of the long drawers, revealing bits of fluff, a packet of drawing pins and a Christie's *Yearbook*. Then he pushed the drawer closed and turned away from her. She was aware of his irritation. Then, he seemed to pull himself out of some inner thought to direct his concentration upon her. 'I'll see you on Sunday week. Would you like me to pick you up, or can you make your way to the marina?'

She hesitated, aware she'd not yet agreed to accept his invitation. 'I'll meet you at the marina.' That way, she could always change her mind.

'Nine o'clock sharp – so we can catch the tide.' He paused, fixing her with perceptive eyes. 'Sure you want to come?'

'If I can't make it I'll let you know.'

His half smile acknowledged her dilemma.

Next morning Mr Benson telephoned to say he would not be back in time to see her before the weekend and was planning to go to Dublin for a sale at the beginning of the following week, provided she could manage without him. She said she could manage fine and told him about Howden's interest in the bureau. 'I'll give him a ring,' he said tersely.

As she put down the telephone, it rang again almost immediately. 'Let's have lunch together,' Mark said. Surprised at how pleased she was to hear his voice, she agreed to meet him in the saloon bar of the White Horse. He was standing at the bar, when she arrived at one o'clock. 'Hi.' His smile seemed a touch embarrassed. He was probably visualising, as she was, their hasty coupling beneath the oak tree. He doesn't know what to make of me, she thought, giving him a friendly smile. 'How are you?'

'Hot. What would you like to drink?'

'Ginger beer with lots of ice please.'

'And to eat? I'm having a ploughman's.'

'That'll do me fine, thank you.'

Mark ordered their food from the barmaid, collected her drink and brought it to her table.

'How was the course?' she asked.

'OK, but I'm glad to be back.'

'There's no-o place like home,' she droned. And then she found herself saying – though subconsciously it must have been in her mind all along – 'I'm thinking of going to Bradstone this weekend – to have a look at the place where I was born. My old home. Why don't you come with me?'

'I'm having Sunday lunch with my parents. We could go in the afternoon.'

'Don't let me disrupt your Sunday.'

'You won't. Tell you what, come and have lunch first – meet my parents. And then I'll take you to Bradstone.' He sounded pleased with his idea.

'If you're sure,' said Frances dubiously, wondering if she was quite ready to meet Mark's parents.

'Of course I'm sure.'

'Thank you.' Just as she was beaming at him and thinking he was good-looking and kind and not smug at all, the door swung open and Carla Holmes burst in, trailing coloured scarves and borne along in a vapour of musky scent. She immediately spotted Frances and Mark, and homed in on their table. 'Hello you two. Having a cosy lunch?'

Mark looked more disconcerted than pleased, as Carla laid a bony hand upon his shoulder. 'Please don't get up,' she said.

'Let me get you a drink, Carla.'

'Thank you – I'll have my usual.'

While Mark went to the bar, Carla pulled up a chair and sat down beside Frances, and took out a packet of king-size Dunhills. 'Cigarette?'

'I don't smoke,' said Frances.

'Shortens your life,' said Mark, setting down a double gin and tonic.

'Only by about seven years, and who wants to be eighty?' Carla breathed smoke out through her nostrils and curled her fingers round the glass of gin and tonic.

'That looks nice.' Two plates holding slabs of cheddar, mini French sticks, sprigs of watercress and dollops of pickle arrived on the table. 'Could I have one of those please?' She flashed a wide smile at the waitress. 'But just a small piece of cheese – Brie if you have it – thank you.'

Arrogant bitch, thought Frances. Was she really the intimate friend of Mark's she claimed to be?

Thereafter, Carla dominated their lunch. She talked to Mark about people Frances hadn't even heard of, drank two more double gins and smoked four cigarettes, with no regard to the direction the smoke was taking. Frances, stoically eating her lunch, was relieved to note that Mark had difficulty in responding to Carla's non-stop chatter. He looked morose and uncomfortable. After drinking a cup of coffee, Frances thought to escape in the ladies room. But, to her dismay, Carla turned up just as she was washing her hands. 'He's such a love, isn't he,' she said applying lipstick.

'Mark? Yes, he's a good friend.'

'Nothing more?' Carla wiped lipstick from her front teeth with a tissue.

Frances didn't respond. My mother would call you vulgar, she thought, flapping her fingers beneath the hand dryer.

'Well, I'm afraid you'll find him a bit of a disappointment in that area,' said Carla. 'The spirit is willing but ...'

She's put out that Mark is taking an interest in me, thought Frances. She doesn't want him herself, now she's involved with Vic. But she doesn't want me to have him. She glanced in the mirror, flicked a curl into place and said firmly, 'Carla, I really must get a move on – I should have been back at work five minutes ago. Bye.'

Back in the bar, Mark was settling the bill.

'I must rush.' She kissed him quickly on the cheek.

'Right. I'll pick you up on Sunday about twelve,' he said. 'Sorry about ...'

'Thank you for the lunch.' She felt compassion towards him. How come Mark had got mixed up with such an unpleasant woman? Years older than him. Predatory. She must have hunted him down for his youthful good looks. His naivety. Perhaps it was he who had tired of her. And now she was getting her own back? I'll probably never know the truth of it, thought Frances. And do I really want to?

Chapter Thirteen

Frances was up early next morning, as Ted the builder was due to come and investigate the state of the attic floorboards, where he suspected the presence of dry rot. He arrived at eight o'clock, just as she was finishing her cornflakes. She made coffee. 'I hope this isn't going to cost too much.'

'Can't tell yet.'

'It didn't show up on the survey.'

'Sue yer surveyor,' said Ted.

'Oh dear – will it be that expensive?'

'You're never done with an old house,' he said lugubriously, stirring sugar into his coffee.

Ten minutes later they were up in the attic. 'See here – just under the winder.' Ted demonstrated the fragility of a skirting-board by jabbing a screwdriver right through it. 'Dry rot keep away from the light. Go through brickwork like lightning after the next bit of wood. I seen mushrooms the size of dinner plates.' He eased up a floorboard with his screwdriver and shoved his hand underneath. 'Let's hope yer joists run right.'

Frances watched as he worked along the bottom of the window. 'It's in the ends of the boards – see.' They were whitish and friable. 'But yer joists are sound.'

'So it won't be too expensive,' ventured Frances nervously.

'I know a bloke what'll do a good job very reasonable. And give you a twenty-year guarantee.' Ted went on peering under the raised floorboards with his torch. 'Not too bad.' He stood up and handed her the torch. 'You have a look.'

She got down on her knees and shone the torch in the dusty space between the joists and the floorboards. Tentatively, she poked her hand in there and touched solid wood: a joist? and then as her fingers scrabbled around in the dust, they encountered a small collection of loose objects. 'There's something down here,' she said grasping the nearest object and pulling it out. It was a burned down candle. Another lay near it. She scrabbled around in the dust a bit more and came up with an old-fashioned chamber candlestick. 'See what I've found. There's a hidy hole under this board.' The candlestick was black with tarnish but it appeared to be made of brass and was gracefully shaped. How long had it lain there? She imagined a little house-maid, lighting her way up to her truckle bed beneath the oak beams. The dust, which smelled sickly sweet and was thick with fluff, yielded up several more objects: an ancient box of matches, a stoneware jar and something small wrapped in black tissue paper.

'Funny what you can find laying about in a old house,' said Ted. 'I've come across all sorts.'

'Hidden treasure.' Frances unwrapped the tissue from the small object. In her hand lay what appeared to be a miniature portrait. Set in a black frame, perhaps a couple of inches in circumference, dirt encrusted, was the dimly discernible portrait of a lady. 'Goodness – it really is hidden treasure.' Straining her eyes, Frances felt a jab of excitement.

Ted peered over her shoulder. 'I wonder who put that there.'

'I wonder,' said Frances.

When Ted had gone, she brought out her mother's magnifying glass and examined her find. Staring up at her like a tiny ghost, through the crust of dirt, was a young woman. She had a pointed face, black eyes, and her crimped brown hair sprang from a high pale forehead. The curve of her minute mouth suggested a smile. Her dress looked Elizabethan: a tightly fitting embroidered bodice and around her neck, Frances could make out the delicate tracery of a stiff lace ruff. Tilting the miniature beneath the magnifying glass she could just discern an inscription in faint goldish letters: Anno Dm. 1573. Was it authentic? If so, it could be really valuable. And how did it come to be there – lying in its shroud of black tissue beneath the floorboards of a farmhouse attic? Who had hidden it there? Or lost it there even? It was small enough to drop unnoticed

111

between a gap in a rotten floorboard. And when? She felt herself grow hot with excitement, as the blood seemed to rush more swiftly through her veins, more closely to the surface of her skin. It's mine now, she thought. I found it on my property. Finders keepers. But it's probably some old Victorian fake. Even so, it must be worth something. Perhaps enough to pay for the dry rot treatment? Mr Benson would probably know what it was worth. If not, he'd tell her who to ask. With a handkerchief, she tried gently to rub away some of the dirt.

For the rest of the day, as Frances carried out her household tasks, she thought about the unknown lady whose smile, though dimly seen, seemed so knowing. In the evening, she sat alone in her sitting room, the miniature in her hand. Darkness fell, and beneath a reading lamp, the sloe eyes in the tiny face appeared to glow with life, the suggested details of the dress become more apparent, the delicate tracery of the ruff around her throat grow more discerned than imagined, complex as a spider's web. When she went to bed, she took the miniature with her and laid it on her bedside table.

The rose outside her bedroom casement tapped against the glass. Nearby a screech owl sent out its unnerving cry and away in the distance she heard the low growl of a car engine. I have to get over being frightened at night, she told herself, going down to double-check the locks, and shooting the bolts as an extra precaution. Back in her bed her mind was too stimulated to allow sleep. At three o'clock she went down and made a pot of tea. She sat drinking it in the kitchen, listening to her own breathing and trying not to imagine a dark figure creeping round her house, his fingers feeling soundlessly for a loose window catch. She turned on the radio, flooding the room with the reassuring presence of a late-night disc jockey and his anodyne music. Eventually, she dozed off in the chair and only awoke when the radio emitted a high-pitched inter-mittent peep, signalling some early morning Open University programme. She switched it off and hauled herself upstairs to bed to sleep for another couple of hours. When she woke again, she felt unrefreshed and not at all ready to meet Mark's parents for the first time. What should she wear for Sunday lunch with Mark's mother and father? Probably not shorts, although it was going to be a hot day. In the end she decided upon her favourite blue cotton dress with a jacket.

Eating her usual bowl of cornflakes and drinking a cup of strong black coffee, she stared at the miniature lying on the table in front of her. She took it in her hand and ran her finger round the smooth circle of dark wood. Was it ebony? Mark would be here soon. What would he make of it? There he was now – through the window she saw his blue Audi bumping along the track. Without conscious thought, she found herself slipping the miniature inside the cornflake packet, which she put away in the cupboard. Somehow, she felt the need to keep her Elizabethan lady to herself for a little while longer.

Mark's parents lived in a village a few miles south of Fressenworth.

A tall beech hedge shielded their substantial redbrick Victorian house from the road. Mark turned the car into the gate and parked on the sweep of gravel in front of the house. On the back seat lay a bin liner containing Mark's dirty washing. 'You're spoilt,' she teased, when she saw it. 'I suppose you exchange that for a pile of nice clean shirts and a tin of homemade chocolate cake.' Mark just smiled and picked up the bin liner. Frances imagined a plump mother with apple-cheeks, twinkling eyes and a bustling manner.

The front door opened on their approach.

'Mum and Dad, this is Frances,' said Mark.

'Hello my dear – we're so pleased you could come.'

'Thank you for asking me.' Frances took the brisk hand offered her. Mark's mother was not at all the comfortable motherly type she had imagined. She was slim and smartly, if rather severely dressed in navy blue. Her dark hair, threaded with metallic grey, was styled in a simple bob. Her eyes, when she looked into Frances's, were full of curiosity.

Mark got his good looks from his father, a big burly man with a thatch of grey hair and kind eyes. 'Come in, come in,' he placed a warm square hand on Frances's shoulder.

Soon they were all seated in a long light room with French windows opening into the garden. The lawn, close-cut and striped, was bordered by colourful flower beds and various differently shaped beds punctured its emerald surface. Frances accepted a glass of white wine.

'And what do you do, my dear?' asked Mark's mother.

'I'm working for Mr Benson – Benson Antiques.'

'We bought a corner cupboard from him. Oh yes – and a rather nice chest of drawers. But I thought that Margaret person worked there. Isn't that right Mark? Slightly shady character I always think. Don't know why.'

'Margaret left all of a sudden, rather mysteriously,' said Frances, 'although Mr Benson expects her back.'

'I did tell you, Mother.' Mark sounded a touch irritated.

'It was lucky for me,' said Frances, feeling awkward, 'I was beginning to think I'd never find a job in Fressenworth.'

'So you haven't been here for long then?'

'No. I used to work in London.'

'London. Well, you have to be a certain type to get on in London. It didn't suit Mark at all. We had to fetch him back in a hurry.'

'Mother – it wasn't quite like that.' Mark looked embarrassed.

'He was much younger then, of course.'

She talks about her son as if he isn't present, thought Frances, imagining sessions with schoolteachers and doctors, Mark and his mother. The mother doing all the talking while the child stood uncomfortably silent. 'Mark is having trouble with his sums. Mark has a pain in his tummy.'

Mark's father said very little, quietly filling their glasses, allowing his wife to take charge of the conversation. She continued to ask Frances the kind of direct questions that require direct replies. It felt like an interrogation, though not an unfriendly one. It was as if any potential girlfriend of her son required intense scrutiny, before normal conversation could be undergone. Frances felt an embarrassment on the part of both the son and the father. Eventually, Mark's mother said, 'Come and give me a hand in the kitchen David.'

When they were alone, Mark said, 'I'm afraid my mother does go on a bit – but she means well.'

Frances smiled. 'I'm sure she does. I didn't know you used to work in London. I remember you saying – ages ago – that you'd been away from Suffolk for a while – but you never said where.'

114

'After I was qualified I got a job with a firm of valuers in the City. But it didn't work out.'

'London can be great. But I wouldn't go back there now.'

'There was a vacancy in Dad's firm. It was a bit wimpish I suppose – but it seemed the obvious thing to take it.'

'Of course it did.'

'Come through to the dining room.' Mark's father appeared carrying a decanter of red wine.

The solid mahogany Victorian dining table was set with crystal glasses, silver cutlery and gold-rimmed white china ware. Silver candelabra, furnished with unlit red candles, stood proudly on the mirrored surface, along with a bowl of pink roses and four spotlessly bright silver vegetable tureens with lids. A substantial mahogany sideboard held a dish containing a joint of pork crowned with dark brown crackling. The formality of the surroundings made Frances feel uncomfortably like a guest of honour.

Mark's mother was sharpening the carving knife. 'We always have a roast on Sundays. I'm afraid I'm a stickler for tradition. Keep Sunday special, you know. Church in the morning – and David read the lesson today, didn't you dear? And then home for a proper Sunday lunch. It's a bit more work, but I've always considered it well worth the effort. Tradition's important, don't you think?' She paused, carving knife in mid-air, and directed a beaming smile at Frances. 'I hope you like pork. Mark loves the crackling, don't you dear. Shall I carve some for you, Frances? I can't believe you're the kind of person who thinks they'll die if they eat a little fat?'

'Er no – I mean yes, I'd love some crackling thank you.'

Mr Edwards handed Frances a plate of neatly overlapped slices of meat, topped with a chunk of crackling. 'Help yourself to vegetables, and apple sauce and gravy.' He smiled genially and removed the lids from the vegetable tureens, revealing roast potatoes, new potatoes, carrots and peas. 'I grew them myself, so I know they're fresh.'

'They look delicious,' said Frances. And they were, as was the whole meal, throughout which, she found herself telling Mr and Mr Edwards about her decision to come and live in Suffolk, the county of her birth, about finding Willow Farm, through Mark, and buying it despite his efforts to persuade her

115

otherwise. 'I suppose he was right to try and put me off – it needs so much doing to it – and it's miles from anywhere, but I love it really.'

'You get attached to houses,' said Mark's mother. 'Take this place – too big for us now, but we can't find anything we like better. It's our family home. And David won't leave his garden, will you dear. We came when Mark was six, and Joanna four. Joanna's married now – she lives in Leeds. And Mark has his own little flat in Fressenworth. But I always say they'll have to carry me out of here feet first, don't I dear.'

Mr Edwards just smiled. Mark silently continued to cut his meat. Watching him, Frances thought, he had nice hands, not too large, well-shaped, sunburned hands. She remembered the feel of those hands moving over her body as she lay with him beneath the oak tree: a million miles away it seemed. Did she still want him? Did he want her? She wondered what he was thinking about, and tried to catch his eye, but he didn't look up.

Pudding was strawberries 'home grown' with meringues and cream. After coffee in the sitting room, David Edwards said, 'Let me show you my garden, Frances.'

'Off you go my dear,' said his wife, 'Mark will help with the washing up.'

Out in the sunlit garden, the lawn glowed so brightly green and looked so perfectly smooth, she felt she ought not to be walking on it.

'I mow twice a week – and feed it of course.' He bent to part a few blades of grass, presumably on the look out for a rogue weed. 'And this is my herbaceous border.' His large hands were tender as he touched flowerheads, and pointed out favourite plants. 'My snapdragons – used to fascinate me as a child, with their funny little mouths. Columbines – so dainty don't you think? Red-hot pokers, peonies, sweet William.'

'These are delphiniums, aren't they. What a wonderful rich colour,' said Frances.

'Yes – they've put on a good show for me this year. I think there's no more beautiful blue.'

She told him of her ambitions for her own garden, and was touched by his enthusiastic suggestions. She thought he seemed a very pleasant man, Mark's father. Clearly the two of them had a happy working relationship and it was easy to see why Mark had decided to leave London. But how had his mother put it? 'We had to fetch him back'. What a demeaning thing to say in front of a potential girlfriend. Poor Mark.

In the vegetable garden, hidden behind a tall, neatly clipped privet hedge, there were rows of potatoes and peas, onions and lettuces, courgettes and carrots. There were scarlet flowering runner beans, blackcurrant bushes and bushes of green gooseberries. Protected by the netting of a fruit cage there were raspberry canes, and on the ground below, bedded in straw, were the strawberries – plump, ripe and shiny red.

'It's wonderful. Your garden is superb.'

'I just love growing things. I often think if I hadn't been an auctioneer, I'd have been a market gardener.' He picked a pea pod, broke it open and offered her the row of peas as if they were a string of perfectly matched pearls.

'Thank you.' She took a pea, bit into its sweet, crunchy greenness, and thought of all the hours he must spend out here on his own.

He said, 'I'm glad you've come to Fressenworth, Frances. It's company for Mark. I hope you'll stay with Mr Benson. He's a nice old boy. But that Margaret – she's a bad lot you know – she and her flashy friend. Though Mark would tell you otherwise. And now you must have some strawberries to take home.' He took a plastic bag from his pocket and bent to lay back the netting that covered the soft red fruit.

Who on earth was Margaret's flashy friend? Vic Howden? But then 'Mark would tell you otherwise' didn't make sense. Some female friend? Carla? Mark knew Carla all right. But Carla and Margaret were rivals not friends. Margaret must hate Carla.

117

Chapter Fourteen

By late afternoon, Frances was walking along the esplanade at Bradstone, Mark at her side. Down on the beach everyone was enjoying the sunshine. They were eating picnics, building sand-castles, playing ball games or just lying around. The sea was deep blue. A few pleasure boats bounced noisily on its calm surface out of range of the swimmers who splashed about in the shallows shouting and laughing.

'My father drowned out there,' she said.

Mark laid an arm round her shoulders.

'He'd been ferrying supplies to an oil rig. They said his helicopter dropped like a stone.'

The engine had cut out one dark February morning. The sea would not have sparkled that day. It would have been gun-metal grey and cold as ice.

'They think it was a flock of birds flying into the rotor blades.'

Mark stroked the back of her neck, gently, with the tips of his fingers.

She remembered a bitter wind blowing flakes of snow in her face. She remembered watching her mother being led into a car slowly, carefully, as if she'd been suddenly struck blind. The car moved away. Hunched in the passenger seat, her mother stared out through the window. There was no acknowledgement of her daughter standing there alone. Whatever those staring eyes were seeing, Frances knew it was not herself, left behind on the pavement. Then, the old lady next door took her home and told her that her mother would be back soon, and she remembered knowing something terrible must have happened for her mother to forget so completely about her existence. But no one would tell her what it was. She was five years old.

Today, standing beside Mark, watching all the happy activity, it seemed inappropriate to think of death – and yet entirely appropriate. All appeared safe and commonplace: the picture-book beach scene, the blue and tranquil sea. But a treacherous undertow swirled beneath those dancing waves. Frances caught her breath, suddenly acutely conscious of danger. If you looked for it, you could see it everywhere.

'Sunday,' said Mark, his quiet voice penetrating her sombre thoughts. 'That's why the beach is crowded – during the week it'll be pretty quiet. Once the schools break up it'll be like this all the time – provided the weather holds.'

They were walking past a row of brightly painted beach huts. Open doors revealed tables and chairs and baskets of food, people making sandwiches, cutting cakes, boiling kettles on camping gas-burners. It all looked very homely and comfortable.

'He was tall and fair, my father, and he had a beard.' She could remember the prickle of it against her face. 'He was only thirty-two when he died.' Four years older than she was now. 'I suppose my mother never got over it really.'

'She had you.'

'It's odd – she was so young when she lost him. And very kind – and pretty. She had menfriends but she never wanted to marry again. I used to think it was because she idolised my father. I hope it wasn't because of me.'

'I'm sure it wasn't,' said Mark, bracingly.

Turning away from the beach, they walked through the old part of the town. Memories stirred vaguely like glimpsed colour plates in a flipped-through picture book: a canopied shop front, a shot of the sea from an oblique angle in the High Street, the swell of waves against the supports of the pier. They were still there – the craft associated with North Sea oil; the rig supply ships, the maintenance vessels. While her mind fluttered with half remembered scenes, she listened vaguely to Mark, talking about boats and fishing and historic buildings and pier entertainments, in an effort to divert her from melancholic nostalgia.

119

They walked on to where the old town merged with the new, spreading south along the cliffs. Marine Close, where Frances had spent the first few years of her life, was located on a private housing estate, built in the sixties. The houses were set in crisscrossing avenues, lined with ornamental trees. Constructed of dense yellow brick, they were square, stolid houses with porches and picture windows and garages. Some had verandahs and sunrooms, garden statuary and very small ponds.

'Marine Close is a cul-de-sac. It's a turning at the end of Pennybright Avenue – I've always remembered that name,' said Frances as they passed front gardens bright with geraniums and fuschias and roses. There were a few people about, mowing the lawn or doing a bit of weeding. A small boy pedalled a tricycle round and round a circular flower bed. A tabby cat basked on a doorstep.

As they walked along Pennybright Avenue, at right-angles to the seafront, Frances dashed ahead, 'I think I can see the turning. Yes, here it is. Look for No. 7.'

The bungalows in Marine Close were built of the same yellow brick as the houses in the Avenues. Net curtains festooned their large windows; their gardens were neat and colourful. One boasted a pond, with a stone heron standing beside it. They all shone with the same well-cared for air of modest prosperity. All except No. 7. No. 7 had dirty Venetian blinds at its picture window. The dark green paint was peeling away from its front door. The garden was knee-high with rank grass and thistles and dense with daisies and dandelions. Spindly pink roses struggled to raise their heads above the groundsel and dead-nettle choking the one flowerbed. The wicket gate hung precariously on broken hinges.

'Oh no.' Tears burned her eyes. 'My poor mother. It's as if her sadness has stayed in the house, like a ghost.'

'No Frances – you're letting your imagination run away with you. I'm sure your house has had lots of owners since you, who have all looked after it well. I expect the present one is away – or ill – or something. It's not in bad repair, you know, just a bit neglected.'

She laid a hand on the lopsided gate. 'I shouldn't have come. Whatever I was looking for, I haven't found it.'

'I suppose you were looking for a happy childhood. But the only things you remember when you're very young are the big events. Those were sad ones for you, and finding your old home in this state has strengthened those sad feelings. You had happy times, of course you did, but you can't remember them. I think it's best to try and forget the past. Live for the day.' He took hold of her hand. 'Let's go and have a cup of tea.'

How could a cup of tea soothe the ache she felt inside? She dropped her hand from the gate and allowed him to lead her away from the sad house.

On the clifftop above the pier, the turrets and cupolas of the Grand Hotel glowed in the evening sun. Attracted by its air of shabby Victorian grandeur, Frances and Mark headed towards it. In its glassed-in verandah facing the sea, they ordered tea. Frances, trying to shake off the lonely feeling that had overwhelmed her at the sight of the sad house, looked at Mark, sitting opposite her, and remembered the day they first met. They'd had tea that day – at the Copper Kettle in Fressenworth. Mark had just shown her round Willow Farm. It was the start of her new life. She thought of all the things that had happened since then and a stream of images floated before her inner eye: the tense, fumy atmosphere in the cabin of Howden's boat, Margaret's high-heeled shoes, Mr Benson's grey eyes looking coolly at her over the top of his half glasses, Howden's hot black eyes tempting her, Mark trembling in her arms, and, yesterday, finding the miniature in the dust beneath the attic floorboards. The smile on the tiny painted face of the Elizabethan lady had been at the back of her mind all day, sweet as an unexplored pleasure, a secret luxury. And now she wanted to share the secret with Mark. How would he react when she showed it to him? would he feel intrigued and excited like she did? Or would he dismiss it as a worthless trinket? She watched him now, calmly drinking his tea and was filled with a sudden rush of affection. She wanted to tell him how much she appreciated his kindness; to make him feel valued. She leaned forward and touched his hand, 'You've been really kind today, Mark – I didn't expect to be so upset – having you with me helped a lot.'

'I'm glad.' He smiled gently.

'And thank you for taking me to meet your parents. It was a lovely lunch.' And then a little devil inside made her say, 'You've forgiven me now, haven't you Mark – for making a fool of myself at Royton Park?'

She realised her mistake as soon as she saw the gentle smile flee from his face to be replaced by a stern tightening of the lips and narrowing of the eyes. 'For getting involved with those crooks? I don't know.'

'It won't happen again.'

'I should think not.'

She thought, there's no need to take quite such a holier than thou attitude, and felt justified in pressing on. 'But all the same, why can't auctioneers advise realistic reserves? Mr Benson says sale catalogues aren't always terribly accurate.'

He put his cup down on its saucer with heavy deliberation. 'Let me tell you a story. When I was first at Draper's, I handled a house clearance sale. There were one or two decent pieces. I put reserves on – overdid it a bit but I was young and inexperienced. None of those lots got sold and the next sale I ran was boycotted by the dealers.'

'There you are then – you're making a fuss about nothing.'

'I'm not complaining about a handful of dealers not bidding against each other for the few decent pieces in the local sale-room. That's light years away from Howden's organised Settlement. You got yourself working with the real Heavies.'

'I don't approve of the man any more than you do.'

'You went out to dinner with him, though, didn't you.' His voice was vibrant with suppressed emotion.

How did he know about that, she wondered, taken aback by what was not far from malevolence in his eyes. She thought, how quickly the atmosphere between us has changed – and it's all my fault.

'Mark – you've got hold of the wrong end of the stick. The reason I went out to dinner with Vic Howden was to try and get him to talk about Margaret.'

'What on earth for?'

'I want to find out what's happened to her – where she is. I think there's unfinished business between her and Howden. Margaret used to buy stuff for him at sales – I think she got herself in a muddle between him and Benson. She was clearly side-dealing. Benson hates Howden just like you do. Maybe she bought something on Benson's behalf that Howden wanted – or maybe she bought something for Howden and somehow Benson got it. Howden's always poking around in the shop – as if he was looking for something.'

'It's pointless – all this speculation about Margaret – she's gone.'

She tried to explain, knowing as she talked that she wasn't convincing him. 'You'll think it odd, but I have this funny feeling about Margaret while I'm sitting in her chair, answering her phone, touching the furniture she touched. I feel close to her.'

'Frances, she's not worth worrying about.'

'I know she isn't exactly straight, but she couldn't help it you see. She was deeply involved with Vic Howden.'

Mark leaned forward, challenging her with exasperation. 'What is it about that vile man? You're intrigued by him too, I know you are.'

'Rubbish. I can't stand him. I just feel affected by the connection between him and Margaret. Maybe I can help her. I have this premonition that one day she'll turn up – out of the blue – and she'll want me to do something for her.'

'Like give her back her job? Unless of course she's dead.' The flippancy of his tone could not save the word from dropping like a stone between them.

'I don't believe that.' Frances recoiled. 'And anyway, I've had enough of thinking about people being dead. You don't accept my reasons for seeing Vic Howden do you?'

'People's motives aren't always clear – even to themselves.'

'Look Mark – I'm not interested in Vic Howden – not in the way you imagine – but since we're on the subject of relationships – what's the position between you and Carla?'

'Nothing that need concern you,' he said shortly.

Remembering Mark's father's enigmatic remark, she said, 'I've an idea that Carla and Margaret are friends. Is that right?'

'Everyone knows everyone in Fressenworth.'

'Birds of a feather, I suppose,' she said, 'But now Carla has taken Vic Howden away from Margaret, I don't suppose they'll be doing much flocking together.'

123

'Where did you get that from?'

'Margaret.'

'Don't be ridiculous.'

'Sorry Mark – it was a silly way of putting it. There's a lot I want to tell you about – only I've been waiting for the right moment.'

'Frances – I'm not interested in idle gossip.'

'It's not gossip. I need to talk to you.'

The seriousness of her tone got through to him and he sighed and said, 'I could do with some fresh air – let's get out of here.'

They walked along the beach, deserted now, but bearing the scars of the day's activity: trampled sand, collapsing sandcastles, an empty Coca-Cola can, sheets of newspaper, an abandoned deck-chair. Beneath Frances's bare feet, the large pebbles felt smooth and faintly warm from the sun. The tide was high: waves broke with a subdued roar on the shingle.

'It's frightening – the size and force of those waves – even in this light wind.'

'There's a terrifically strong current: the beach shelves very steeply just here – see – it's dangerous, specially on a falling tide.'

The crunch of their feet on the shingle sounded companionable, measured and even, like the breaking waves. The regularity was soothing. Planning what she would say to Mark, she slipped her hand into his. A couple of miles up the coast the beam of a lighthouse flashed.

'Let's sit down a minute.' Taking off his jacket, Mark spread it on the stones. In front of them, each wave curled, slowly at first, before gathering speed to crash in a cloud of spray, its undertow sucking back the pebbles with a rumble. Mark picked up a flat shell and skipped it over the running foam. 'What is it you want to tell me then?'

Steeling herself, she told him about what had happened on board Howden's boat, glossing over the details of Settlement, in particular her own part in this, and concentrating on the finding of Margaret's shoe. She told him about the note, with its message to Howden, concealed inside.

Mark had listened without interrupting and was sitting very

124

still. 'Well – so Margaret's cleared off with some mysterious person, possibly because she was upset on account of Vic Howden possibly having an affair with Carla – but I don't see how it affects you.'

In the silence that followed, it seemed the crash of the breaking waves had a threatening note.

'Do you mind about Carla?'

'I'm not interested in discussing Carla. I'm here with *you* aren't I.' He threw a couple of stones into the curve of a wave with a loose flick of his wrist. 'Perhaps you're attracted to that ghastly man on account of his age. When you were telling me about your father today, I realised how much you'd missed by not having him.'

No response to this theory sprang to mind. She shifted her position on the shingle, which was beginning to feel cold and hard. Far above, the evening star sprang into view, a sudden spark of silver in the darkening sky. 'Why do you think Margaret's shoe was behind those books?'

'Who knows?'

'You don't wear high heels on a boat. She would have changed out of them when she came on board. How did the note get inside the shoe? The other shoe was in the shop.'

'I don't understand why you took it.'

'I just did. And what about NH? Who is NH? Do you have any idea?'

'Maybe he isn't important. Someone offering her a way out of some mess she was in – caught between Howden and Benson. A catalyst to start a new life – like you did.'

'I hope so. I hope she's alive and happy somewhere with him, and not all alone and dead.'

'It's a possibility. She could have collapsed in some out-of-the-way place – or had a fatal accident. Or been murdered.'

'Don't say it.'

'The newspapers are full of stories of women being raped and strangled. She could have been dumped in a ditch or buried in a wood.'

'They do say most murderers are known to their victims,' said Frances, the sound of her tremulous voice almost obliterated by the crash of a breaking wave.

125

Chapter Fifteen

When they arrived back at Willow Farm, everything seemed very quiet and still. She thought, when you've been away from your home, even for a day, it looks deserted when you return. The dark, uncurtained windows threw out no welcome. She shivered.

'Are you all right?' Mark put a hand on her arm.

She clung to him. 'I can't sleep,' she said. 'Country sounds seem so loud and unexpected – I suppose it's because there are so few of them. In a town there's always the background noise of the traffic.'

He put an arm round her. 'I'll see you in.'

She unlocked the front door and they went through into the kitchen. 'Can I make you a coffee?'

'Neither of us will sleep if we drink coffee,' he replied, looking at her steadily.

From its hunting ground, way over the fields, the screech owl sent out its unnerving cry. She jumped, and clutched at his hand.

'You are in a bit of a state,' he said, 'Would you like me to stay?'

'Please.' She was flooded with relief.

'Where shall I sleep?'

She wanted the comfort so badly – and where was the harm? She stretched out her hand.

Sunlight was filtering through the curtains when Frances woke. She slid carefully out of bed, leaving Mark lying there. His limbs were perfectly relaxed, his sleeping face tranquil. She thought, how young he looks, and pulled the sheet up over his naked chest, gently, the way a mother tucks bedclothes round a sleeping child.

Down in the kitchen she made a pot of tea. When she was with Felix it was he who had made tea in the morning and brought it to her in bed. Felix was surprisingly domesticated. Felix was dark and slightly built – and expert. She might never feel for anyone what she'd felt for Felix. It was wrong to compare them. But, in bed with Mark there had been a kind of nervous haste, a sense of intensity without exuberance. She did not want to think of Carla's cryptic remarks. But she wondered if Mark had been badly hurt by a woman.

She opened the pine cupboard and took out the packet of cornflakes. She put her hand inside and felt for the miniature. There it was, wrapped in its covering of tissue paper. She closed the cornflake packet and put it on the table, along with cereal bowls, sugar and milk.

She took two cups of tea upstairs. Mark was sitting up in bed, stretching and yawning. 'I'll have a bath,' she said, 'while you drink your tea.'

There was a moment of awkwardness, during which they smiled shyly at each other. Putting the cup down on the bedside table, she bent and kissed him on the side of his mouth, her lips encountering the edge of his overnight beard. 'I'm glad you stayed.'

'So am I.' He smiled confidently, freely, and clasped her hand. 'I don't suppose you've got a razor have you?'

'Look in the bathroom cabinet.'

She drew back the curtains and gazed out at the summer landscape. The great fields of barley were turning dusty-gold. Soon it would be harvest time. Then it would be autumn. The fields would be ploughed; the leaves would wither and fall. And winter would come. I'll be fine by then, she told herself, properly settled in. The dry rot will have been dealt with, the farmhouse will be fully decorated. Margaret will have returned. And if I lose my job, it won't matter because perhaps the miniature will have made me rich. She leaned out of the casement window. 'I'll have to do something about that rose – it taps against the glass and wakes me at night.'

'Just wants cutting back. I'll do it sometime.'

'Thanks. It's a beautiful day. Everything seems better in daylight.'

'Everything will be fine.' He sipped his tea.

She bathed and dressed. 'Boiled egg for breakfast?'

'That would be nice.' He slid out of bed and went into the bathroom she had just vacated.

Sharing bed and bath with someone is so intimate, she thought, looking at his naked back view and noticing the way he loped across her carpet with his large white feet. What if he was there all the time? She was not sure she would want a man to be there all the time.

In the kitchen she put the eggs on to boil and plugged in the kettle.

Mark appeared, washed and shaved. He sat down at the table.

'Help yourself to cornflakes.' She watched carefully as he poured the cereal into his bowl. The miniature, wrapped in its black tissue paper slid out with the cornflakes. Mark's hand stopped in mid air. 'What on earth's that?'

'A surprise gift of course,' she said. 'Unwrap it.'

Mark put down the cornflake packet and picked up the small object on his plate. Very slowly he removed the tissue paper. 'My God!' He stared down at it, still as stone. And then he said in his quiet, careful voice, 'Where did this come from?'

'I found it in the attic yesterday. Ted had to take up the floorboards – to look at the dry rot. And it was hidden under there.'

For a while, Mark said nothing. He just held the tiny portrait in his hands and stared intently at it. When he looked up at Frances, his eyes behind the barrier of his spectacles looked disorientated, as if he'd been knocked off balance by a blow to the head. 'But this cornflake packet? Why is it in this cornflake packet?'

'I put it there of course.'

'What an extraordinary thing to do. It could be valuable. You amaze me.'

'It's perfectly safe in a cornflake packet,' she said, 'I'm not going to throw it out by mistake. Do you really think it's valuable, Mark? I've been looking forward to showing it to you. I wanted it to be a surprise.'

128

'It's certainly a surprise,' he said, turning the miniature over in his hand, examining the back and running a finger round the frame. 'It needs cleaning.'

'Wouldn't it be wonderful if it was really old – an authentic Elizabethan miniature,' said Frances, putting out her hand and reclaiming it.

'You need to get an expert on miniatures to take a look at it. Even if it's fake, it's a very pretty thing.'

'It must belong to me, mustn't it? Or could it be treasure trove?'

'It was found in your house. I imagine it belongs to you.'

'But I wonder who put it under those floorboards.'

'We'll probably never know. Do you want me to take care of it – get someone to value it for you?'

She hesitated, unwilling to part with her Elizabethan lady.

Seeing her reluctance, he said, 'I'd put it in the office safe.'

'I'd really rather like to show it to Mr Benson first – he'll be back next week.'

'You're sure?'

'Yes – thank you all the same.'

'Well – look after it then.'

'Of course,' she said, slipping the tiny portrait back into the cornflake packet. 'It'll be quite safe in there.'

'If you say so.' His smile expressed affectionate incredulity. Then, looking at his watch, he said, 'My goodness is that the time? I'll be late for work. I'll phone – see you during the week.'

'I must go too – and open up the shop,' said Frances. 'Thank you for yesterday, Mark. And I'm glad you stayed last night.'

'Thank *you*,' he said, and bent to kiss her on the lips.

Half way through the morning Mr Benson telephoned from Heathrow. He was waiting for his flight to Dublin to be called. 'I hope to be back on Wednesday – but I may not see you till Thursday. I'll telephone and let you know where you can get hold of me – as soon as I arrive.' And then his money ran out.

She typed some invoices and did the filing. By mid afternoon, only three customers had passed through the shop. And none of them bought anything. There seemed to be a lot of time for thinking, all alone in the hot, dead afternoon. No one else came. She wouldn't go and talk to Sidney, unwilling to face his customary hostility. The miniature occupied her mind. It was as if that tiny face had carved itself in relief, like a cameo on to the surface of her brain. And, as usual, she thought about Margaret. Where was she? Why had she not been in touch? Perhaps Mr Benson knew more than he was letting on. Surely someone in Fressenworth must have some clue as to her whereabouts. Was the timing important? Was there a reason she had chosen to go away just after the Woodton Hall sale? Frances opened Margaret's blue book and turned to the last entry. There it was, in Margaret's black-inked spidery handwriting: Woodton Hall Sale 26 March. Nearly three months ago.

Lot 233 Sec. Bookcase £5,000 H.
Lot 300 Pr. Vict. Rosewood Cabs. £4,500 H.
Lot 410 George III Mah. Tallboy £1,800 H.
Lot 420 Mah. Pembroke Table £2,100 H.
Lot 436 Dutch Mah. Armoire £3,100 H
Lot 450 Mah. Wine Cooler £1,500 H.
Lot 461 Sundry framed prints £50 H!!!!

There must be something about this list, about Margaret's last sale that was significant.

Lot 450, the mahogany wine cooler. Howden had that delivered to his boat. She was concentrating so hard, she forgot to breathe. Lot 461 sundry framed prints for £50. A row of exclamation marks scrawled after the letter H. Frances had a vague recollection concerning a box of prints. During the cleaning and tidying process of Benson's shop, she had put several things – classed by herself as junk – down in the cellar. She locked the shop door and gingerly descended the cellar's crumbling stone steps. The light was poor; one weak electric bulb hanging unshaded from a fraying flex. She knocked her head on this and set it swinging so that her shadow lunged around the decaying stone walls like a shadow boxer. She poked around among the pile of damp cardboard boxes containing mouldy curtains, unmatched china plates and chipped ornaments, redundant light-fittings and miscellaneous cutlery. Eventually, she found the box she was looking for, lying beside the blackened remains of a brass bedstead and a load of ship's lanterns.

A sound in the shop above, someone rattling the locked door made her start in alarm. She stood for a moment, the box of prints in her hand, listening. Then she climbed the precarious steps and went back into the front showroom. Someone was walking away from the shop door. She decided not to open up. It was nearly five o'clock and once Sidney had gone home, she would be alone. She went systematically through the box. It was just a box full of broken picture frames and fly-blown hunting prints, unworthy of those flamboyant exclamation marks. Her head felt as if something very small and fleet of foot was scurrying round and round inside. She took out the cardboard box containing Margaret's possessions. Quickly, furtively, Frances kicked off her sandals and slipped her feet into Margaret's high-heeled black patent leather shoes. She stood up and walked round the showroom, the stiletto heels tap-tapping on the wooden floor. What did it feel like to be Margaret? 'Tell me where you are Margaret,' said Frances aloud in the empty showroom. She took out the small handkerchiefs, opened the pot of green eye-shadow. Her heart began to bump unevenly as she picked up the bunch of keys. Standing there in Margaret's shoes, with Margaret's keys in her hand, Frances knew exactly what she was going to do. Hot with excitement she took off the shoes and put them back in the box with the rest of Margaret's possessions. Except the keys. She locked the shop, set the alarms and hurled herself into the car, all in the space of a few scrambled minutes, lest she should lose the nerve to go ahead with her plan of action. It didn't occur to her to doubt the identity of the keys. They were indelibly stamped with the essence of Margaret – like all of her possessions.

Girdlestone was no more than a hamlet – a few miles further south than the village where Mark's parents lived. There was no shop, and no public house, just a few houses grouped around a small green. Surely a neighbour would have some idea of Margaret's whereabouts? As she parked her car, a white BMW drew up at one of the houses and a young man and a woman got out. Londoners, visiting their holiday home, thought Frances, as she watched them carrying suitcases up the path. They'd be no use. Probably never heard of Margaret.

She walked purposefully towards a row of cottages set beside the green. They were pretty, period cottages and they had names painted on their gates. End Cottage, White Cottage, Gardener's Cottage: no Forgetmenot Cottage. Looking around, she noticed a track at the back of the green, and just visible behind a large chestnut tree, two detached cottages with thatched roofs. She crossed over to them. Neither cottage had a name painted on its gate. But the further one had forgetmenots flowing over its path of crazy paving and cushioning the hollyoaks, foxgloves, lupins and poppies crammed in its front garden. She knew immediately that this was where Margaret lived. The overhanging eaves of the thatched roof gave an air of protective privacy to the whitewashed walls and small case-ment windows. At first sight, the garden appeared to be burgeoning out of control so crammed with flowers was the flowerbed which took up half of it. But as she opened the gate and set foot on the crazy-paving path, Frances could see very few weeds among the confusion of colour, and someone had mown the small square of grass the other side of the path and trimmed its edges. The clematis scrambling over the porch and reaching for the windows, had flowered and been pruned.

Trying to look as if she had right of entry, Frances approached the front door, which was of stained wood and had a horseshoe hanging on a nail above it. She took Margaret's keys out of her pocket and fitted one of them into the mortice lock. It turned sweetly. This was so easy. Her pulse was racing, as she slipped the yale key into its lock and turned it. She pushed open the door and stumbled over a pile of unopened mail, straight into a square room with a brick floor. She saw a pine table, chairs and a small oak dresser. There were willow-patterned plates on the dresser rack and the dresser base was cluttered with a dusty jumble of antique bottles, pot-lids, picture postcards, bone-white sea shells, china ornaments and stoneware jars containing long-dead flowers. She stood there for a minute, taking all this in, her heart beating unsteadily, sweat breaking out in her palms. Margaret could be somewhere in here. Dead.

At the back of the room she'd just entered, she saw a door.

This led to a small bathroom. The bath was green with limescale and the room smelled dank. Next, she found the kitchen, through another door on the left-hand side of the first room. It was long and narrow, and rather dark, with one small grimy window, a flagstone floor and cupboards amateurishly drag-painted in varying shades of dark green. An unhygienic-looking electric cooker stood in an alcove where there must once have been an old-fashioned range. Pots and pans and a dusty bunch of herbs hung from hooks on the ceiling and on walls.

She went back into the first room and from there, through another door on the opposite side to the kitchen, into the sitting room. A square wood-burning stove stood in the open fireplace, along with a stack of logs. Through the small casement window a beam of evening sunlight penetrated the dusty gloom and illuminated the piles of books, old magazines and sale catalogues lying around on the worn Turkey carpet. There was a saggy leather sofa draped with an oriental shawl, and several ancient-looking leather armchairs.

Now the bedroom, she thought, apprehensively. Behind another door at the back of the sitting room a steep and narrow staircase led to Margaret's bedroom, which was long and light and must once have been two rooms. The bed was empty, starkly covered with a not very clean white chenille bedspread. Frances let out a gusty sigh of relief, and imagined Margaret lying down there again, alive. She brushed her fingers over the thick, soft fabric, and hated being an intruder.

Thin oriental rugs lay on the painted floorboards. The doors of a carved oak cupboard hung open, exposing Margaret's clothes hanging on a rail in there. With fingers grown suddenly supersensitive, Frances felt the roughness of a tweed skirt, touched the furry slub of a woollen jacket. The open drawer of a chest revealed slippery pastel-coloured underwear. I shouldn't be doing this, she thought. I'd hate anyone poking around among my things. 'I'm sorry Margaret,' she said out loud. 'Where are you? Just give me a clue.' She glanced over at Margaret's dressing-table, and among the pots and tubes of make-up, she saw a framed photograph. Swiftly, she stepped across the room and took it in her hand. It was a photograph of two very young children: a boy and a girl. The boy had brown curls and a smiling freckled face. The little girl was smaller and looked younger. Her straight dark hair was cut with a fringe and her eyes were solemn. She was Margaret. Flawless, innocent. The little boy must be her brother. With a sudden feeling of sadness, Frances replaced the photograph, walked over to the window, and stood looking out. Maybe Margaret left in a hurry, but she had arranged for someone to keep her garden under control, ready for her return, she thought, looking down at a blaze of red poppies.

After a while, full of unease, Frances went back down the stairs to the sitting room. She sat on one of the leather chairs, making the dust fly up. Bending down, she peered at the pile of papers and magazines on the floor and saw something so surprising that all the air in her lungs expelled itself in a gasp of amazement.

Draper and Edwards, Auctioneers and Estate Agents.

The heading at the top of the sheet of paper leaped out at her. Even more so the black typescript below:

WILLOW FARM
16th century. Small Suffolk Farmhouse. Unmodernised.

She picked the paper up off the floor and read the particulars of her house, exactly as she herself had read them four months earlier. How odd, she thought. Why on earth didn't Mark tell me Margaret was interested in Willow Farm? She folded the paper and put it in her pocket. Willow Farm was no longer for sale.

She closed and locked the door, which half an hour ago, she'd unlocked, fearful of what she might find. Thank God, she'd been spared that nightmare explanation of Margaret's whereabouts, but now she was leaving Forgetmenot Cottage with more unanswered questions.

Frances walked down the path, away from the abandoned house, alive with the spirit of Margaret, and was just closing the wooden gate, when the front door of the other cottage was pulled open and an old lady hobbled out. She was wearing slippers and a pinafore apron and leaning on a stick. 'She's not here,' she said in a wavery voice. 'Margaret's not here. What do you want?'

'I'm sorry,' said Frances, 'I don't mean to alarm you. I'm a friend of Margaret's and I've been rather anxious about her. I haven't heard from her for so long, you see. I wonder if you know where she is?'

The old lady's rheumy eyes regarded Frances suspiciously. With knobbed arthritic fingers, she brushed back a wisp of white hair which was escaping from the untidy knot on the back of her neck. Her face was seamed and webbed with wrinkles. Frances thought she looked incredibly old.

'Went away didn't she.'

'I know. But can you tell me where she's gone?'

'Never said.'

'But she told you she was going away?'

'She come and go a lot. Don't take much notice.' She peered closer at Frances and her eyes were still full of suspicion. 'I haven't seen you before. How do I know you're a friend of Margaret's? How did you get into her house? How do I know you aren't a burglar.'

'I work with her employer, Mr Benson. He has a key,' said Frances firmly, hoping that the name Benson would mean something.

'Hmmn.' The old lady appeared to be considering the next move. She shuffled a little nearer to Frances, tapping forward with her stick. 'Come to think of it, she did tell me, she'd be going away. I forget you know. I'm old, see. Very old. My daughter she come when she can. But her Len. Me and her Len don't get on. Never should have married him. Won't take me in. Wouldn't want it. But I'm not going into no home. I'm staying here.' She poked her stick at a weed. 'That's what I tell them. They can't make you. I'll go soon enough when I'm dead.' She gave a catarrhal chuckle. 'She's a flighty piece that Margaret. Men! Well I liked a man in my time. Never married you know – so she said. Went away with a man.'

'A man? What did he look like?'

'Getting dark wasn't it. My daughter says I should wear my glasses. Had a fall – when I was wearing my glasses.' She slashed at another weed with her stick. 'I wear 'em to do the pools.'

N.H., Frances was thinking. Evidence of his existence.

135

'Tell me what you can remember about him. Was he young? Old? Tall, short?'

'I just hear his voice. Like I said, it was getting dark. Well fairly dark. Went off in a car didn't they.'

'What sort of car.'

She appeared to be considering the car. 'Bigger than what hers is. That one's hers.' She pointed a wavering finger to a dirty-looking Ford Escort under the chestnut tree.

So, Margaret had left her house and her car, and driven away with N. H. without telling anyone when she was coming back. Frances thought about Margaret and men. The old lady could be imagining men. Making things up. She had a sly look about her, but that might just be the acquired cunning of extreme old age.

'Margaret must have a gardener,' said Frances, turning back to look at the riot of colour in Margaret's garden, at the neat lawn. 'Does he come regularly?'

'Drop of rain and he don't turn up. Bloke with a beard. Looks like one of them hippies. He did come Saturday. Done the grass and trickolated the flowerbed. I see him put a note through the door. I expect he want paying.' She sniffed and lifted a corner of her pinafore to wipe her nose.

'She's always nice with me, you know. We been neighbours for ten years. I'll be glad when there's a light next door again.'

'I heard she was thinking of moving.'

'What'd she want to do that for.' She swiped at a dandelion with her stick, peering closely at Frances, her watery blue eyes suddenly sharp. 'You don't think she's been kidnapped do you? Young girl went missing down Fressenworth way last year. Walked home from one of them discos. Found on the golf course with the back of her head stove in.'

'I'm sure Margaret's all right,' said Frances with more conviction than she felt. 'She went away with a friend. She'll be back soon. Please let me know if you have any news of her. Here's my name and address.' She printed them in large letters on a scrap of paper and gave it to the old lady. 'Thank you for talking to me.'

'Yes well – it's time for my programme.' The old lady turned round and shuffled back into her house with surprising speed.

*

Driving home, full of unease, Frances thought, this has gone on long enough – it's time to find out what has happened to Margaret. Mr Benson will be back soon. If he really doesn't know what is going on, Margaret must be reported missing. She telephoned Mark, but there was no reply from his home number. Next morning she called him at work and invited him to supper. 'Why don't you come here,' he said, 'I've got one of Mum's fish pies.'

'I expect she meant that just for you,' she said, laughing.

'Well if so she's overestimated my appetite. See you after work.'

In the afternoon, Mr Benson turned up without warning. He was unusually talkative and appeared to appreciate her competence in looking after things in his absence. He said 'Thank you my dear,' several times and also, 'I'll have to see what I can do ... (Did he mean he was about to give her a rise? Or take her on permanently?) Before disappearing into his office, he told her, with engaging enthusiasm, and gratifying confidence in her developing ability to appreciate good quality antiques, about the very large mahogany breakfront bookcase he had bought at the Dublin sale along with a nineteenth-century Mason's dinner service.

She took him a cup of tea and set it down on the desk. He was absorbed in a sale catalogue. 'Thank you my dear.'

She hesitated, hovered, stayed. 'Mr Benson, may I talk to you a moment?'

'Yes?' He looked up, keeping his place in the catalogue with a forefinger.

But instead of telling him about the miniature, as she had intended, she found herself saying, 'It's about Margaret.'

'Well?'

'I've been here three months. You said I could stay till Margaret came back. Is she ever coming back, Mr Benson?'

Silence.

Motionless, his finger on the catalogue, holding the place open, he said, quietly, 'I imagine so.'

'You told me you were expecting her.'

His hand seemed to do a little jump on the open catalogue and she noticed how the knuckles were enlarged, bony and

137

white. He would not expect her to have any interest in Margaret, other than with regard to the job. 'And if she doesn't return, does that mean you might want me to stay permanently?'

'Certainly I would.' He sounded relieved.

'And in the meantime, do I just hang around and hope she doesn't turn up?'

He shut the catalogue, picked up his teacup and took a sip. 'I'm sorry if it puts you in an awkward position. I appreciate everything you're doing for me.'

According to that old lady, thought Frances, Margaret went away in a car with a man, who might or might not have been N. H. She watched Mr Benson take another sip of tea. 'But where is she? Where is Margaret? She could be dead for all I know.'

He set down his cup with a clatter, slopping tea and his empty hand on the desk top twitched.

In the tense silence that followed, she found herself thinking, reassuringly, he's a frail old man – surely he wouldn't harm a fly.

Finally, he said in a colourless voice, 'She just went away. All of a sudden.'

Should she tell him about Margaret's note to Vic? About N. H.? Perhaps he knew Margaret had gone away with a man?

'She telephoned me at home. Something urgent had come up. She apologised – for leaving me in the lurch. Said she'd be back. But she didn't say when.' He paused and clasped and unclasped his hands agitatedly. 'To tell the truth, my dear, I am a little worried that it's been so long. Without even a telephone call. As far as you are concerned, I regret that I'm unable to clarify your position. But I would like to point out, it was you and not me, who suggested you work here. And very grateful I've been.' He looked up at her and managed one of his wintery smiles.

'Mr Benson, I feel I must tell you – yesterday I went to Margaret's house. She'd left her keys in the desk, so it was easy to get in. I found no clue as to where she might be, but her neighbour told me Margaret had gone away in a car with a man.'

The smile faded from his face. 'I see.'

138

'Who could that be?'

He shook his head.

'She was very thick with Vic Howden.'

He made an angry noise in the back of his throat.

'She was side-dealing wasn't she, Mr Benson.'

'She gave me little cause to complain,' he said brusquely. 'When I first came to work for you all sorts of odd people turned up looking for her, or telephoned to speak to her. And we both know she operated very successfully in a Dealers Ring. But what about a boyfriend? The neighbour mentioned men. She hinted Margaret had a lot of men. Apart from Vic Howden, do you know who else there might be?' *Gone away with N.H.* It was too complicated to explain all that.

'You'd hardly expect me to be part of Margaret's private life now would you my dear?'

'Mr Benson – don't you think it's time we tried to find out what has happened to her?'

Benson's old face took on a faint hue of pink. He pressed his thin lips together. 'The matter will be put in hand. Now – do I hear the bell? Perhaps you'd be good enough to see who it is.' He turned back to his catalogue. 'And I'd be grateful if you'd close the door behind you.'

I haven't managed to tell him about my miniature, said Frances to herself, and all because of you, Margaret.

Mark's flat was one of those purpose-built modern, character-less slots for living in, inhabited by single people who are at work all day, and out enjoying themselves at night. The sort of place that cannot be described as a home. The pale emulsioned walls, the speckled fitted carpet, the glass-topped coffee table, the two-seater sofa and matching easy chairs, the clinical fitted kitchen, the austere bathroom, all signalled low-maintenance, practical living, minimum effort and no heart.

'Drink?'

'Please.'

Mark took a bottle of white wine out of the fridge, opened it and poured two glasses. She noticed the fish pie, standing at the ready beside the microwave along with a packet of frozen peas. 'Come and sit down.'

She sipped her wine and took a few cashew nuts from the

139

bowl on the glass-topped table.

'Did you show the miniature to Tommy Benson?' asked Mark.

'He's away till the end of the week – didn't I tell you? I'll have to wait till he gets back. I'm worried that it might be treasure trove you know Mark. But it'll probably turn out to be a fake so it won't really matter.'

'Don't be so pessimistic.'

She finished her first glass, and while Mark topped it, said, 'I had a little adventure yesterday. I decided to try and find out a bit more about Margaret.'

'Really?'

'So I went to her house.'

'You went to her *house*? Good Lord – what an extraordinary thing to do – what did you find?'

'Well not Margaret. I didn't really expect to – but at least she wasn't lying there dead.'

'You mean you went inside? How did you get in?'

'She'd left some keys in the shop. It was easy as pie. I don't know why I didn't think of doing it before. Or why you didn't. You must know where Margaret lives.'

'I'm not in the least interested in Margaret's whereabouts. For reasons of her own she's chosen to disappear for a while.'

'Carla seemed to think she'd gone for good. Perhaps she knows something we don't know.'

'Frances, I have to admit to being quite shocked. You could be had up for trespassing.'

She ignored his censorious tone and continued, 'I met Margaret's neighbour. She was reasonably friendly – in the end. She hasn't heard from Margaret, although she remembered her saying she was going away. Also, and this is really interesting, she said she saw Margaret going off with a man – in a car.'

'Did she really.'

'So do you think it could have been this N.H. chap?'

'Seems logical,' said Mark thoughtfully.

'She was incredibly old and doddery, but I don't think she was making it up. Also, Mark, you never told me Margaret was interested in buying Willow Farm. Why didn't you tell me that Mark?'

"What makes you think Margaret was interested in buying

Willow Farm?' he asked in a quiet careful voice.

'While I was there, in her house, I found the particulars of *my* farmhouse, on *your* firm's headed paper. And you really didn't know about that?'

'Certainly not. It's news to me, Frances. Maybe she's on the mailing list, and one of the secretaries sent it out to her.' He appeared to be turning something over in his mind and after a minute or two, with a sudden small exclamation, he tapped his forefinger on the coffee table and said, 'Tell you what though, I've just thought of something. That swine Vic Howden was interested in your place. I didn't take him round myself, but someone did. God knows what he wanted it for.'

How odd, she thought, and through her mind flashed the memory of Vic coming to collect her for dinner, and looking round the farmhouse as if he was familiar with it. She'd even asked him if he knew the place, and he'd said something noncommittal. 'I see,' she said, 'I suppose that could explain it – we know all about the connection between Margaret and Vic, don't we Mark.'

'Yes,' he said shortly. 'And now can we talk about something more interesting.'

At the end of the evening, after they'd eaten the fish pie and drunk some more wine, they went to bed. He was excited but gauche, heavy handed but vigorous. She could not tell how much he really cared for her and thought, maybe this will feel right – in time. And then, he stroked her face with trembling fingers and begged her to stay all night.

Over breakfast of coffee and toast in the practical, comfortless kitchen, Mark said, 'By the way – I forgot to tell you – my parents thought you were great.'

'I liked them too – particularly your dad.'

'They want you to come and have lunch again this Sunday.'

Sunday, something was happening this Sunday – what was it? Vic. Vic was expecting her to go out for a trip on his boat. She hadn't actually made up her mind to go, but the prospect was undeniably exciting. And now there was the business of Vic's interest in Willow Farm – of Margaret's interest in Willow Farm. She might learn something more. It was all too

141

tempting.

'That's very kind of them – of you – but I'm not sure if I'm doing something.'

'Oh that's a shame – can't you get out of it?'

'I'll see.'

'What are you doing anyway?'

How could she tell him about Vic? He hated Vic. He'd be livid.

'You're not having anything more to do with that bloody man I hope?'

She'd have to own up. He'd only find out anyway – if she went. 'He's asked me on his boat – but I haven't said I'll go.'

'But you will though, won't you.' His voice was tense and tight with fury.

'It'll be an opportunity to ask him why he was interested in Willow Farm. And he might explain Margaret's involvement.'

'Who are you kidding?'

'I know what I'm doing.'

'You're either incredibly naïve or a bloody liar.'

'Mark – don't be cross – it's silly. Please. I haven't said I'll go.'

'Do what you want. But I should be careful if I were you. He's dangerous, that man.'

'I can look after myself.'

'Can you really?'

'Don't be like that, Mark. Look – let's not have a fight about it – we've both got to get to work. Come and have supper tonight – we'll have a proper talk.'

'I can't – I've got a meeting with a client. I'm pretty busy this week Frances. I'll see you after the weekend. We'll have a talk then.'

'I'm sorry.' She looked at his flushed, angry face. 'Please try to understand.'

'Oh I do,' he said, and his voice was full of pain. 'I understand only too well.

Chapter Sixteen

Frances arrived at the marina at exactly nine o'clock. She was in a buoyant, reckless mood. The river glittered in the sun and small white clouds skidded across the sky as if they were wads of cottonwool, polishing it more brightly blue. The wind clattered shrouds against aluminium masts and whistled in the rigging as boats came and went, their crew jumping about with mooring ropes and fenders. The marina had an air of camaraderie, pleasant anticipation and healthy activity, very different from how it had been on that other clandestine occasion. As she thought of it and of him, she spotted Howden, waiting for her on the pontoon. He looked relaxed, standing with his hands in the pockets of his blue trousers, a striped Breton pullover emphasising the thickness of his chest. From her vantage point in the car park above, she thought he looked rather ridiculous. How was it at other times he could seem threatening? She started down the path towards him and, as he saw her approach, he began to walk along the pontoon to meet her, nodding greetings to neighbouring boat owners on the way.

'Well done.' His hand brushed hers as he took her duffel bag and led her back along the pontoon, which swayed beneath their feet. 'I'm glad you're on time. We should leave straight away if we want to make use of the tide.'

As she stepped aboard *Calypso*, she saw once again, in her imagination, that diverse group of men gathered round the table in the saloon, pitting their wits against each other on an April evening.

'Do we have company? Any of your friends coming along?'

Howden slung her bag down on one of the bunks in the saloon. 'No my dear: I'm afraid you're stuck with me.' He looked her full in the eyes. She stared him out. The safe family atmosphere all around made the darker side of Howden's nature and her own imaginings about what he might be capable of hardly credible. She smiled, not caring if he thought her provocative.

In a few moments he had started up the engine and, under his direction, she cast off the mooring ropes and very soon they were heading downriver. Looking back at their spreading wake, listening to the deep-throated purr of the diesel engine, watching Vic Howden controlling the wheel with his fingertips, Frances thought there was something to be said for being rich.

In half an hour they had reached the mouth of the river and were motoring past cranes and gantries and moored container vessels and fishing boats. A passenger ferry having made the crossing from Holland entered the river. She felt vulnerable as a piece of flotsam, dwarfed by the sheer cliff of steel, an object of curiosity for the passengers lining the rail.

After a while, Howden said, 'Can you take the wheel while I hoist the sails. Just hold it steady and point out to sea.'

She braced herself against the motion of the boat which pitched and rolled in the heavy swell at the harbour's mouth and then the sails filled and the vessel settled to a more even surging, rocking motion. He took the wheel from her and switched off the engine. From her seat in the cockpit, she watched the heaving, foam-streaked water and listened to the rushing sound of their progress through it. The wind was strong enough to blow the tops off the waves and the spindrift sparkled in the sun.

'Where are we going?'

'How about Holland?'

'You're joking of course.'

'I was – but it's not far – we could be over in ten hours.'

'No thanks.'

He was watching her closely, as if he was testing her. 'I thought you had a taste for adventure.'

'I do – but perhaps not today,' she said, enjoying the salt wind on her cheek and in her hair, but fighting to suppress the hint of nausea stirring in her belly.

His eyes were inescapable. Well – he was only an ageing womaniser, she told herself.

'We need to change course – take care of the jib for me please.' He showed her how to free the jib sheet on the leeward side of the boat and winch it in on the other side as they turned through the eye of the wind. She knew perfectly well, from her dinghy sailing days, how it should be done, but it amused her to pretend incompetence.

They sailed up the coast in fine style, the boat broad-reaching in the strong onshore wind. In two hours they were off the mouth of the River Alde. The wind was blowing across the narrow entrance. She saw surf breaking on the sandbanks either side of the channel which was filled with choppy water.

'See the entrance buoys,' said Howden. 'Port and starboard. Red and green. We keep the green one to the right as we go in. And I have to approach at the correct angle to avoid the sandbanks. See I'm lining the boat up on those two triangles on the shore – have to get one behind the other before I can turn for the entrance. It's tricky – there's not a lot of water, and the tide runs very fast. Each year the sandbar moves a little – and so the channel is never quite the same. Sometimes they have to move the buoys and alter the position of the markers on the shore.' He furled the foresail, hauled in the mainsail and switched on the engine. 'That dial is the depth sounder – can you watch it for me please. It tells us how much water we've got beneath the keel. Shout if it registers less than a metre.'

They negotiated the sandbar successfully, although at one point Frances shouted that the depth was decreasing with alarming rapidity, and so entered the river.

There was a baby seal lying on the beach by the high water mark. He saw her looking at it. 'Dead,' he said.

'Oh.' She had been about to make some comment, thinking the little creature was basking in the sun, but with his words she recognised the unmistakable stillness of death.

The river wound between banks of shingle which turned into mud further inland, and soon they were motoring between quiet marshes populated by grazing cattle and birds. In an hour they were anchored in a deserted creek off the main river, shielded a little from the wind by the low land-mass that separated them from the sea. In the cockpit it was sunny and

145

sheltered. Howden brought out a bottle of champagne and two glasses. She accepted the champagne which heightened her feeling of exhilaration engendered by the sound and feel of the wind during their swift sail along the coast, the brightness and warmth of the sun, the sight of the glass-green waves and the vast panorama of cloud-strewn sky and desolate marshland.

After a while, Howden went down into the cabin and reappeared with a plate of smoked salmon, brown bread and butter and a quartered lemon.

As he stood behind her, pouring champagne into her glass, she was unsure whether it was the touch of the wind, or the imagined caress of his fingers but, beneath her hair on the back of her neck, the skin began to prickle. He sat down opposite her. The silence between them was exaggerated by the squabbling of a flock of oyster-catchers. She must say something. What should they talk about? Antiques? Mr Benson? Margaret, always at the back of her mind, waited for an introduction.

Watching Howden's blunt-fingered hands as he laid a piece of smoked salmon on to a slice of bread, she imagined the intimacy of those hands upon her. His body pressing against hers would be like suffocating.

She squeezed lemon on to her smoked salmon, and bit into it. Her mouth was filled with the fishy, oily softness. 'Delicious.'

'I get it from a local chap who smokes his own. Have some more.' He passed the plate to her and she took another piece in her fingers.

There was silence while they ate. He watched her. She watched him back. His hair, habitually sleek, had been tousled by the wind. His eyes were narrowed against the glare of the sun, his skin made ruddy by the effect of both sun and wind. His Breton shirt had rucked up out of his trousers – when he stretched, she caught a glimpse of a hirsute torso – there was mud on his blue trousers and on his sailing shoes. He looked relaxed, younger, rougher. No longer clad in a tailormade suit, bereft of his gold watch and his silk shirt, here was the rough-hewn carcase of the man, stripped of his glossy veneer.

To break the silence, she said, 'Mr Benson went to a sale in Dublin last week. Did you go to it?'

'No. I had to see a customer in Belgium. I left a price on a few things, but I didn't get them. Incidentally, talking of Benson – did he give you a price for the bureau?'

'The bureau?'

'You haven't forgotten?'

'Oh – the red walnut bureau in his office. I told him you were interested. He said he'd ring you.'

'Well, he didn't, but no matter. Have some more bubbly.' He poured from the bottle.

'Let's drink a toast,' she said, raising her glass.

'Who shall we drink to?'

'To Margaret.' She drank, watching Howden.

He shrugged his shoulders and raised his glass. 'OK. Here's to you Margaret.'

'Do you think she'll come back Vic?'

'Who knows,' he said calmly. 'Margaret is a law unto herself.'

'Mr Benson seldom talks about her but he's admitted to being worried. I think he'd expected her back by now.' She paused and then added recklessly, 'He doesn't like her connection with you.'

Howden said nothing, but she felt him grow tense.

'I rather want to meet Margaret – even though it'll put me out of a job. I know so much about her.'

'Do you now.'

An uneasy silence fell. She wished he would stop looking at her. She wished she didn't like him looking at her.

Above their heads an enormous black-backed gull swooped down to the surface of the creek, its hooked beak poised like a spear. There was a splash and a widening ring of ripples. Twenty yards away a young shelduck surfaced.

'Missed him,' said Howden.

The great gull had risen up and was circling overhead.

'He'll try again.'

Beneath its enemy, the young shelduck paddled frantically. Again the gull swooped. Again the little duck dived in the nick of time.

'Can't we do something?'

'Like what?'

'Frighten off the gull; rescue the duck.'

147

'The duck's had it – here you see nature red in tooth and claw – that little shelduck doesn't stand a chance.'

And so it proved. Eventually, the exhausted creature could dive no more. The gull plucked the limp form from the surface of the water and a moment later could be seen, with blood-stained beak, dragging out its entrails on the river bank.

'Nature's cruel.' He smiled, stood up and came round behind her, empty champagne bottle in hand. With the fingers of the other hand he followed her spine from the nape of her neck down to the small of her back. The heat and pressure of his fingers seemed to ignite her spinal cord transmitting a surge of sexual desire through every nerve in her body.

She heard a splash as he tossed the empty bottle overboard. Then, seemingly clamped to his hand, she was led down into his cabin. He pulled back the blue duvet, and the flat white sheet, stretching out before them, was the last thing she remembered seeing because his fingers were unzipping her jeans.

She thought she knew about sex. She thought Felix had taught her to love, but never had she imagined she could be so transported.

Her body became disconnected from her mind, which recoiled from its carnal desires. She felt how he wanted her. At the extremes his arms were tight as a band of iron, his fingers light as a butterfly's wing. He didn't hurt her. There was only the exquisite pain of sensual pleasure. It wasn't simply that he was a master of the erotic: he seemed to draw from her an equally rapacious eroticism. She knew what he needed. Instinct led her to limits of touch and taste that she never imag-ined lay within her. The outside world was irrelevant. Their absorption with each other was total. She could not say what was most vital: sensitivity of hands, softness of tongue, thrust of penis, salt flavour of flesh. It was the entity of the two of them, bound together by the intensity of their senses and, for her, the terrible excitement of exploring some potent, uncon-trollable danger. She heard herself cry out again and again. His voice in her ear murmured endearments, entreaties, repeated her name.

How long it all took, she did not know. Time was immater-ial. In the end, she more or less passed out on the rumpled bed against the heat of his body. She awoke alone to the lap of water against the hull.

Her mind was dazed. She could have thought herself dreaming, were it not for the feel of her body, still heavy with the imprint of the man. She lay and listened to the water lapping against the hull. Later, she would try to rationalise. For now, the experience was too profound and disturbing to allow analysis. She forced her eyes lazily round the cabin. Where was Howden? She listened for any sound of him and after a while heard the sudden slosh of a bucket of thrown water, followed by the rhythmic swishing of a brush against a hard surface. He must be scrubbing the decks. It seemed too ordinary to be true. She sat up on the bed, stretched her arms above her head and her eye chanced upon the row of books behind which she had found Margaret's shoe. An image of Margaret in her place, doing precisely what she was doing now, shot into her mind. And then into her mind leaped another image of Margaret – entwined with Howden. It was not an image she cared to linger on. It was easier to revert to thinking about Margaret's shoe and wondering how it could have got behind those books, and whether Howden had noticed its absence.

She thought of Margaret writing that note to Vic. Would she post it? Or leave it somewhere for him to find? Here – in the boat, on the saloon table? Held down by the shoe? She would have come alone; or with N.H. even. She'd have had access to the boat. They'd been lovers after all, she and Vic. Frances imagined Vic reading Margaret's note. Stuffing it angrily inside the shoe and shoving it out of sight behind the books.

She slid off the bed, stood up and found her hand straying towards *Whitaker's Almanack*. She pulled it out. As she did so, a slim hardback book feel over, lacking support from the *Almanack*. She picked it up and felt a little shock as she read the title: *The Art of the Portrait Miniaturist*. She steadied herself and began to turn the pages, her eyes greedily taking in the colour plates that stared up at her. There were portraits of bewigged aristocratic gentlemen, of ladies with porcelain complexions and slender necks, of curiously elderly looking children. Her hand stayed itself at the portrait of a young woman. She had a high white forehead and elaborately dressed hair. She wore Elizabethan dress. Beneath the colour plate were the words: 'Jane Boughton, on vellum, inscribed and dated 1574.' And then, in capital letters NICHOLAS HILLIARD': underlined in blue biro.

Frances gave a little gasp and her fingers clutched at the book. Nicholas Hilliard 1574. 'Anno Dm. 1573.' – discernible through the magnifying glass. Nicholas Hilliard. It was like switching on a light in a dark room. The furniture had been there all the time, only you couldn't see it. And now the illumination was too stark, too unforgiving.

She sat on the bunk in Howden's boat, listening to the sound of water lapping the hull, to the wind flap-flapping a loose end of rope against the mast, to the rhythmic swish, swish of Howden's broom on the teak deck, and she saw herself pulling a crumpled sheet of paper from a high-heeled shoe. As if it lay before her now, she saw the scrawled, defiant message, 'Vic – Have gone away with N.H.'

Frances stared at Jane Boughton. No one could fail to be struck by the similarity between this wonderfully painted likeness of a radiant young woman, and that other minute face, faintly seen through a film of dirt, but crafted, surely, with equal flair and confidence. If intuition was leading her to the right conclusions, N.H. (Nicholas Hilliard) – long-dead portrait miniaturist of genius was here, in the presence of the portrait, found under the floorboards in her own house and currently concealed in a cornflake packet. He was no flesh-and-blood man living – somewhere in this world – with Margaret.

All at once, she was aware that the sound of scrubbing had ceased. Was it possible that ...? She glanced nervously towards the cabin door, encountering her reflection, which flashed wildly at her from the large mirror on the built-in dressing table. Her hair was disordered, her eyes blazed strangely, her cheeks were white as the sheet she had lain upon with Howden, and she was naked. The door moved so softly she didn't hear it, just saw it swinging inwards as she stood there, paralysed by the horror of her imaginings, the open book in her hand.

'I wondered if you were awake.'

Still she could not move. Howden came near. 'Pretty, isn't it,' he said, touching the colour plate with his forefinger.

'Clever chap that Nicholas Hilliard. If the camera hadn't been invented, maybe you could still find someone who could paint like that.'

'Maybe.' Life returned to her paralysed limbs. She closed the book and replaced it as nonchalantly as she could manage. Vic was fully dressed in his sailing clothes, even down to lace-up plimsolls. She felt exposed in her nakedness. There was a flicker of amusement around his mouth, but his eyes were knowing. He stretched out his hand and with the flat of his palm he stroked her left breast, trailing his fingers gently down over the nipple, which hardened instantly. 'You have beautiful breasts.'

'I'll get dressed now,' she said, 'and then I'll join you in the cockpit.'

'I'll leave you to it then.' He brushed her other breast with the lightest of fingers before leaving the cabin.

Her hands were shaking as she pulled on her jeans and tee-shirt.

In the dazzling sunshine, the black-backed gull was circling another young shelduck and Vic Howden was smiling at her. She tried to smile back. Did he sense the horror that flooded her mind? What was his connection with 'her' miniature. He couldn't know she had found it under the floorboards of Willow Farm. And he didn't know *she* knew that, according to Mark, he'd looked round the place when it was up for sale. Margaret had the particulars of the farmhouse; had most probably looked at it herself – could have gone there with Vic. Margaret is dead. I know that now, thought Frances. And her gut contracted with the awful finality of it.

Vic said, in a brisk, cheerful voice, 'We must leave in a moment of two – the wind is freshening and I want to sail back on the tide. Take the wheel while I get up the anchor.'

She longed to be safely home and alone: away from those hands that had such power over her, those treacherous tempting eyes, that suffocating body. Green waves broke on the sandbanks at the mouth of the river, the air was damp with spindrift: unconcerned, the great gulls scavenged on the shingle banks in the breaking surf.

They shot along the coast, the tide under them, the wind on the beam.

151

Vic was drinking. He'd wedged a bottle of red wine in an open locker. He offered Frances an empty glass – 'Help yourself to some vino.'

'No thanks.' Crouching in a corner of the cockpit, she urged the boat to sail faster.

'You seem nervous,' he said suddenly. 'What's worrying you?'

'Nothing. I'm fine.'

'No you're not. Something's upset you. I wonder what it can be?' He tipped wine into his glass, spilling some of the red liquid on his trousers. After he'd take a gulp, he said, 'When I came into the cabin just now, you were staring at the picture of that Hilliard miniature, but you looked as if you'd seen a ghost. Why?'

'You startled me – coming in so suddenly.'

'You know something, don't you. What do you know, Frances?'

'Nothing. I've no idea what you're talking about.'

'It was you took that shoe wasn't it? I wondered – but of course it had to be you, didn't it.'

'What shoe?'

'Margaret's shoe. From behind those books. You must have read her note. *Gone away with N.H.* That's what she said, didn't she. Lousy bitch. But how did you know what she meant? How did you cotton on to that? Anyone'ed think you'd seen it. What do you know about miniatures?'

'Nothing. I've no idea what you're talking about.'

'Don't lie to me.' He took a slug of wine. There was a cruel sneer on his sensual lips and a vicious gleam in his protuberant eyes. 'It's mine you know.'

She clenched her fists to stop her hands from shaking. 'What is yours?' She said slowly, watching his face.

'The Hilliard of course –well I'm pretty sure it's a Hilliard. She stole it. She shouldn't have done that. I found it for fuck's sake. I looked after her all right – I thought I could trust her. I should have gone to that sale myself.' He was flushed and windswept, his eyes screwed up against the glare of the sun.

There was no need to prompt him. She might well have not been there as he continued to rant, almost to himself. 'I didn't think she'd put two and two together like that. I'd have seen her all right. I always have. I found it – with my knowledge, my expertise. They all missed it – that idiot Draper and your wimp of a boyfriend. But I knew what it was. I've earned it. It's mine. And she stole it, the evil bitch. She shouldn't have done that.'

He took another swig of wine. She was appalled by the sight of the red lips that had touched her so intimately. The horror in her mind defined itself. Can it be that I have made love to a murderer? She was gripped by a grossly arousing spasm of fear.

He'd killed her – in a rage. For taking the miniature. *How did it get under the floorboards at Willow Farm?* Margaret? She'd come back for it – *if she was alive. Willow Farm.* Vic had been round *Willow Farm.* A crawling sensation spread over the surface of her skin as she thought of Margaret's last sale: of the box of prints; of the wine cooler.

All of a sudden Howden seemed to become aware of her. 'You do know something, don't you. You're always on about Margaret – asking me where I think she is – you know something about that miniature. What is it? Tell me Frances.'

'I know nothing.'

'I don't believe you. Come on – tell me.' He put out a hand to grab her. Eluding him she sprang up on to the deck, moving rapidly along it out of reach of those strong hands. With relief she saw how quickly the coast was flashing by. The wind strained the mainsail, bellied out the huge foresail, towering above her like a white mountain. Howden shouted something unintelligible. A violent movement glimpsed in the corner of her eye made her turn and glance back – Howden was spinning the wheel – in the nick of time she flung herself flat as the great boom came crashing over in a shuddering jibe. The boat veered, she clung to the guard rail, heard Howden shout something else – heard the canvas crack like gunshot as the vessel broached side on to the wind and a wave swept over the bow. In the cockpit Howden fought to bring the boat under control.

'You could have killed me,' she yelled.

'Didn't you hear me shout to you to get down? The depth dropped to nil. I had to turn or we'd have gone aground. You could have been stuck out here all night. How would you like that? Come down here. It's safer in the cockpit.'

153

'No.'

'I can't talk to you up there.'

'Too bad.'

'I'll have to come up to you then, won't I.'

She saw he was setting the self-steering mechanism. Below her the cold green water glittered in the sun.

'You look terrified. What's the problem?' He began to clamber up on to the deck.

She backed away, moving further forward along the cabin top.

'I'm not going to hurt you.' He stretched out his arm.

'You just tried to kill me,' she yelled. 'I don't trust you. Keep away from me.'

'Why should I kill you, you silly girl?'

'Because I believe you killed Margaret.' Frightened as she was, the accusation could not be held back. Words shot out like foam spewing from a champagne bottle when the cork is released.

'Why should I kill Margaret?' He was nearer now. She dodged behind the mainsail.

'For the miniature.'

'But I haven't *got* the miniature.'

'She wouldn't give it to you. You tried to make her though, didn't you?' The rash words went on spewing out. 'But you couldn't get the better of her. She's in that wine cooler at the bottom of the sea isn't she?'

He began to laugh. White spittle flecked his red lips, tears streamed from his narrowed eyes, his thick body shook with a paroxysm of mirth. 'You're mad my little friend. You're stark staring mad. Come here.'

He came swaying along the deck – hands out, reaching for her. She thought, he's going for my neck. 'No.' Her scream, more piercing than the cries of the cruising gulls, was shredded by the wind. 'Keep away from me.' She had reached the very bow of the boat. Her heart was banging so hard she thought it might burst her ribcage. Empowered by her fear of him, she slithered from the cabin top and dodged back along the deck inside the foresail. He was close behind her. She felt his hand grabbing for her waist. He was breathing heavily, still laughing. 'Playing silly games are you.' He lunged forward –

154

trapped her by the elbow. With all her strength she wrenched away from him, stumbled over a rope and fell headlong against the guard rail. He crashed down behind her. She kicked out and her feet found their soft target. Then there were glimpses of rushing water inches from her face as the boat, hit by a squall, heeled steeply. Lighter and nimbler than Howden, she managed to cling on. He must have been winded by the fall, and by her kicking feet. His inert body started to slip between the stanchions. Slowly it fell, hit the water with a mighty splash and went down like a stone.

The shock of the cold revived him, and after a few seconds he came spluttering to the surface. 'What the hell do you think you're doing?' She could just make out the darkness of his desperate eyes in his contorted face. Could she watch him drown? The vessel, still steered by the auto helm, was speeding away. Howden, floundering in the sea, grew smaller and smaller.

'Come back.'

'I can't,' she yelled.

'Engine ... sails down.' She could just hear his words above the gusting wind and the rushing water, as he tried to struggle after the boat. It wouldn't be her fault if he drowned. She turned away from the dark patch in the water, searched the horizon, and saw, some way along the coast, the gantries and cranes of Harwich harbour and far out to sea a cross-Channel ferry.

If she allowed Vic Howden to die, what sort of person would that make her? Could she watch a human creature drown? A man with whom she had lain in lust all afternoon? A man who had released the fearsome depths of her own nature? Fragments of his yelled instructions reached her, distorted by the wind. With clumsy haste, she unfastened a yellow life belt from its position on the rail and threw it astern. She saw him struggle towards it as the boat sailed ahead. Would he be able to reach it? How long would he last clinging to a life belt? Her eye lit upon the inflatable dinghy held on its davits over the stern of the boat. If she dropped it into the water, perhaps he could climb in. Quickly, she examined the mechanism that held the dinghy in place. After agonising moments, she managed to release it and watched it splash down into the water, still attached to the vessel by its painter. She untied the painter and it too dropped into the water. Then the dinghy seemed to shoot backwards, as Frances, alone in Howden's vessel, streamed on towards Harwich. Astern, she could just make out the yellow life belt bobbing up on the waves. Of Howden's dark shape there was no sign.

He had seemed to fall in slow motion. When he surfaced, his dark hair was plastered to his skull, his open mouth gasped for air, his arms flailed and the vibrancy of fear underlay the anger in his voice. Even in summertime, the North Sea was bitterly cold.

Calypso was sailing parallel to the coast, the onshore wind on the beam. It ought to be simple enough to turn and go back for him, taking the wind on the other beam.

She unhooked the auto helm and swung the wheel, turning the boat through the eye of the wind and freeing the jib sheet on the leeward side. As she put the helm over, the jib flapped across. She winched in and secured it, leaving the mainsail to take care of itself. She could no longer see the yellow life belt, but she was able to spot the dinghy bobbing among the waves caught in the current. She steered towards it. Howden and the life belt would be further along, swept up the coast by the tide. She grabbed the binoculars and put them to her eyes. At that moment there was a bleep bleep from the navigation equipment. Alarmed, she laid down the binoculars and examined the bank of dials in front of her. Noughts flashed on the depth sounder. In a panic, she spun the wheel trying to turn the boat back on its original course. There was a grinding bump, the sails stalled and the vessel came to a heart-stopping halt. She had driven herself on to a sandbank.

Desperately, she wrestled with the wheel. The wind in the sails was heeling the boat. Perhaps it would heel it enough to free the keel. Which way did the sandbank run? Distractedly she rushed from side to side. And then she remembered how Howden had yelled at her to take down the sails and put the engine on. She released the jib sheet and eventually, by hauling on the self-furling mechanism, managed to furl the foresail. Which was the main halyard? Feeling the sweat breaking out all over her body, she climbed up on to the cabin top, straining her eyes, in the hope of enlightenment, at the differently coloured ropes running up the mast. By the process of elimination, she hit upon the right one, released it and the boom crashed on to the cabin top followed by billowing acres of canvas. Somehow she bundled the huge sail away, using the ties attached to the boom and then she collapsed in the cockpit, trembling with exhaustion, tears streaming down her face. There was no point trying to start the engine now. Here she was, marooned on a sandbank, alone on a falling tide. Submerged in the North Sea, Howden's lungs would fill with cold salt water. His bloated body would be washed ashore somewhere – anywhere – some time – any time. A sob rose in her throat. The light was fading. Soon it would be dark.

And then, she remembered the radio. She stumbled down into the cabin. It was already switched on: she could hear two fishermen talking to each other. She picked up the mouthpiece. 'Help – man overboard between Harwich and the mouth of the Alde. Please come – help – help.' Her voice sounded thin and wavery, like that of a frightened child pretending to be grown-up.

She had no idea whether anyone heard her, but she repeated the message and then went up on deck again. The empty wine bottle had dribbled a trail of dark red over the floor of the cockpit. She grasped the bottle by its neck and threw it, with considerable force overboard. All around her, the water level was dropping. Waves slapped against the lower section of the hull. The boat had settled with a list to starboard.

She tried to think what to do. She knew they had come out of the Alde on a falling tide, with just enough water to get across the sandbar. The tide was still ebbing. She would be stuck here until the water had risen high enough to float her off: probably about the middle of the night. She wondered, should she try and put an anchor down? It seemed too difficult an undertaking. Darkness was creeping all round her with malevolent arms. The damp cold air seemed to stifle. Her skin was clammy from left-over sweat. She shook uncontrollably. 'Pull yourself together,' she said aloud. 'You're perfectly safe.'

She went down into the cabin and found a thick sweater of Vic's, a sleeping bag and a bottle of gin. She had another go on the radio. And then she went up again and huddled in the

157

cockpit staring out into the night. Lights sprang up on the distant shore and she thought, I'm not alone in the world. There's life out there – people watching television, eating supper, going to bed. Along the coast, the lights of Harwich harbour twinkled enticingly. There were lights out at sea. Lights everywhere: flashing lights, constant lights, red lights, green lights, white lights. I'm wearing a murderer's sweater, she thought. Maybe he's dead now. The thought gave her no pleasure. But, sipping Vic's gin, gradually she warmed to the relief of being alive herself, as she watched the dark water and waited for the tide to rise.

Chapter Seventeen

In the early hours of the morning, the flooding tide washed *Calypso* off her sandbank. Overnight, the wind had swung and was now coming from the west and so, held offshore, the boat drifted south with the tidal flow.

Frances, waking with the sun, from an exhausted, alcohol-induced sleep, found herself to be some way out to sea, with Harwich harbour still in view. With the horrible realisation that this was indeed no nightmare, but real life, she looked helplessly about her at the heaving water. Vic – alive or dead – would have been swept far away and there was no point in trying to look for him now. It would be too difficult to raise the sails; she must get back to harbour under power and contact the police.

The ignition key was in its place, but nothing happened when she turned it to try and start the engine. Carefully, she examined the display panel and saw a prominent red button. She pressed this, and to her relief, the engine fired. The gear lever was easy enough to operate, being a simple matter of pushing it forward to go ahead, centring it for neutral and pushing it back for reverse. The depth sounder indicated three metres. Dead ahead of her was a tall navigation buoy with two upward pointing triangles on top of it. She had a nasty feeling this must mark the end of a sandbank, but had no idea which way the bank ran. She decided to head out to sea, which seemed safest, and had the satisfaction of watching the depth increase rapidly, and then, when she judged there to be no danger of running aground again, she turned the boat to run parallel with the shore and made for Harwich. A cross-

Channel ferry loomed on the horizon, bound for the same destination.

Through the binoculars, she managed to pick out the large green buoy which marked the right-hand edge of the channel. Green for starboard, red for port, she told herself – if you were going into harbour. Oh – how she longed to be home. Saved from this inhospitable element, far from the terrible happenings of the last twenty-four hours. On the other hand, reaching shore would bring them in close – make the nightmare real. Out here, in limbo, she was saved from facing the consequences of her actions.

It seemed a long way upriver to the marina and when she got there she nearly demolished a quay heading. But helpful men appeared from nowhere to fend her off, shout instructions, take charge of the warps and secure the vessel.

Firm ground was hard and unforgiving. Her legs felt like lengths of elastic, hardly capable of supporting her. One of the men, middle-aged with a monklike fringe of soft grey hair, and kind brown eyes in a weatherbeaten face, reacting to her obvious distress, stretched out his arms and she collapsed into them.

'Vic,' she gasped, 'Vic went overboard.'

'When?'

'I tried to go back for him, but I hit a sandbank – I spent all night on a sandbank. I put out a message on the radio but I don't know if anyone heard.'

The man pressed a large red handkerchief into her hand. 'Try and tell us when he went in and where.'

'Yesterday evening – about seven – between the Alde and Harwich.' She managed to blurt it out, between gulping sobs.

'We'll call the coastguard. We can do that from the marina office. Jimmy, keep an eye on things here will you,' he said to a young man who had been among the group helping her in with the boat. 'Come along my dear.'

Relaxing into the strong curve of his arm, she wanted, very much, someone always to look after her.

He took over, talking to the coastguard while she stood hopelessly by the telephone. When he'd finished, he said, 'You need to report to the police at Harwich. Don't worry – I'll take you there.'

'You're very kind. Thank you – thank you.' She scrubbed at her eyes and blew her nose on his handkerchief, which smelled of tobacco.

The policeman had sandy hair and freckles and the pinkish skin which goes with that hair colouring. Even to Frances, he seemed very young. Concentrating on those freckles in order not to remember the sight of Vic's thickset body slipping slowly into the waves, she said unsteadily, 'We hit a squall – the boom crashed over – he slipped – and then he was gone.'

'What time did this happen?'

'Around seven o'clock. We were on our way back to Harwich from the Alde.' She stopped, gulping back tears, 'I turned to try and pick him up – but I went aground on a sandbank and didn't get off till this morning.'

'Yesterday? This happened yesterday?'

'Yes. Yes.' Did they need to sound so surprised?

While the policeman was writing all this down, two other people came into the room, both in navy blue uniform. One was the coastguard; the other was a policewoman.

'Force five out there yesterday from the south-east, good visibility, choppy sea.' The policeman looked at the coastguard, who nodded.

'As soon as he went I dropped a life belt – and the dinghy. He was swept away by the tide – so fast.'

The kind man with the soft grey hair, whose name was Ken, said, 'She put out a radio message.' He laid a warm hand on her shoulder.

The policeman went on writing and then he said, 'I'll leave you to read this through, and then please sign it.'

They all left the room except for the policewoman, who smiled at her and said, 'You mustn't worry – they'll do all they can you know.'

She could hardly manage to write her name and was shivering with cold, despite the bulk of Vic's sweater which, being far too large, hung down past her knees.

After a while, they all came back into the room and Ken said, 'I'm going to take you home now – everything will be all right, you'll see.'

'What about my car? My car is at the marina. I must pick it up.'

'We'll go back and get my son – he can follow us. You're in no fit state to drive.'

'We'll let you know,' said the policeman, 'as soon as there's any news.' His expression seemed to be one of encouragement rather than condemnation.

Jimmy, who was about eighteen and looked just like a young version of Ken with brown hair, took the keys of her Peugeot, and Ken settled her into the passenger seat of his comfortable Rover, with tenderness, as if she were an invalid. When they got going, he turned on the heater. 'Warming up a bit now?' he asked.

'You're very kind. I don't know what I'd have done without you.'

'Our pleasure, my dear. You needed a bit of a hand – you're all in.'

She watched mindlessly as the countryside flashed by in a blur. 'Do you think he's drowned?'

'My dear, you did all that you could. It's very hard to get someone back on board once they've gone over.'

'It's probably my fault.'

'How could it be your fault? No one's to blame in an accident.'

I was trying to save myself, she thought. It could have been me – dying out there all alone in the cold sea. He's a murderer – he deserves to die. But a voice inside her head was saying, very quietly 'not by my hand please God'. What would this kind man think of her if he knew what had really happened? What would he say, if she told him the truth?

They drew up at Willow Farm.

'Are you sure you'll be all right?' Ken's warm brown eyes were full of concern. 'Shall we come in with you?'

'I'm fine. Please – you've done more than enough. All I want to do now is have a hot bath and get some sleep,' she said, suddenly unable to bear his kind-hearted innocence. And then, with a sudden flash of inspiration, she added, 'Don't worry – I'll get hold of my boyfriend.'

This seemed to reassure him. 'If you're really sure ...' He

162

scribbled his name and address on a scrap of paper. 'I'm here if you need me – and in any case – let me know how things are.' Then he gave her a hug and his son shook her hand and handed her the keys of her car.

'How can I thank you,' she said, hardly able to see him, her eyes were so full of tears. And then they were gone and she was standing alone, waving at the receding car.

Some people were so good.

Some were bad – like Vic. Vic was a murderer. If Vic hadn't been drowned it would have been her: dying all alone in the cold North Sea – just like her father had.

She unlocked the door, went through to the kitchen and was brought to a stunned halt by the scene of devastation that met her eyes. On the table stood the cornflake packet; beside it a mountain of cornflakes. In a blind panic she rushed over, plunged her hand into the empty packet, scrabbled among the scattered cornflakes, tore open the packet and its plastic liner, and confirmed that the miniature had gone.

'Oh my God!' Her anguished cry bounced off the walls of the plundered kitchen. It seemed there was no waking from this nightmare. Desperately, she cast around her at the cupboard doors all swinging open, at the dried food emptied from jars and packets, at the ransacked refrigerator, the lidless pots of yoghurt lined up on the table along with a mound of tea tipped from the caddy, at the crockery stacked on the floor, at her pink cyclamen, neatly uprooted from its pot. Someone had been through her kitchen, searching every inch of it with scientific precision.

She stumbled through the rest of the house in a daze. The cloakroom window had been forced. Splintered wood littered the floor. There was no room that had not been examined with meticulous attention to detail. Furniture had been pushed aside, drawers emptied, their contents placed, not untidily it was true, upon the floor. Books had been removed from shelves and stood in piles on the floor. With a sense of dread, she went upstairs. On the bed lay her open jewel case. Scattered around it were a few remaining trinkets. Gone were her gold chains, the gold watch her mother had given her for her twenty-first birthday, the seed pearls that had been a christening present. Worst of all, gone was her mother's

163

engagement ring: a solitaire diamond. Frances flung herself down on the bed and wept.

The telephone started to ring. The police, she thought, made a grab for the receiver beside her bed, and gasped something into it.

'Are you all right my dear?' Mr Benson's voice sounded querulous. 'I've been trying to get you all morning.'

'I can't ... I can't ...' Her brain could not form words for her tongue to utter.

'It's all right my dear – I don't expect you to come in if you're unwell – and you do sound – unwell.'

A sob was forcing its way up her throat. 'Yes, I am – unwell – extremely unwell.'

'I'm sorry to hear that.'

The sob erupted with a shudder.

'Have you called the doctor?' He sounded quite worried. 'If you haven't already, certainly you must do that my dear. Ring me back and let me know how you are – and if there's anything I can do, you must tell me.'

'Thank you Mr Benson.'

'Don't worry if you can't get in tomorrow – but I'd be glad if you'd let me know. I'll say goodbye now.' And he rang off.

She surveyed the chaos that was her home, and balked at calling the police just yet. She'd had enough of police stations. How could she explain about the miniature? But her precious jewellery – she must do everything possible to retrieve that. She started to cry again as she thought of the few pieces of jewellery that were her last link with her mother. Apart from the engagement ring, which she had worn every day, there was an enamel bracelet and an antique amethyst pendant, and a cameo brooch.

Overcome with exhaustion, she slumped into a chair.

If Howden had drowned, would the police find anything suspicious about such a death? No one could know they had grappled – that she had kicked out at him. He'd fallen over-board: she hadn't pushed him. Perhaps she should have told the policeman what had really happened. If he was dead, he couldn't be accused of killing Margaret, whose undiscovered body in its wine-cooler coffin lay – somewhere – on the sea bed. Had he bludgeoned her to death? Or did he strangle her with those powerful hands? With a shiver of horror, she remembered herself and Vic – their two bodies locked together in the mutual pursuit of ecstasy. But when he made love to her, she hadn't known he was a murderer.

Any minute now, a policeman could appear with a warrant for her arrest: to take her in for questioning. Unable to bear the oppression of being alone, enveloped in a fog of fear and uncertainty, mentally and physically drained, she dialled Mark's number. It was all too much. Mark would never understand, but she must talk to someone, even if that someone, having listened to her tale, no longer wanted to be her friend. If she'd let Mark take care of the miniature, as he'd suggested, it would not now be stolen. If she'd never gone on Vic's boat, none of this would have happened. Despair overwhelmed her.

'I'm afraid Mr Edwards is out of the office all day,' said the receptionist in her special telephone voice.

'Please tell him I called.'

'I'll leave a message on his desk, but I'm not expecting him back until tomorrow.'

'I see – thank you very much.' Replacing the receiver, Frances felt more desolate than ever. She stared at the chaos the intruder had left behind. The thought of alien hands among her possessions, going through her drawers, touching her clothes, poking fingers into her food, made her retch. She picked up the telephone book, and looked up the number of the local police station. 'I've been burgled,' she said into the receiver. 'Could someone come right away please.'

165

Chapter Eighteen

The policeman introduced himself as Inspector Robertson. He had a craggy face and eyes of a washed-out blue. He looked tired. Probably about due for retirement, thought Frances as, wearily, he took down descriptions of her jewellery. When she tried to explain about the miniature he seemed to perk up a little, though his face remained deadpan. 'Found by you under the floorboards. Portrait of young lady, possibly by a sixteenth-century artist called Nicholas Hilliard. Stolen from cornflake packet.'

'It must belong to me, mustn't it? If it was found on my property?'

'Concealed there by a person, or persons unknown.'

'Not exactly. I think I know who put it there, either on purpose or accidentally. But I believe her to be dead.'

'You found the article recently, but you believe it to have been placed there some while ago by a person now deceased?' His voice betrayed no lack of credence.

'I think it was put there very recently by a woman named Margaret Weston who used to work for Mr Benson the antique dealer. She's disappeared.' As Frances tried to explain her theory about Margaret and the miniature without mentioning Vic, who after all might be dead, Inspector Robertson wrote stolidly in his notebook. Eventually, he said he would circulate descriptions of the stolen articles and she shouldn't lose heart as there was a reasonable chance of them being recovered. She didn't believe him.

After he'd gone, she thought she'd better do something about clearing up the horrible mess in the kitchen. It made her feel sick – the sight of all that spoiled food. She threw it in the dustbin. Then, vigorously, she scrubbed the table and the floor and poured disinfectant down the sink. The concentrated fury of her physical activity seemed to calm her distracted mind. Next, she tidied the sitting room, restored to order the emptied drawers, arranged books on the shelves.

Upstairs, promising herself the final reward of a hot, scented bath, she was replacing her cosmetics in the cabinet when there came a knocking on the front door. She went slowly down the stairs.

The young policeman with sandy hair stood on the step. 'May I come in?'

'Er yes,' she said nervously.

'Inspector Watkins.' He took off his hat. 'I wanted to come and tell you myself.' He followed her into the sitting room. 'It's good news, Miss Lambert. I'm here to put your mind at rest. Mr Howden has been rescued.' He beamed at her.

She didn't know what she felt.

'He was picked up by a fishing boat. They're keeping him in hospital overnight, but I understand he'll be allowed home tomorrow.'

Still beaming expectantly, he waited for her to express her joy.

When the turmoil in her head flattened out, she realised part of her was glad Vic wasn't dead. She wanted him brought to justice in the proper manner. She did not want his death on her conscience, but felt a frisson of terror at the thought of Vic alive. She should have told the truth. How could she now accuse Vic of assaulting her and murdering Margaret? She'd avoided explaining exactly what had happened on board *Calypso*, for reasons of self-protection. If Vic had drowned, she might have been asked some awkward questions. And a dead murderer could not be brought to justice.

'They say he's in reasonable shape. You'll be able to see for yourself. Suffering a little from hypothermia – he'd managed to climb into the dinghy. That's what saved him. It was a sensible thing – dropping that dinghy. You did well,' he said approvingly.

'It's such a relief.' She forced herself to sound grateful, happy. 'I can't tell you. Can he remember how it happened?'

167

'He wasn't in a fit state to say a lot.' An amused expression flickered over Inspector Watkins's pinkish face. 'I can tell you one thing – he was worried about his boat. Very relieved to hear you'd brought her in safely.'

'Hmmn.' Perhaps it would be better to make a further statement? Now she'd told the other policeman about Margaret and the miniature, Vic's connection with it could be shown to be relevant. And what about the wine cooler? Margaret's coffin. Lying somewhere on the sea bed. Someone should question Vic about the wine cooler. She was too tired to think straight. She yearned to lose herself in sleep for a very long time. 'Thank you for coming Inspector Watkins. You'll have to excuse me if I'm a bit confused. When I got home this morning, I discovered I'd been burgled. So, you see, you are the second policeman whose paid me a visit today.'

'That's a bit of real bad luck.'

'They took a ring I was very fond of.' Her voice shook.

'I do hope we recover it for you Miss Lambert,' said Inspector Watkins looking grave.

'Yes. It's been very upsetting. All this happening.'

'At least you know your friend is safe.'

Those words rang ominously in her head after he'd gone. Vic might be safe. But how safe was she? He couldn't turn up tonight, because he was in hospital. But there was tomorrow and all the days to follow. Her fears about being alone in the farmhouse had become real rather than imagined: focused, not random.

She was in bed when Mark telephoned. 'I had a message to call you.' He sounded reserved and formal.

'Oh Mark – please – could we meet. I've been having such an awful time. I need a friend.'

More softly, he said, 'Come to supper tomorrow – I'll pick you up after work.'

'I won't be at work. Can you come here?'

'What's the problem Frances – you sound very upset.'

'I can't talk about it now – I'm too tired and too confused. I have to get some sleep. Just come and see me as soon as you can.'

'Of course – sleep well.'

168

She slumped back against the pillows and tried to blot out the sounds of the night. The owl seemed to be off hunting elsewhere, but a light breeze caused the climbing rose to beat out its unnerving tap-tap against the casement. It pervaded her sleep, provoking all manner of strange sounds, human cries, dissenting voices, thunder claps, and a curious rushing noise. Towards dawn, a tidal wave, sleek and bright, rose to engulf her. She awoke, drenched in sweat.

At eight am she telephoned Mr Benson and told him she wasn't well enough to come to work, but she'd be in next day. She called Ted and he came and fixed the cloakroom window and fitted some extra security locks. 'Stone the crows,' he remarked when she told him the miniature had been stolen, along with her jewellery. Then he went through a list of local people, unknown to her who had all been burgled recently. 'Can't sleep easy these days can we?' He shook his head sadly. 'Terrible times we live in. When I was a nipper, my mum never even used to lock the door.'

She was grateful for his company, his sympathy, his irritating loquacity.

Alone again, she wandered from room to room in distress, for Willow Farm was no longer the safe haven she had imagined when first she glimpsed it through the windscreen of Mark's car. She nibbled at biscuits, made cups of coffee, slurped wine in desperation. But nothing seemed familiar, nothing seemed real.

When Mark arrived in the evening she flung herself into his arms. 'I'm so glad you're here.' She buried her face in his chest.

'Steady on – you nearly knocked me over – what on earth's happened?' He held her close and produced a handkerchief.

'I thought I was going to die – I've been burgled – the miniature's gone – oh Mark.'

'There there.' He soothed her as he would a child, smoothing her hair, wiping her cheeks.

Once in Mark's flat, she felt herself settle, become more normal. In this anonymous place there were no unexplained creaks and tappings; no loose floorboards, no insinuating draughts. Here, the double-glazed windows were insulation against disturbing noise and cool night air. The smooth pale walls, the soft carpet, the chair that cradled her, the unassuming pictures all combined to make her feel nothing bad could ever happen here.

He opened a bottle of wine. 'Now – tell me what's been going on. No rush. In your own time.'

He seemed steady as a rock, as he listened attentively to what she had to say.

He had no problem accepting Howden had tried to attack her. At this point she felt the tension in his stillness, his pressed-together lips, his eyes boring through the transparent barrier of his spectacles. She waited for him to say 'You should never have gone with the bloody man in the first place.' But, to her surprise, he merely said, in his quiet voice. 'Thank God you're all right.'

Talking too fast as if to make up for all her mistakes as well as acknowledge them, she said, 'I should have given the miniature to you, Mark, and then it wouldn't have got stolen.'

'Oh – it's easy to be wise after the event.'

'If Howden's to be believed, he spotted the value of the thing and got Margaret to buy it for him at auction. He said the auctioneer missed it – you and Mr Draper. Do you remember the Woodton Hall sale, Mark?'

'Not really.'

'The Hilliard must have been in the box of prints.'

'Since it's been stolen we can only guess if it really was a Hilliard,' he said stiffly.

She knew better than to say any more about auctioneers and valuations. 'The thing I'm really upset about is losing my mother's engagement ring. It means a lot to me, that ring.' Her voice wobbled.

'I'm sorry.'

'It's like losing a last link with my mum. It meant so much to her. I can see it on her hand now. She wore it all the time – even in hospital – when it was far too big for her poor finger.' She gulped back a sob.

Mark reached over and pulled her into his arms. He stroked her unruly hair and kissed the top of her head. 'Don't give up hope. Maybe it will turn up. The police will circulate the jewellers. What does it look like?'

'A solitaire diamond. Not very large. But it was a good one. My father wanted my mother to have the best, you see. I'd do anything to have it back. I mind much more about that than about the miniature – even if the miniature might be worth thousands and thousands.' She paused, leaning against him, breathing his comforting warmth. 'You know, it's very odd, my house was searched so thoroughly – it's almost as if the person who did it knew the miniature was there somewhere.' She looked up at Mark's suntanned face with its clearcut features, into his eyes full of concern, gazing into hers, rather blindly because he'd taken his glasses off. 'But you are the only person I told about it.'

Mark blinked, as if to clear his myopic vision, and inclined his head a little. 'Are you sure?'

'Yes.' She disengaged herself from his arms, sat up and drank a mouthful of wine.

Calmly, he said, 'Whoever turned over your house could easily have come across the miniature by accident. People do hide things in unusual places – thieves know that.'

'I suppose so.'

'Have you told the police you're suspicious of Howden?'

'Not yet.'

'Perhaps Margaret isn't really dead. Perhaps she'll come back looking for the miniature.'

'I suppose you can't accuse anyone of murder until you find a body.'

'Probably not. Come on Frances – let's have supper.'

'One of your Mum's fish pies?'

'Pasta – and I made the sauce myself.'

She stayed the night. She felt safe, lying chastely beside Mark, far away from her violated home.

Mr Benson said, 'The police were here yesterday, asking more questions about Margaret.' He looked thoughtfully at her. 'Are you sure you're well enough to be back at work.'

'I'm not ill, Mr Benson. When you telephoned I was extremely upset. I'd just been burgled. And there seems to be some connection with Margaret.' Once more she embarked upon the story of the miniature and Margaret and Vic Howden.

Benson did not comment, as she talked, trying to unravel for herself as much as for him, the intricacies of her tale.

When she had finished, he said dryly. 'I must say this all sounds most extraordinary,' and passed his hand over his head as if to contain the thoughts inside.

When she finished work that evening, Frances went to the police station and asked to see Inspector Robertson. 'No luck yet, I'm afraid – we're doing our best,' he said.

'I haven't come about my jewellery. I need to make another statement,' she said, and set about making a clean breast of everything. She told him what had truly happened on board *Calypso*, and said he should confer with Inspector Watkins of the Harwich harbour police. She said she suspected Vic Howden to have some connection with Margaret's disappearance and suggested they question him about a wine cooler purchased at Woodton Hall sale on 26 March, at the same time as the miniature.

Inspector Robertson looked even more tired than he had done yesterday. But by the time she had finished her statement, she thought she detected a small flame of energy flickering in the washed-out blue of those eyes, although his immobile face gave nothing away. Finally, she said, 'I'm frightened of Mr Howden, you see. And I live alone.'

She spent one more night with Mark and then she steeled herself and returned to Willow Farm. Kind as Mark was, she needed time on her own, and the longer she put off going home, the more difficult it would be. Unburdening herself to the police had helped, providing a kind of insurance – rather like taking out a life policy. They knew Vic had been to Willow Farm when it was up for sale; that Margaret had the details in her house; that the miniature had been found there. They knew of his long-term connections with the absent Margaret. They knew about the wine cooler. Their knowledge was her protection. She prayed they'd arrest him. Lock him up. If not, would he come looking for her? Seeking revenge for what happened on board *Calypso*? She wedged a chair under the handle of her bedroom door and lay rigid in the silence, straining her ears for unfamiliar sounds. When finally she slept, she dreamed of

Vic. She dreamed he was kissing her naked body all over as she lay supine, paralysed on the bunk on his boat. Unable to resist arousal, she was held prisoner until, miraculously recovering the movement in her limbs, she forced herself to thrust him from her. She drove him out of the cabin and up on to the deck. Endowed with superhuman strength, she flung him over the side of the boat where the waves were reaching up for him. He struggled alongside with flailing arms and began to beat upon the hull. His lips were moving but no sound came from them. Then, slowly, he slipped beneath the surface. Her eyes were able to follow his bare, muscular body down, down through the green water to the bottom. And there, resting on the sea bed, was the wine cooler. Like a lost treasure chest. As Vic's descending feet touched it, the lid burst open. A naked woman with wild accusing eyes issued forth; white as chalk, black hair plastered against her skull. Grappling together, the two bodies shot towards the surface. Paralysed Frances opened her mouth to scream – 'Margaret' – and woke to the feeble croak of her own voice.

It stayed with her for two days, the horror of that dream.

She went on waiting for something to happen. Mr Benson was curt and uncommunicative. It grew very hot. Women wore the lightest possible summer dresses, men discovered short-sleeved shirts. Some people talked doomily about global warming. Others said if this was global warming they welcomed it.

She could not fault Mark, who was kind and attentive. 'I don't like you being on your own at night,' he said. Why do I not feel more for him, she asked herself. He is kind, good-looking, intelligent, reliable. *Boring*, a little voice whispered in her head. But no, that was unfair. Mark was conventional rather than boring. The fault must lie with her. Was there something in her background, some psychological reason why she should not feel more responsive towards someone who was so eminently suitable? Would she always need the energy and duplicitous charm of a Felix? The evil charisma of a Vic? Every now and again, however much she didn't want it to, that lost afternoon with Vic Howden sneaked back into her mind in little surges and her muscles would clench, her mouth would moisten and her breath would catch. But she was still afraid of

173

him. Still believed him capable of murder. Still barricaded herself in her bedroom at night.

Inspector Robertson telephoned. 'Can you come down to the station, Miss Lambert. We might have some good news for you.'

Full of anticipation, she rushed down to the police station, and was asked to examine a ring.

'It appears to answer the description of the diamond solitaire ring stolen from your house,' said Inspector Robertson. There on the table lay her mother's engagement ring. She thought, I'm not dreaming. I'm really here. A wave of happiness washed through her. She picked up the ring and slipped it on her finger.

'Yes,' she said, 'It's definitely mine. I can't thank you enough Inspector.'

'I'm pleased it turned up,' he said.

'How did you find it? Where was it?'

'It came in to the station.'

'I'd like to thank whoever found it. Give them some reward. This ring is very precious to me.'

'We don't know who it was. The ring was just posted through the door.'

'Oh dear – what a shame! I wish I could tell them how happy they've made me. But it's good to know there are some honest people around, isn't it Inspector? I can hardly believe it.'

'No sign of the rest of your jewellery – or the miniature I'm afraid.'

'Never mind – this is all that really matters. She moved her hand, making the diamond sparkle in the light.

She telephoned Mark and asked him to come to supper and stay the night. 'I've got something to tell you,' she said. 'And please bring whatever's needed to cut down that rose. It's tap-tapping gives me nightmares.'

He turned up with pruning shears and a collapsible ladder.

'Look!' She held out her hand, displaying the ring.

'You've got it back! Oh Frances I'm so glad.' He laid down his gardening equipment and rushed over to give her hug. She kissed the soft skin of his neck just beneath his jaw.

'I've just collected it from the police station. Some anonymous person sent it in. I shall wear it always now.'

'How amazingly wonderful.' He took her hand in his and touched the precious stone on the third finger of her left hand. 'You're engaged,' he said, 'You must marry me now.' It was said as a joke, but he was watching her face carefully.

'I'm not sure I'm suited to marriage.' She gazed at the ring, closely encircling her finger. It seemed to bring her mother almost as close.

'No sign of the miniature?'

'No – but as I told Inspector Robertson – this is the most important thing. It's a miracle to have it back. See how it sparkles!'

Next morning as Frances sat at the typewriter, trying to concentrate on typing invoices, a florist's van drew up outside. A young woman with long blonde hair got out cradling an enormous spray of cut flowers. She entered the shop. 'Miss Lambert?'

'That's me,' said Frances.

The flowers were laid upon her startled arms. 'Beautiful aren't they,' said the girl.

Staring down at them, Frances thought, how extravagant. Red roses – symbol of romance. Surely Mark wasn't serious about marriage? The velvety blooms were beaded with drops of water, like morning dew, wrapped in a rustling caul of cellophane and tied with wide white ribbons.

'Thank you,' she called to the girl, who was just leaving. She lay the roses on her desk, opened the small envelope attached to them and took out a white card. The handwriting was bold – and forward sloping. It said, 'Great fuck. Pity about everything else.'

The entire surface of her skin flushed a burning red. She tore the card in half, tore it again, and again, and dropped it in the wastepaper basket. The roses were so dark they were almost black. They had green leaves, no scent, and the thorns had been removed. She could not bring herself to destroy them.

175

Chapter Nineteen

The heat-wave continued. The still, hot days passed, pregnant with issues not come to full term. Each day, Frances expected Vic to turn up, burning for vengeance. But nothing happened. Her fears for herself began to subside. Her concern for Margaret had been off-loaded on to the police. There was nothing to be done.

Mark invited her to Sunday lunch with his parents. 'They really took to you, Frances, and Dad's got you some plants.'

She hesitated. 'It's very kind of them. But ...' She did not want to sit at that formal dining table, subjected to the scrutiny of Mark's opinionated mother, offering herself up to the prospect of endless Sunday lunches, playing the role of 'Mark's girlfriend'. She was not ready for all that.

'*But* you don't want to come.' He looked crestfallen.

'Of course I'd love to come but I've things I need to do at home.'

'I see.'

Ashamed, succumbing to his injured tone, she said quickly, 'Tell you what – why don't you all come and have lunch with me at Willow Farm?'

He brightened immediately. 'Are you sure? I'll bring the wine.'

Knowing a traditional roast meal was expected, despite the summer heat, she bought sirloin of beef.

On Sunday morning, she laid the table with her blue and white willow-pattern plates and filled a pottery vase with some of the blue irises which grew in a clump down by the pond.

She prepared new potatoes and broad beans and made the batter for the Yorkshire pudding. Beef, according to Mother's Constance Spry cookery book, should be roasted in a hot oven, and needed fifteen minutes to the pound, if you liked it rare, which, according to Constance Spry, is how beef should be served. Slivers of fresh horseradish were recommended, but Frances had to make do with a jar of sauce. Treacle tart for pudding – bought from the home-made cake shop.

She had just slipped the meat into the oven when they arrived in David Edwards' green Rover. She went outside to greet them. Elizabeth Edwards stepped out of the front passenger seat, wearing white linen trousers, a red silk shirt and dark glasses, her black and silver hair, sleek as a helmet. Her husband, smiling broadly, was comfortably approachable in rather baggy denims.

Mark emerged from the back, carrying two bottles of wine.

'How very kind of you, my dear.' Mark's mother removed her dark glasses and looked around her interestedly. 'This is a treat.'

Mark's father was off-loading a large bunch of sweet peas and plants in pots, from the boot of the car. He presented the sweet peas to Frances, who thanked him profusely. 'And I've brought you some delphiniums – I raised them from seed – should have been planted out last month. But if you put them in now, they'll flower next year.'

'How lovely – I remember the ones in your garden – that wonderful deep blue – thank you.'

'And some bulbs. Autumn crocuses. Put them in now too – and they'll bloom in September. And these peonies – I've so many. It's a bit early to move them, but they should be all right.'

'And a little rosemary bush,' said Elizabeth Edwards. 'I told David to bring you one of those – he's always taking cuttings. And roast lamb isn't roast lamb without a sprig of rosemary. But do give it plenty of water. David was always starting little gardens for Joanna and Mark when they were children, and they never remembered to water them. So of course everything died.'

'Come and sit down on the terrace and have a drink,' said Frances, sneaking a look at her watch. The beef should be ready in three quarters of an hour.

'How charming.' Mrs Edwards gazed all around her before lowering herself gracefully into a cane chair putting her dark glasses back on. 'Why don't you open that wine for us dear,' she said to Mark who was standing around, a bottle of wine in each hand. And then she turned to Frances and said, 'We were so sorry to hear about your burglary. What a horrid thing to happen. I do hope you didn't lose too much.'

'Oh – Mark told you! Well – at least I got my ring back.' Frances held out her hand, and the diamond sparkled in the sunlight.

'Wasn't that a lucky thing,' said Mr Edwards, 'Mark keeps us informed you know.' He smiled at his son, who was pouring red wine into glasses.

'There's some white in the fridge,' Frances said, watching Mrs Edwards refuse a glass of red.

'I thought claret with the beef,' said Mark.

'You know I always like chilled dry white as an apéritif,' said his mother, patting him on the arm.

Frances escaped to the kitchen to fetch the Australian Chardonnay. When she got back to the terrace, Mark and his father were talking about a Victorian school in a nearby village which had become redundant and was about to be put up for sale by the Council. 'Grade II listed building,' said Mark. 'Flint, with a deep pitched roof and a little bell tower. Someone could do something imaginative with it.'

'Let's hope they do. Let's hope someone buys it and it doesn't just fall into disrepair and have to be demolished.'

'It's a bargain actually.'

'That seems to be the only way to sell anything round here,' said Mrs Edwards bitterly. 'Too cheap. Oh dear – the trials of the provincial estate agent.' She sighed.

'I don't think things are any better in London,' said Mark, tersely.

'You've made this place very attractive, my dear.' Mark's father's even voice dissipated the tension building between mother and son. 'And the builder's made a good job of the terrace.'

'Yes, Mark found Ted for me. He's been brilliant,' said Frances. 'Mark, why don't you show your parents what we've

178

done here, while I see to things in the kitchen.'

'Let me give you a hand,' said Mark's mother.

'No, really, I can manage,' said Frances, recoiling at the idea of Elizabeth Edwards overseeing her cooking.

The beef looked fine when she got it out of the oven; crisp and brown on the outside. With luck, it would be pink and moist inside. She let it rest while she drained the vegetables and made the gravy and listened to Mark giving his parents a conducted tour of Willow Farm. Then, there was no keeping Mark's mother out of the kitchen. Her inquisitive eyes darted over the old-fashioned solid-fuel stove – (which made the room extremely hot) – the deep enamel sink, stacked with dirty saucepans, the pot basil which needed watering, the jumble of ornaments and mementos on the dresser. Under that discomforting eye, Frances got a rather flat Yorkshire pudding out of the oven. With heavy tact, Elizabeth Edwards turned towards the roast sirloin, waiting on the large willow-pattern dish, oozing a little reddish juice. 'Would you like me to carve?'

Frances, remembering the woman's adept wielding of the carving knife in her own home, decided to relinquish her tenuous advantage as hostess and submit to a takeover. 'Yes please – I've sharpened the knife.'

Her meal was praised politely by Mark's mother, and over-enthusiastically by Mark and his father, who each had two helpings of meat and vegetables and drank most of the wine. The treacle tart was also well received by the men. 'Only a tiny piece my dear' – Mrs Edwards tapped her enviably flat stomach – 'And no cream for me thank you.'

After coffee in the sunshine, David Edwards helped Frances plant the delphiniums and peonies and the bulbs in the flowerbed below the terrace, and the rosemary in the little bed outside the back door, where there was already some mint growing. And then they wandered companionably round the garden. She showed him the wisteria she'd planted against the front of the house, and the clematis at the back.

'Be a good idea to put a few shrubs in in the autumn,' he said, 'Mainly shrubs and annuals are the thing when you don't have much time. If you're clever you can get colour all year.'

'I'd like purple lilac – for the spring.'

179

'Yes. I'm not sure you have the right soil for rhododendrons and azaleas, but you could grow ceanothus and choisya – that has a lovely scent – and buddleia to encourage the butterflies and pyracantha for the berries in the autumn.'

She took him down to the pond. 'There were masses of daffodils here when I first came, and I love this willow herb and the bulrushes. I know it's all a bit overgrown, and needs dredging, but I want to keep it looking fairly wild – it's a natural pond after all. There are lots of fish.'

'You could have water-lilies – and different kinds of fern,' he said enthusiastically. 'These irises are lovely.' He stooped to examine the clump growing by the edge of the water. 'You had some in a vase on the table.'

Slightly raised voices sounded from the terrace.

David Edwards sighed. 'My wife can be a little managing, I'm afraid. Especially where Mark is concerned. She's always had very high hopes for him. Being the only boy. She had a good career herself – in fashion. With one of the big London stores. Gave it all up when we married. But there you are – Mark's a bright enough chap as you well know, but he's got no driving ambition. He takes after me. Prefers a quiet life. I was pleased when he came back to join the family firm. We work well together, Mark and I.'

He took a knife from his pocket and probed the soil beneath the irises. 'You need to divide these – I'll show you how.'

Daringly, Frances said, 'When we last met, we were talking about Margaret, and you said something about a friend of hers who was also a friend of Mark's. I got the impression you weren't too keen on her. Did you mean Carla Holmes?'

'Probably. Carla Holmes is a colourful lady with a not very good reputation, I'm afraid,' said David Edwards mildly. 'But – well – there are not many youngish people around here and you don't choose your children's friends do you? You can't run their lives. Make them be what they're not. I tell that to Liz.' He cut into the clump of irises and lifted up a rhizome with a new iris growing from it. 'Plant that over there, by the weeping willow, plus a few more, and you'll soon have another clump.' He regarded her with steady blue eyes. 'I hope you're happy here, Frances. I hope you'll stay with us all. And it's good for Mark to have a friend of his own age. He doesn't always have

180

it very easy.' He bent down to the irises, knife poised.

At that moment there came the sound of rapid footsteps and Mark burst through the low branches of willow. He was panting and red in the face. 'What are you saying? Why are you talking about me? I can't stand people talking about me behind my back.'

David Edwards straightened up, knife and rhizome in hand. 'Steady on old chap,' he said. We were just having a friendly chat – nothing to worry about.' He put out a hand and laid it on his son's shoulder, as if to control the violent trembling that had taken hold of Mark's body.

'What are you doing hiding away down here? What have you been saying?' Twisting his shoulder, Mark grabbed his father's hand, knocking the knife to the ground. He pulled him away from the pond and up the bank.

Alarmed by Mark's bewildering outburst, Frances waited for a while and then followed father and son slowly up the grassy slope. When she got to the top, David Edwards had a firm hand on his son's shoulder, and was talking to him in a low voice. She could not hear what was said. The high colour had drained from Mark's face and his arms hung slackly by his side. He looked like a chastised adolescent.

Up on the terrace, Elizabeth Edwards was lounging in a cane chair, legs stretched out in front of her, gazing with concentration at the business section of the *Sunday Times*. What had been going on between those two, wondered Frances uneasily? What unnatural hold had that overbearing woman maintained on her son, in order to provoke such disturbing behaviour?

181

Chapter Twenty

Late one afternoon, when Mr Benson was out, Vic Howden pushed open the showroom door. The shock of his physical presence clamped her to the chair. Her fearful mind recoiled from him. Her intemperate sex pulsed in recognition. She wished a thicket of brambles would spring up between them, barring his access. But there was nothing to impede his progress across the wooden floor towards her. Carla Holmes followed him in. She succeeded in conveying the impression she and Howden were an established couple. She did this not by laying a hand on his arm, or calling him 'darling', but in a casual way seemed to align her body with his and without even looking at him, subtly implied an intimate awareness.

'Hello,' Frances said feebly. 'How are you?'

'Not done for yet as you can see.' His tone was jovial, his expression bland. 'Fortunately he's very strong,' chipped in Carla. 'What a terrible accident.' She turned possessive eyes full upon him, like the proud owner of a racehorse that's come in first over heavy going.

This is bizarre, thought Frances. I don't believe this. For days she'd been preparing herself for Howden's murderous rage or, at the very least, righteous indignation. Could it be that he had no recollection of their tussle on *Calypso*'s deck, of the blow she'd aimed at him with her feet? Or was there some other reason for his apparent lack of antagonism? The distraction of Carla? But his relationship with Carla was hardly in the first flush. It was surely not the root of Howden's sanguine air, the relaxed drop of the shoulders, the secretive, satisfied set of his full lips? She realised that for the first time she could remember, on entering the shop, he wasn't automatically looking around him.

'Win some. Lose some.' Howden smiled into her eyes. She hated him.

'The lowboy,' said Carla, impatiently.

'Carla wants some advice on the walnut lowboy in the back showroom,' said Howden. 'Come along my dear.' He took her arm. 'Let's take a look.'

'Let me know if you need any help,' said Frances, confused and angry.

She could hear them moving around, talking softly. Eventually, she went through and found Carla measuring a wardrobe and Howden examining a recently purchased marble-topped console table. Howden looked up as she entered, 'She likes the lowboy.' Carla nodded. 'And I like the table.'

Then, directing the full sensuality of his glossy eyes into hers, he said, 'By the way, Frances – about that wine-cooler – I sold it on to a chap from Essex. Keeps his boat in the marina. The police have checked it out. Thought you'd like to know.'

Unbidden, the memory of that dream flooded her mind. Margaret's bloodless flesh and wild accusing eyes. Margaret and Vic, locked in combat, rising through green water towards her. Vic's knowing hands on her own body. She shook her head as if to chase the vivid pictures from her mind.

'And not even a bottle of bubbly inside.'

She could not bear to remain close to him. 'Excuse me – I think I heard the door bell.' She shot back into the front showroom. She was trembling. He was so patronising, so pleased with himself; so bloody arrogant. But he'd not shut Margaret's dead body inside the wine-cooler and dumped it in the sea. The wine-cooler was, at this moment, looking decorative in the sitting room of a yacht owner from Essex. This did not exonerate him from murder. And the fact he'd been questioned by the police meant they were on to him, which was some small comfort.

They came and stood by her desk. Carla smug, Vic casual. 'Tell Tommy I'll give him a ring about the lowboy and the table.'

They left and she watched Vic open the passenger door of

the Mercedes for Carla, who slid herself inside exposing plenty of thigh. Thick as thieves, she thought. Vic and Carla. Dreadful Carla with her showy clothes, her over-shapely legs, her beastly bouncy hair, her horrible round eyes and that confident air of superiority. Carla and Vic. Carla and Mark. There was something bothering her about the connections between these three people. But it was all too unpleasant to think about. Forget Carla, she told herself. She's just an old tart, who seduces young men and gets her claws into rich old ones.

She got out a duster and began, vigorously, to polish her desk. But she could not stop thinking about Vic and the more she thought about him, the odder his behaviour seemed. Why was he not angrier with her? He'd nearly lost his life. And there he was, walking into the shop as if nothing had happened. Something was giving him reason to be pleased with himself. His whole bearing appeared complacent rather than threatening. Was it safe to feel relief?

At six o'clock Frances went to the White Horse in search of Mark. Shamefaced, he had apologised for his outburst on Sunday. 'Sometimes I'm afraid I behave very childishly, when my mother's around,' he'd said next day. Frances, missing her badly, thought how fortunate she'd been in her own mother, and decided to try to forget the unpleasant episode down by the pond. Poor Mark. She felt sorry for him, but at least he had the comfort of a very understanding father. And so, they had fallen into the habit of meeting for a drink after work. Then they would make supper at Willow Farm or at Mark's flat. Observing the rituals of normal life – working, socialising, the preparation and consumption of food was comforting.

Mark was standing at the bar. 'Hi Frances.' He smiled. 'My God it's hot – my shirt's sticking to me.' His face was damp.

'I always feel sorry for you men,' said Frances. 'I couldn't bear to wear trousers and lace-up shoes and socks in this weather.'

'Shorts and sandals – that'd be nice. Tropical kit for heat-waves.'

'Still, you can take off all your clothes when you get home.'

'We both can.' He grinned. 'What can I get you?'

'Double ginger-beer with ice, please.'

'My jacket's over there – why don't you go and sit down and I'll bring the drinks.'

'OK.' She made her way over to a table in the corner where she could see Mark's jacket hanging over a chair. She was just sitting down when Carla Holmes came into the bar. Carla pranced over to insert coins into the cigarette machine, which regurgitated a packet of Dunhills. She put the cigarettes in her bag and went over to the bar, where Mark was still waiting to be served. She touched his arm. He turned. She stood on tiptoe and kissed him on the mouth. He looked surprised but seemed to welcome her kiss, and then Frances saw him glance guiltily over to where she sat waiting. Carla murmured something and then she swished out of the bar in her short flouncy skirt on her spiky heels. At the door, she turned and waggled her fingers jauntily at Mark.

They know each other extremely well, those two, thought Frances, whatever Mark might say. He's intrigued by her and she can't resist giving him the come-on. A little voice in her head whispered, he's still seeing her. In spite of you. And why should she mind? But she did. Carla prancing about between Mark and Vic.

Mark and Vic. It's different for me, thought Frances. Vic was an aberration. Mark appeared at the table with their drinks.

'Carla seemed very pleased to see you. All over you in fact.'

'You exaggerate.'

'She came into the shop an hour ago with Vic. Very friendly they were.'

He went still and tense, as if nerve and muscle had gone into spasm.

'You hate it when I mention Vic, don't you.'

'Why do it then?'

'Well – it's quite interesting really. As I said, he came in to the shop with your friend Carla today. And it was very odd. I'd expected him to be really mad with me for nearly drowning him. But he wasn't. It was almost as if he had some reason to be pleased about something. I've been puzzling over what it could be. The police have obviously been talking to him. They've checked up on the wine-cooler and that's OK, so he's happy about that. But there's something more. They're so

185

thick – Carla and Vic. Like conspirators. And now Carla is all over you. I know there's some connection.'

'You're talking nonsense. Have a proper drink. Let me get you a glass of wine.'

'No, it's far too hot. Don't go away. I want to talk about this. Mark – have you been seeing Carla?'

'Does it matter if I have?'

'Only that she's so thick with Vic. And she's making up to you for a reason. When did you last see her?'

'Just now,' he said flippantly.

'You know what I mean. It's up to you, of course. It's your business who you see. But there's something not quite right about all this. Vic and Carla. Carla and you.'

'And you,' he ground out in a fierce and trembling undertone. 'You and Vic. Did you think he was a murderer when you let him fuck you?'

She was glad that the pub was crowded, grateful for the sheltering noise of convivial drinkers and of the music thumping out of the sound system. Behind his spectacles, Mark's eyes burned like hot coals. The glass in his hand shook, spilling drops of beer on the table. 'How do you think I felt when you went off with that bastard? I knew you were all alone on his boat. And you fancied him like hell – I knew that. What do you think that did to me.'

She would admit nothing to Mark. It was bad enough admitting it to herself.

'I couldn't get it out of my mind – the thought of you letting him to it to you. I went out for a drink that night. And Carla was there. We had a few. I needed to talk to someone.'

'And you talked about me.'

'I was upset. I got drunk.'

I wouldn't betray you, she thought, talk about you intimately with someone else, spill secrets. 'What about Margaret?' Did you talk about Margaret? I think it's very peculiar Carla doesn't know where she is.'

He poured the rest of his beer down his throat and wiped his mouth with the back of his hand. 'I suppose she might have made some remark about not being surprised Margaret had cleared off. Margaret was side-dealing of course – got herself into difficulties caught between Benson and Howden.'

186

'What else?'

'I don't know – I can't remember.' He stared into his empty tankard. 'Really – what does it matter?'

The thing that was nagging her about the connection between Mark and Carla and Vic – and – yes – Margaret – began to slide into focus in her brain. There was a sudden flash, like a match struck, with a rasp and a flare – and she had it. She made the connection. 'Did you tell Carla about the miniature?'

'Why should I do that?'

'I don't know – just for something to talk about I suppose.'

'I might have. I can't remember. I was drunk.'

She was racing away with it now – with her bright new theory. 'If you told Carla about the miniature – and she knew about Margaret walking off with what could well be a valuable Hilliard – which she probably did – being so thick with Vic – she could have put two and two together. However it got there, she could have assumed it to be the same miniature. She knew Vic was mad to get his hands on it. And so she stole it back for him. I bet it was her who broke into my house.'

Mark said, 'That's a very interesting theory. I need another drink. Let me get you one.'

'Oh all right. But don't be long.'

He got to his feet and went over to the bar. He returned with a pint of beer and a glass of wine, looking thoughtful.

'It would explain why Vic seemed so pleased with himself,' she said. 'What could it be worth, do you think? If it really was a genuine Hilliard?'

'Oh I dunno – a hundred grand – probably more.'

'So what do you think, Mark? Do you believe my theory is possible? More to the point, did you say anything to Carla about the miniature?'

'I wish I could remember.' He leaned his head in his hands and seemed to be looking for inspiration in the beer mat. After a while he said, quietly, 'Yes. I suppose it's possible.'

'Oh Mark, you *are* an idiot.'

'Look, Frances – at the time we didn't know what it was – we still don't know how it got there. And anyway, it was pretty careless of you to leave it in that stupid cornflake packet. I offered to look after it for you.'

'Thanks a bunch.'

'What do you expect me to do now? Accuse Carla of breaking into your house and stealing the miniature?'

'We need to get it back.'

'If you want to know – I'm sick to death of the whole thing. They're a load of crooks – out to get something for nothing.'

'Blame the cataloguer for giving them the opportunity. I suppose you'd like to see the miniature returned to its original owner and put up for sale again so the auctioneer could make big bucks out of it along with the fool who didn't have the intellect to appreciate the quality of the thing he'd got, or the sense to get it valued by an expert.'

Mark stiffened. She knew it was wrong of her – to criticise auctioneers for lack of expertise. But why should she make allowances? She was angry with him. He had let her down.

'I'd better be going,' he said, staring into his beer.

'Me too.'

He shot a quick, wounded look at her. 'Do you want to come with me?'

'I have to get used to being on my own.'

At least the nights were very short, she told herself, unable to sleep, upset by the rift with Mark. It would heal, she knew, but it made her feel uncomfortable, raw as a newly shorn sheep, trying to adapt to the loss of its protective coat. But there were not many hours of darkness in which to toss and turn, in that shadowy land between sleep and waking – all the events of the last days weaving through her mind like a piece of improvised jazz, the underlying melody forming and reforming, giving her no rest. The heat made it worse. With only a thin sheet for cover, still her naked body was bathed in perspiration. By quarter to six she'd had enough of lying in bed. She got up, slipped on her track suit and went outside. Because of the drought, her garden was like a desert. As was her habit every morning before going to work, she collected her watering can and set off towards the pond. The hard baked earth would suck up moisture like a giant sponge. She made her way across the terrace, over the tinder-dry lawn and down the bank of shrivelled grass where cowslips and daffodils had danced in the spring. Even at this hour, the sun beat strongly on her bare head. She usually made three trips with the watering can, in an attempt to save the lives of her most valued plants: the needy clematis, the delphiniums and peonies and the rosemary bush given to her by Mark's father, the young wisteria.

Dried mud edged the pond. Each day, the brown water seemed less. Each day she had to go deeper to fill the can.

The leaves of the willow and alder leaning over the pond, rustled a little in the faint breath of an early morning breeze, and dappled the surface of the water with shifting lozenges of light and shade. As she bent down with the can, keeping an eye out for the fish, small black shadows streaming through the suspension of mud and water, she noticed a grid-like pattern beneath the surface. A trick of the light perhaps, the sun piercing the network of leaves. As she watched curiously, the pattern seemed to become more distinct, until it leaped out at her like one of those three dimensional pictures emerging from a page of coloured dots. As you stare through the densely packed dots with unfocused eyes, shapes begin to assemble themselves. Carefully you bring your eyes back into focus, and there it is, springing from the page, a fully formed, three-dimensional image of mountain peaks or many petalled flowers.

There was definitely something lying in the mud, made visible by the drop in water level. She could see long straight lines – a square or rectangular shape. Straining her eyes she thought she really must have the pond dredged. Clear it of old boots and buckets with holes in them, rusting pieces of iron-mongery, bicycle wheels – the sort of stuff that traditionally gets chucked into ponds to lurk unseen in the mud, contaminating the water. Then she would stock it with exotic fish; grow water lilies instead of pond weed.

She rolled up the legs of her track suit and waded a little way into the water, her feet sinking into the soft mud. Was it a piece of metal? She thought she could see knobs and curlicues. The corner of something? An iron bed frame? A piece of farm equipment? A gate? Gingerly, she waded further in, flinching from the slimy fingers of mud crawling up her shins. Yes – it was a gate – quite large – cast-iron. It had a familiar look about it. Perhaps it was partner to her own remaining gate, presently propped up against the side of the house while she decided what to do with it. Why would anyone want to chuck a gate into a pond? Another couple of steps, and turbid water had crept over her knees and was soaking her track-suit trousers. She flung the can back on to the bank, plunged her hands under the water, reached out and managed to touch the corner of the gate. It felt cold and hard and rough against the sensitive pads of her fingertips. She pushed gently. It didn't move, but the surface of the water rippled slightly and as it did so she noticed something pale on the underside of the gate. And then something else – dark – a piece of cloth. The ripples flattened out. The wind swept a willow branch aside and the sun shining directly down on the water highlighted a long, shadow beneath the gate. With absolute clarity, for a sharp, horrifying moment she saw that the dark patches were clothing. That the nearest pale bit was a skeletal human hand. That the larger pale bit with black holes in it and black strands floating round it, was a human face.

Her cry of terror sent the birds fleeing from the trees. She turned and fought her way through the clinging mud and contaminated water to the bank. Clutching the trunk of the willow tree, bent double, she retched and retched on her empty stomach.

Chapter Twenty-One

Frances was waiting for Mark to come back from work. Curled up on the squashy sofa in his sitting room, she thought there was nothing in the world she wanted to do. Her body seemed pressed down by a great weight: it was almost too much effort to go through to the kitchen and make herself a cup of coffee. The shock of it, she supposed, had used up all her energy. Adrenaline pumped into the blood stream precipitates flight. She'd had an excess of that recently. And now she seemed to be in a state of semi collapse. Almost comatose, like a hibernating mammal. Until today, she'd not even been to work because Mr Benson had closed the shop, out of respect for Margaret.

She'd been here for three days. Mark had fetched her from Willow Farm. After the police had taken Margaret away, she telephoned him, forgetting they'd not parted on the best of terms the night before.

'Hello Frances.' Even in her distraught state, she registered the coolness of tone. Her own voice could not be controlled: it wobbled and squeaked like a pubescent boy's on the verge of breaking. 'I've found Margaret.'

In the silence that followed, she felt the shock waves pounding back at her. Then he asked in his quiet voice, 'Where? Where is she?'

'In my pond. Under my gate. The police have just taken her away. She's dead, of course.' Frances was sobbing. Great gulping hiccuping sobs. After a while he said quietly, 'Poor Frances. I'm very sorry.'

'Oh Mark – you never wanted me to buy Willow Farm in the first place. Maybe I should have listened to you.'

'You never do. You fall for dreams. Look – you shouldn't be out there alone. Would you like me to come?'

'I can't stay here. Can I come to you for a little while?'

'Of course.'

And so, she packed a case, turned her back on her home and fled to reliable Mark, to be comforted by his warm arms and soothed by the undemanding atmosphere of his silent flat. While he was at work, she would sit for hours at his white formica kitchen table, and watch the slow-moving hands of his black-faced clock, or she would curl up on the squashy leather sofa in his bland sitting room with the television on. She had no appreciation of what she was watching but the transmitted images on the screen helped to prevent her own ineradicable images from filling up her brain.

The horror of that pale mass gradually assembling itself into a face. Black holes – a glimpse of yellow bone – the dark strands that were her hair. If only they were no more real to her than those screened images.

She fled stumbling and gasping up the bank of shrivelled grass, over the slippery lawn, across the terrace and back to the house: grabbed the telephone. She was trembling so violently words scrambled themselves in her head, her tongue seemed too big for her mouth, her lungs supplied air in erratic gusts. But somehow she managed to convey to the police her urgent need of their presence.

After that, everything happened very quickly. She might have been watching a speeded-up cine film in which she was one of the characters: a disconnected, traumatised observer, watching herself watching as they raised the body from the mud. They put it on a stretcher, covered it with plastic and took it away in a black police van with no windows. She watched it rolling down the lane and she thought, I never heard your voice, Margaret, and now I never will. But this is not the last of you. For you have haunted my place of work, my home, my thoughts. You cannot be part of my future. But I will never be free of you.

When the van had disappeared from view, she went down and looked at Margaret's temporary grave. There were footprints and splashes of mud all around the edge, and the disturbed water was brown as molasses. The bed of the pond would be shifting, closing over, filling the newly made space down there. My pond, she thought. Can I bear to go on owning it? There was her gate, lying heavily on the grass, coated in slime.

The sun still shone, beating down on her back and on her bare head. She had stood here, quite content, listening to the sound of the breeze in the willow and alder, enjoying the soft rustle of the leaves, admiring the effect of dappled shade on water – only a few hours ago. But it seemed more like a hundred years. This place was made strange for ever. Once more she stumbled back to the house and grabbed the telephone. This time she called Mark.

Now she sat in the quietness of Mark's sitting room, drinking coffee which had gone cold because she'd forgotten about it, and she thought of Mr Benson. Mr Benson had been the one to identify the body. Poor man. Where would he go for comfort? He no longer had a wife, and his only daughter lived in America. He shut the shop for the rest of the week and stayed at home. She tried to offer words of comfort, but he seemed dazed, unresponsive. Coming to terms with the finality of it. Margaret would never walk into his showroom, touch the smooth planes and intricate carvings of his antique furniture, she wouldn't sit at her desk, lay warm fingers on her typewriter keyboard, scrawl figures in her little blue book. All this time, while Frances sat at Margaret's desk, typed on Margaret's typewriter, dealt with Margaret's customers, Margaret had lain in the mud at Willow Farm.

Knowing Margaret would never come back was not the same thing as being confronted with the horror of her decaying body. Mr Benson returned from the morgue white as chalk. His eyes held the brightness of tears and his hands were shaking. 'I'm afraid there's no doubt. They said the the mud and cold water had helped to preserve her. But the fish,' he stopped and his thin lips trembled, 'Poor soul.'

She couldn't stop thinking of the photograph in Margaret's bedroom. Of the unblemished face of the little dark-haired girl. As the days crawled by, the man who was once the little boy, posing beside the childish Margaret, arrived from Australia. He'd not been in touch with his sister, bar an annual Christmas card, for ten years. He took Margaret's keys and stayed in Forgetmenot Cottage, a flabby middle-aged man with very little hair, waiting for the inquest to be over so he could give his sister a decent burial and get back to normal life.

Margaret had been strangled.

The police were to be seen everywhere. It was the lead story in the local newspapers: the murder of Margaret Weston the main subject of discussion in the public houses, the shops and homes of the people of Fressenworth. Frances waited for news that Vic Howden had been arrested. How could he not be guilty? Margaret, the miniature, Willow Farm. They were all connected.

Perhaps he hadn't meant to kill her? Perhaps he meant only to frighten her? Frances was aware of a desperate attempt to make herself feel better about her own reprehensible lust for a murderer.

When Mark came home, she was still curled up on the sofa. He got a bottle of wine from the fridge and poured two glasses. 'How was your day?'

'Unreal.'

The showroom seemed more redolent than ever of Margaret's ghost. The police took away Margaret's shoes and the box containing her few possessions. But removing Margaret's possessions did not excise her presence.

It was impossible to do any business. When the showroom was not full of policemen, asking questions, examining things, it was bursting with voyeurs, pretending to be customers.

The dealers came in, all of them except for Vic. Trevor and Ronnie, Billy and Dick and Patrick. As if responding to some bush telegraph, they appeared on the first day the shop was opened. They came separately and hung around her desk asking, with ghoulish interest, for details and exclaiming at the horror of it. Ronnie said portentously, 'I suspected it all along. Lotta enemies had Margaret.' Trevor said, ' I dunno – always thought Margaret could get away with anything. Not the sort to get knocked off.' Patrick said 'It's a terrible thing

– women on their own are a target for nutters. They may never find him.'

Frances thought about Margaret's enemies. About her side-dealing. About the strange telephone calls and odd people coming in to see her, during the first few weeks she'd done Margaret's job for her. If not Vic, consider one of the other dealers. Any of them could have harboured a grudge. What about Patrick? Callous and clever – a connection with Carla. Ronnie? A vicious streak. Billy? The drunkard. Dick? Sharp as a weasel, avaricious. Any of them could have known about the Hilliard and wanted it for themselves.

Murderers live among us. Until they are unveiled we think of them as ordinary people, living unexceptional lives. Are we all capable of killing? Not me, thought Frances, who couldn't bear to lay a mousetrap, abhorred the shooting of pheasants for sport. I don't believe I could ever kill anyone. But someone killed Margaret.

Mr Benson remained in his room all day.

Frances and Mark finished the bottle of wine and sat down to a ready meal of microwaved chicken chasseur. She seemed to have lost her sense of taste. She stopped trying to force down the meat fibres and pappy rice. 'You know Mark, I wonder they haven't arrested Vic. They're investigating a murder now, not just looking for a missing person.'

Mark did not reply, stolidly forking food into his mouth.

'Do you think I should tell them I suspect Carla of stealing the miniature for Vic.'

'Frankly no. The police have got things in hand. Aren't you tired of playing amateur sleuth?'

'I suppose it's more important to nail the man Margaret went off with after that sale. Surely it must have been Vic. Unless there's some other man in Margaret's life. The old lady next door says they drove away in a car.'

'How reliable is that old lady?'

'She seemed pretty *compos mentis*. Does the football pools.'

'Hmmn. You know it's quite possible Margaret was attacked and murdered by someone totally unknown to her – or to anyone. Some itinerant. Because she happened to be in the wrong place at the wrong time.'

195

'That's what Patrick said. But what was she doing at Willow Farm?'

'She could have been killed somewhere else and dumped in your pond.'

Frances opened her mouth to say something else, but as she did so, Mark with great suddenness, clattered his knife and fork down on his plate and, raising his hands in agitation, yelled, 'My God, Frances – haven't you had enough of all this. I'm sick and tired of you going on and on about Margaret. Can't we forget about her now and get on with our own lives. She's dead. It's over.'

Chastened by his outburst, she said quietly. 'It's not over.'

'Well as far as I'm concerned, it is.' He pushed back his chair and got abruptly to his feet. 'Do you want coffee?'

'If you're making it.'

She said nothing more as he put the kettle on and prepared the coffee. When he came back to the table with their two cups, he said, 'We both need a holiday. Why don't we drive down to the south coast – or up north if you prefer.'

'I don't know if I *can* go away at the moment. I'm not sure I'm *allowed* to.'

'We'd check it out with the police – tell them where we were.'

'It's a nice idea.' What would it be like – going away with Mark? She could not help remembering the rapture of snatched days and nights with Felix. Tried not to imagine the horrible excitement of lying with Vic. There's definitely something wrong with me, she thought. I'm perverse and immature. Why am I not delighted at the idea of spending time alone with Mark?

Later, in bed he said, 'I love you, Frances. Please come away with me.'

And then, suddenly, she was having sex with a stranger. She could not believe this was Mark. Gone was his lack of assurance, his apprehension, his fearful, clumsy tenderness. His love-making was violent in its insistence. He seemed possessed by a feverish need to imprint every inch of her body with his. He was sweating and shaking with uncontainable emotion. She was frightened by his ardour, unable to match it.

In the morning he pleaded with her, 'Just a few days – I know a lovely little place near Exmouth. It will do you good. Please.'

Uneasily, she agreed. She did not want to mislead him. I can't love you, she thought. But I'll always be your friend.

'We'll go after work tonight. I'll make the booking this morning.'

Mr Benson, still inarticulate with shock, hardly seemed to notice when she asked him if she could take some leave. He stared at her sadly. 'Of course, of course, whatever you wish.'

'I'll clear it with the police – and I'll keep in touch.'

Frances got back to the flat before Mark. She started to pack the few clothes she had brought with her, unwilling to go home for more. It had been another hot, humid day. She stripped off her limp dress and underwear, went into the bathroom, stepped into the shower and turned the spray on full. On the way out, she stubbed her big toe quite badly on the ledge of the shower cubicle. Blood welled from underneath the nail, which hung loose. She wrapped a towel round herself and hobbled over to the mirror-fronted cabinet. But there was no Elastoplast to be found among the shaving gear and tubes of Alka Seltzer. She wrapped toilet paper round her toe and hobbled into the bedroom, to look for some in Mark's bedside cupboard. She opened the little drawer and scrabbled about among the packets of condoms, handkerchiefs and spare spectacle cases. Blood seeping through the toilet paper threatened to stain the carpet. Hurriedly, she grabbed a large handkerchief from the back of the drawer disturbing the neat pile of condom packets. She twisted the handkerchief round her toe and as she was closing the drawer she noticed something protruding from one of the packets. It wasn't a condom. It was the end of a slender gold chain. Mystified, she pulled it out and recognised it immediately. It was one of her own gold necklaces. But all six of them had been stolen from Willow Farm. She put out her hand to investigate the drawer further and as she did so, Mark came into the room. Speechlessly, she held out the chain.

He stopped dead and clapped his hand to his mouth. 'Oh my God Frances – I forgot – I found it under the bed last week. I

197

meant to give it back to you. But with everything else – I just forgot. I'm so sorry.'

In a small breathless voice she said, 'But it was stolen – from my house – when the miniature went. There were six of them.'

'You must have been mistaken. This one was definitely under my bed. Hurry up – we need to get a move on if we're going away.' He shut the drawer of his bedside cabinet. 'How are you getting on with your packing?' His lips were white around the edges.

She was shivering, in spite of the oppressive heat. She started to dab herself with the towel.

'What have you done to your foot?'

'I stubbed my toe. I was looking for a plaster.'

'Let me see.'

She sat on the bed and gently he unwrapped the blood-stained handkerchief. Her flesh shrank back from his gentle hands. 'Sorry – I didn't meant to hurt you.' He pressed the torn nail back into its bed and the blood welled from under it. He went to his chest of drawers and brought out a first-aid kit. He extracted a gauze dressing and a reel of adhesive plaster. 'Try and keep still.'

All the time her foot was in his hand, she was trying to remember when last she had worn that particular gold chain. Why should she question him? Why should her skin flinch from the touch of his administering fingers? Why were there goose bumps all over her body?

When he had finished she pulled on trousers and a tee-shirt. He was taking clothes out of the wardrobe and out of his chest of drawers and packing them into his case. 'It'll be great to get away – do you know Devon? We'll take long walks and eat cream teas and drink Devon cider.'

She definitely did not want to drive all the way down to Devon with Mark. Her eyes were drawn, as steel filings to a magnet, towards the closed drawer of his bedside cabinet.

He was watching. 'Ah – yes – we'll need some of those.' He opened the drawer, pulled out packets of Durex and threw them in his case. 'Right – are you ready? Let's go.'

'Actually – I don't feel too good – I think I'll have to lie down.'

198

'Oh dear – it's that nasty toe. Never mind, have a rest – and I'll bring you a cup of tea.' He smiled at her and she could not read the expression in his eyes behind the lens of his spectacles. He picked up the cases. 'I'll stack the car.'

She heard him go downstairs. With the beats of her heart thundering in her head, she crept over to his bedside cabinet and opened the drawer. Nerves taut as piano wire, ears straining for the sound of his return, with desperate fingers she fumbled among the handkerchiefs, spectacle cases and the three remaining packets of condoms. The first two were intact. Her pulse began to slow. She must be mistaken. She must, indeed have dropped one of her gold chains here. The seal on the third packet was broken. Curled inside lay another of her gold chains. Unnameable fears swelled, like the incoming tide rising through sand. She could not move. She knew he was there, standing in the doorway, although she had not heard him come up the stairs. Painfully, she turned her head. His eyes, behind his spectacles, had gone black. His face was grey.

Again, speechlessly, she held out a gold chain. She watched the whiteness round his lips overtake the whole of his face. Silently, they faced each other. Then, the car keys dropped to the floor as his hand released them. He took off his glasses, as if he no longer cared to see her.

In a small voice, which was no more than a breath of air, she whispered, 'It was you – I don't understand. Why?' She saw the beads of sweat spring out on his nose. His eyes seemed to sink back into his head.

'You took my gold chains and my ring.'

No denial burst from his pale lips, which twitched as if they needed to release something.

Aghast, she continued, 'And you gave my ring to the police.'

'You minded so much. About your mother. I couldn't bear you not to have it.'

Painfully, the words forced themselves from her lips, 'While I was on Vic's boat you broke into my house and you stole the miniature and my jewellery. Why?'

He'd been a stranger in the night. He was another stranger now. As he stood there, facing her, his whole body began to tremble. In a voice she did not recognise, he said, 'I had to. You must realise – I had no alternative.'

She didn't want to follow his mind through these dark labyrinths. She didn't want to know the truth of it. She wanted to go home.

He was standing in front of the door; twitching in an oddly regular way. She dared not go near him. As calmly as she could manage, she said, 'Never mind, Mark. It doesn't matter about the miniature – I'm pleased to have my ring back. Let's just forget about all this and go out to the car.'

'I missed it you see – the Hilliard. How can I be expected to recognise something I don't know about?' He seemed to be concentrating not on her, but on what was in his head, as she stood clutching her gold chain. It felt as if her thigh bones had dissolved.

'Please Mark – let's go out to the car.'

'I wouldn't have known about it if Margaret hadn't been so jealous of Carla.'

He stared at her with glazed, inward-looking eyes. 'I was at the sale – you asked me once – and I didn't tell you. But I was there. Draper and me. She came up after and said she wanted to look round your place.'

'You showed Margaret round Willow Farm?'

His face lit up. 'Yes. That's right. She knew Vic was thinking of buying it with Carla. Said she and I had cause to complain. She must have had it with her – but I didn't know.'

'What?'

'The miniature of course. She made me take her there – said she might be able to buy it herself.'

'Willow Farm?'

'Of course.' He was irritable. 'She wanted to put one over on Vic. When I asked her what she'd do for money she told me she'd come into a fortune. "I've pulled off a coup," she said. "At Woodton Hall I bought for fifty quid a miniature which could be worth two hundred grand. I don't suppose you've ever heard of Nicholas Hilliard have you Mark?" Those were her words. Superior bitch.' He was breathing quickly, unevenly. He pulled down his tie, wrenched at his collar, ripping off buttons. 'Vic told her to buy it for him. He didn't tell her what it was. But she guessed. Said she wasn't going to let the bugger have it. I thought she was talking a load of nonsense. "Hilliard – she said, sixteenth-century – didn't even

200

have to put it up at the Knock-Out." And then she said, "Not much cop at cataloguing are you?"' His lips were wet with saliva. He peered blindly at her with myopic eyes. 'I've always tried – all my life to do my best. And it's never been good enough.'

His eyes were bright now – could those be tears? She edged towards the door, blocked by his body. *'Listen* to me. You can't go.'

'We're going *together*, Mark, to Devon.' Her voice sounded faraway. 'Why don't you take the rest of our things out to the car?'

'We were up in the attic. "I'm going away, she said – with my friend Nicholas." Thought it was a huge joke. *"Vic* recognised him. *I* recognised him. But *you didn't."* I felt like a kid back at school. I won't be made a fool of.' And Frances saw the first signs of violence. His leg twitched and he kicked viciously at the skirting board.

'It was all her fault you know. I had to get even. I said her friend Nicholas might bring her in some cash, but he couldn't do for her what Vic could do.' He paused, punched his fist in the air in a gesture of triumph. 'I said Vic wouldn't be doing *that* to her any more because he was doing it to Carla. And hardly surprising.'

He was breathing heavily now. Sweat streaked his face. Her own body was drenched. 'And then it really started.'

'Please Mark. I don't want to hear. Let's go.'

'She said I couldn't do it – you know, *do* it – make love – have sex. His face contorted into something approaching a leer. She said Carla told her. Vic's had them both you know – like he had you. I'll kill him. One day I'll kill him. How could you *hurt me like that.*' His hands tore at his hair. He groaned – gasped for air. Stumbled away from the door, lurched round the room. He looked drunk, deranged. She thought – he'll have a fit. Slowly, slowly, she inched her way towards freedom. 'No you don't.' He moved back: blocked the door. *'Listen* to me.'

'All right.' Humour him. He's mad.

'You know how I've loved you – *she* said I was impotent. She said I was a failure at everything.' His voice dropped sadly. 'It happens. I come up against a wall of glass. I can see through – to

201

the other side. I want to be there. But I haven't the strength. That's what I dream. I can't try any more, you see. I can't get any further. With *anything*.' His voice rose in anger. 'She wouldn't stop. Her voice was punching holes in my head. I said – that's not true.' He raised his head and stared at her. 'I'm good at my job – I can make a woman happy. *Tell* me.'

'Yes, Mark. Yes.'

'Her voice was hammering into my head. I could hear it echo. All round the attic. "Stop" I said, "stop". But she wouldn't.'

He moved towards Frances, blank-eyed as a sleep walker. Hands held out in front as if to protect himself from falling.

'Mark.' He didn't hear her voice. 'Mark – it's all right. Whatever happened – you didn't mean it to.'

'I said show me. "*Look* what you missed". Flashed it in front of my eyes. "*Impotent imbecile.*" I couldn't stand it. Shut up I said. Cruel bitch.'

'Mark stop. Please stop.' She tried to find him. But in those blinded anguished eyes she saw only the horror of what he had done.

'I put my hands out like this.'

Slowly, he laid his hands on her shoulders. She looked up into those terrified, terrifying eyes. 'And then I brought them together like this.'

His hands closed lightly round her neck.

'Mark' she croaked, 'Mark it's me.' His fingers were tightening on her windpipe.

There must come a time when fear is overtaken by the instinct to survive. If you cannot breathe, you lose consciousness. If no air can enter the lungs to oxygenate the blood, to keep the heart beating, you die. Frances tried to fix Mark's eyes with her own. To communicate soundlessly. To signal that this was not Margaret he was strangling. This was Frances, whom he professed to love. But even in her half conscious state, as the breath was slowly being squeezed from her throat, she knew that his eyes did not communicate recognition to his brain. His eyes were seeing what happened months ago in the attic at Willow Farm. And his hands were duplicating their vile act. She saw sweat beading his face, saw the insane eyes of a creature she did not know.

I don't want to die. Every sinew, blood vessel, nerve, brain cell fought for life. She heard a voice, loud as a church bell, clanging in her head. 'Pretend you're dead.' She slackened her open mouth, let her fighting arms drop by her sides, allowed her knees to buckle. The pressure did not cease. She closed her eyes. She heard him cry out – a terrifying animal cry of unbearable anguish. She passed out.

Chapter Twenty-Two

She was alive. The pains all over her body were as nothing. Very carefully, quietly, slowly she got to her feet and listened. Was she alone? Had this terrible thing really happened? Her aching body and burning throat; the bruises circling her neck told her it was no mere nightmare. She crept through the sitting room, bedroom, kitchen, bathroom. Nothing.

She dragged herself to the bed where she had lain with Mark and crouched there quivering like a beaten animal. She pressed her face into the soft pillow, clutched the smooth sheet with her fingers. She was alive, and her life was infinitely more precious than she had realised. 'Thank you God,' she babbled. 'Thank you God for sparing me. I'll be good – I'll live a good life.'

Where was Mark? Would he come back – to check she was dead?

'I must get out of here,' she said aloud. When she tried to stand, her legs couldn't take the weight. Shadows whirled in her head. She fell back on to the bed and thought, 'I need help.' Once again she telephoned the police.

She went home to Willow Farm. Inspector Robertson was concerned and avuncular. But she refused police protection. She did not believe she was in danger.

Murderers revisit the scene of their crime.

Had Mark returned to the flat to find her gone? He must realise, dead, or alive, she, Frances linked him inexorably to Margaret's murder. Nothing he did could preserve him from that conclusion. Besides, he cared for her – he had said he

204

loved her. He wouldn't knowingly harm her. There would be no *point* in harming her.

But he was out of his mind.

Barricaded in her bedroom, she lay awake, still as stone, listening to the night sounds, her mind seething with grotesque images.

Mark was out there somewhere. Where? It seemed his distraught parents had no news of him. She remembered his strange outburst that Sunday down by the pond. And understood it now. It was nothing to do with whatever he and his mother had been arguing about, as she'd assumed at the time. She remembered hearing their raised voices as she and his father stood, chatting amiably, innocently, a few yards from the place where Margaret lay, secretly. Mark had come crashing through the low branches of the willow, propelled not by anger, but by fear. She remembered Elizabeth Edward's words when they'd talked before, about Mark's brief time working in London. *'We had to fetch him back in a hurry.'*

There must always have been some instability. She thought about that domineering woman, Mark's mother, who must surely bear some responsibility for shaping her son's mind. And then she thought, with sorrow, of his gentle good-hearted father. Saw those practical hands showing her the iris rhizome. Those steady blue eyes – *I hope you're happy here – you'll stay with us all – a friend of his own age* – It seemed kinder not to contact them.

On a bleak March evening, Mark, kind, conventional, boring (she'd once thought him *boring!*), Mark collected Margaret from Forgetmenot Cottage, drove her to Willow Farm and choked her to death there.

'I'll always be your friend.'

Would he be convicted of murder? Manslaughter while the balance of his mind was disturbed? She imagined him locked in a bare prison cell. For how long? Twenty years? Would doctors in white coats subject him to psychiatric treatment?

She thought of the impenetrable darkness in Mark's mind. The impossibility of ever really knowing another person. To believe them capable of perpetrating acts unimaginable by yourself was hard enough.

There was a female blackbird in the attic, the day he first

took her there. It flew out through the broken window. No wonder Mark had tried to put her off buying Willow Farm.

He committed murder in my attic.

Then he had dragged her poor body down the winding stair; bumped it all the way across uneven ground to the pond. Requiring some means of keeping her under that dark water, he had coolly made use of one of the cast-iron gates. I remarked on that, thought Frances, feeling sick. The one that was lying in the grass. I said how odd to choose elaborate gates for a simple farmhouse, and what happened to the other one? And Mark didn't turn a hair. Now it is propped up against the side of the house.

He helped me put it there. So heavy.

He must have waded with her to the deepest part. And then he must have dragged the gate out and dropped it over her; the great weight of it pressing her down into the mud. And then, he'd gone away, cleaned himself up, and carried on as normal.

Lying alone in the hot night, Frances thought how deluded she'd been, believing Willow Farm a safe haven. Perhaps safe haven is within yourself – and no place can provide it.

Her story appeared in the newspaper.

Police hunt for Mark Edwards, 28. Wanted for questioning in connection with the murder of Margaret Weston, 42. Mark Edwards is also accused of assaulting his friend Frances Lambert, 28.

He'd know she was alive now.

Mr Benson treated her gently, like a fragile piece of his own porcelain, when she went back to work, a scarf concealing the violet and saffron bruises around her neck.

After four days Inspector Robertson came to Willow Farm to tell her Mark's body had been found in the river Deben. Two teenage boys spotted it as they threw sticks for their dog. Her immediate, overwhelming reaction was one of relief. And she was sick with disgust at herself for feeling it.

During the next two days, she got up in the morning, went to work, came home again, ate baked beans or a boiled egg and went to bed, where, trying to come to terms with her guilt, still she did not sleep. But at least, she consoled herself, Mark wouldn't have to go through the horror of being brought to trial. Of being sentenced. Of being imprisoned.

I won't ever have to see him again. Was it wrong to be glad about that?

She remembered the day they'd walked along the river path. Made love under the oak. There was always something not quite right, she thought. I believe I knew it then. Poor Mark. He hated water. He must have really wanted to die. She wept for him. And she wept for herself.

When she thought about Vic, she went hot with embarrassment for believing him a murderer. For accusing him of murder. What must he think of her? She had not seen him since he came into the shop with Carla in tow. Imagining them together, she experienced an unacknowledgeable twinge of jealousy. Suppressing it, she told herself sternly – simply not being guilty of murder doesn't transform Vic into an acceptable companion. The roses he'd sent had lived for a while, in a glass vase in the showroom. Almost artificial in their perfection.

He came into the shop two days after Mark had been found. He was alone, and so was she, as Mr Benson was previewing a sale. She was listlessly typing invoices.

He nodded at her, and started to prowl round the showroom as usual. She was slightly insulted when he made no attempt to talk to her, to flirt with her. Did she no longer attract him? she tried to concentrate on her typing. Eventually, he came and stood by her desk. 'Well now Frances – how are you?'

'I'm thinking of leaving Fressenworth.' This notion had, in truth, only just leaped into her head.

'Too exciting for you here?'

'And selling Willow Farm. Are you interested – you and Carla?'

'It's not a buyer's market I'm afraid my dear. You'll have to stay for the time being.' He treated her to a lingering look. 'Shame about that upstanding young estate agent. But I always thought there was something funny about his eyes. Too close together. You want to be more careful choosing your boyfriends, my dear.'

She fumed quietly.

207

'I've upset you. Sorry.'

She fiddled with the papers on her desk to conceal her agitation.

'You must have had a very unpleasant time. I shouldn't make light of it.'

'Never mind.'

'Any sign of my miniature?'

'*Your* miniature?'

'I rather think I bought it in the first place.'

'*Margaret* bought it. And *I* found it – on *my* property.'

'Well if it turns up, we'll be able to have a nice little battle over it. That will be good fun.'

'It's probably lost for ever.'

'Shame.' He smiled at her.

Mr Benson said, 'I understand how you must feel, but please don't make any long-term decisions just yet.'

'I've enjoyed working here,' she said, 'But I never expected it to be permanent.'

'You have been very useful. You're learning about the trade. I would be sorry to lose you. At the same time, I can't offer you the kind of opportunities you would get if you did indeed return to London, but that, of course, you understand. I would very much like you to stay on. I'm growing old but I don't want to sell my business. I've no one to leave it to. I could perhaps offer you a partnership in due time.'

'A partnership?' A proper responsible career. Not just a job. Did she want this? 'It's good of you Mr Benson,' she said slowly. 'May I think about it? I don't want to make up my mind in a hurry.'

'Certainly my dear. Please take your time.' He removed his glasses and smiled at her, the brave smile of an old man who does not forget that once he was young and powerful.

The drought broke that evening. By the time Frances was driving home, the sky bulged with clouds that had been building all day. Purple as the bruises on her neck, bilious at the edges they hung menacingly about the cornfields. It grew so dark she had to turn on her headlights. The forked lightning came first, splitting the clouds, then the sheet lightning flash-

208

ing luridly on and off as if a mischievous god was playing with a giant light switch. Almost instantaneously a thunderclap burst directly above her head. It was so loud, she found herself ducking instinctively. Huge drops of rain began to beat on the roof of her car and by the time she reached Willow Farm they had become a torrent. She was drenched in the seconds it took to run from the car to her front door. Inside the house, she watched the exploding sky with awe. She felt how the dusty earth would be soaking up the essential rain, the thirsty animals and trees and plants would be drinking it in. She imagined it beating down on her pond, cleansing the contaminated water, bringing refreshment and new life.

It rained all evening. She made herself a mushroom omelette, drank most of a bottle of wine, and thought about Mr Benson's offer. Could she bear to go on living in a place that had so deluded her. Could she walk up to the attic, and not remember the pressure of those fingers, and know what it felt like to be strangled? To be Margaret? Could she stand by the pond and not remember the long line of Margaret's decaying body, the black holes in her face?

Returning to London was no solution. Perhaps she should make another escape? Go somewhere completely different. Abroad perhaps. But you couldn't keep starting again; you had to stick at something. Fressenworth and Mr Benson were one thing. Willow Farm quite another. They weren't a package deal. She could stay in Fressenworth, work for Mr Benson and sell Willow Farm.

It went on raining all night. She listened to it swishing against the windowpane, beating on the roof, imagined it filling her pond, and reached no decision.

Next morning, as she opened Mr Benson's post, she came across a small package addressed to herself in shaky capital letters. Uneasily, she slit it open. And there, wrapped in black tissue, was the Hilliard miniature. On a square of white paper, in the same shaky capital letters, was only one word. That word was SORRY.